ANDRE GONZALEZ

Angel Assassin

First edition

ISBN: 978-1-951762-40-7

Editing by Stephanie Cohen-Perez
Cover art by 100Covers

This book was professionally typeset on Reedsy.
Find out more at reedsy.com

For Arielle, Felix, and Selena.

"It's so reassuring to have a woman heroine who triumphs with more than just what she has on the outside, who has more to offer the world than just a pretty picture."

—America Ferrera

Contents

GET EXCLUSIVE BONUS STORIES!   iii

Chapter 1   1

Chapter 2   8

Chapter 3   16

Chapter 4   22

Chapter 5   28

Chapter 6   34

Chapter 7   40

Chapter 8   46

Chapter 9   53

Chapter 10   61

Chapter 11   67

Chapter 12   74

Chapter 13   81

Chapter 14   87

Chapter 15   92

Chapter 16   98

Chapter 17   103

Chapter 18   113

Chapter 19   118

Chapter 20   124

Chapter 21   129

Chapter 22   137

Chapter 23   143

Chapter 24   151
Chapter 25   160
Chapter 26   166
Chapter 27   173
Chapter 28   181
Chapter 29   187
Chapter 30   196
Chapter 31   203
Chapter 32   208
Chapter 33   213
Chapter 34   220
Chapter 35   226
Chapter 36   231
Chapter 37   235
Chapter 38   242
Chapter 39   248
Chapter 40   252
Chapter 41   261
READ THE FUTURES REPORT!   268
Author's Note   269
Enjoy this book?   272
Also by Andre Gonzalez   273
About the Author   275

GET EXCLUSIVE BONUS STORIES!

Connecting with readers is the best part of this job. Releasing a book into the world is a truly frightening moment every time it happens! Hearing your feedback, whether good or bad, goes a long way in shaping future projects and helping me grow as a writer. I also like to take readers behind the scenes on occasion and share what is happening in my wild world of writing. If you're interested, please consider joining my mailing list. If you do, I'll send you four FREE novellas as a thank you!

You can get your content **for free,** by signing up at www.andregonzalez.net

Chapter 1

Arielle Lucila jammed her pistol inside the man's gaping mouth. Her arm didn't so much as tremble. Like anyone, the twists and turns of life had shaped her sense of purpose in the world. Pain and tragedy had chipped away at her like a patient sculptor hacking off chunks of marble to create a timeless masterpiece. She was exactly where she was supposed to be.

The man lay flat on his back, his dark skin glistening as sweat covered every inch of his face. It had been a treacherous two-hour manhunt for the Mexican drug lord known as El Guapo. His bloodshot eyes dripped with desperation, begging for mercy.

Arielle had come into this mission on her own, confident she could bring him down along with the rest of his cartel, and securing the perimeter around his mansion in Culiacán, Sinaloa.

She had arrived the night before, scouting the area from a distance with night-vision goggles to familiarize herself with the landscape surrounding the private mansion. An iron fence with spiked tips secured the property, and she had found only one exit along the rear, where El Guapo could slip out in case of an emergency.

Weeks of studying the area with satellite maps left her

1

confident she only needed one other Angel on the mission to watch that rear exit. She never knew who manned that post, nor did it matter. Twenty-one cartel members populated the property, and she killed every single one of them on her own, sniping a cool dozen from a perch in a tree one hundred yards away before moving closer to the mansion. The rest retreated inside.

Arielle always loved that part of the job, seeing several grown men scatter like terrified ants. Maneuvering toward and through the mansion was plenty more difficult thanks to the cameras planted throughout the property, but she had learned the layout like her own home, and was ready for the trapdoors and hiding spots where El Guapo's goons hid to ambush her.

The Road Runners, the secret organization she had joined many years ago, had unlimited resources and had no problem paying off the architect who had created El Guapo's famous mansion for the original blueprints and designs. This mission, like every other before it, proved rather straightforward thanks to the advantage they always had. It almost wasn't fair, until you considered these gifts were used to kill people like El Guapo, with forty known murders under his belt, and hundreds more by the hands of his cartel.

Arielle wasn't driven by hatred, but rather a respect and appreciation for life. Those who used others' lives for their own gain had no reason to exist in her world, and she'd see that none of them could shatter the lives of innocent families again. She knew the pain too well, its scars having hardened her soul in the years since she lost her own family.

She brushed aside those thoughts before they distracted from the task at hand. Not that El Guapo posed a threat—Arielle had shot him once in each leg and crushed his arms with a crowbar. She enjoyed this part of her work, making those who caused so much suffering live through their own moment of personal hell before she turned off their lights.

"I'll admit, this is a beautiful home," Arielle said, forcing the gun deeper into the drug lord's mouth, causing him to gag uncontrollably. "It will need a good cleaning after the mess your people made today, but I think we can turn this into something useful for society, don't you think? Maybe an orphanage, or senior home. I don't know, a rehab center for drug addicts seems appropriate to me."

El Guapo's eyes bulged out of his sockets, begging her to stop, but she saw the look of acceptance and defeat in them. It was a look she knew too well, one that made her heart skip a beat each time she witnessed it. She never saw regret or remorse, but rather, shock. How could someone so powerful and connected end up in such a predicament? Maybe their lives flashed through their minds, or perhaps they calculated how they ended up looking death straight in the eye. She didn't care either way.

Arielle felt the man pushing his tongue against the pistol, trying to force it out of his mouth. "Fighting until the last moment," she observed. "Admirable, but not enough. Do you actually think you're going to walk out of here? Look around—I did this all by myself."

She paused and looked away, inviting El Guapo to do the same. His head dropped to one side, eyes scanning his office where four bodies formed a trail of death from the door to behind his desk.

He grunted, fighting to speak, and Arielle shook her head. "I used to let people like you say some final words, but I've found it to be a waste of time. Let me guess, you want to call me a crazy bitch?" She grinned and pressed the pistol deeper, cutting off the grunts as El Guapo's face reddened, his lips turning a shade of purple while his body convulsed. "You're choking. And unless you can give me one good reason to shoot you instead, I think I'll wait this one out."

The gagging stopped as he fell silent. The only sounds were his hands rapping on the hardwood floor while his entire body tensed. He was only seconds away now. Arielle knew, again, by the distant look in his eyes. They stared in her direction, but focused behind her. *Through* her.

It only took another minute until the convulsions softened and the drug lord lay motionless. His balled fists relaxed, fingers opening into a slight curl. A cloudy haze took over his eyes, prompting Arielle to reach forward to brush his eyelids shut. She kept the pistol in his mouth, not wanting to take any chances—she had made that mistake only once before.

Arielle remained on top of him for the next ninety seconds for good measure, listening for any sounds throughout the house.

Silence.

She had done it. Killed an entire cartel on her own, and the only injury she had to show was a small graze from a bullet that had caught her on the calf.

Two-day recovery, she thought, mind already wondering about the next mission.

She removed the pistol from El Guapo's mouth and stood over his body, still keeping it cocked and aimed at his face. "You sick man. All those children, police officers, and judges you killed. All the people you took advantage of to do your dirty work. You'll get yours wherever you end up."

Arielle lowered the pistol to his chest and fired three rounds, the corpse not so much as flinching as it absorbed each hit. She had once shot a dead drug lord in the face and couldn't stomach the way it looked.

Before she called headquarters to confirm the job was complete, she wanted to browse El Guapo's office. The most powerful man in Mexico surely had something worthwhile for her to keep as a memento. She started at his desk and rummaged through the drawers, finding bundles of cash, forged documents, and plenty of guns and ammunition. She expected as much, but froze after finding a framed picture buried under a mountain of fake passports.

The portrait was slightly grainy, suggesting it had been taken several years prior, and showed a young boy with his parents. Arielle held the portrait next to El Guapo's face and concluded that he was indeed the young child in the photograph.

"Maybe we weren't that different after all," Arielle said. "How many times were you alone in this office and pulled out this picture to have a cry? I do it about once a week still. The pain never fades, does it?"

She stuffed the portrait back into the drawer before any compassion could drip into her mind for the man who had murdered hundreds. Keeping her targets as dehumanized as possible was crucial to her job's success. And her mental health.

Now she wanted to get out as quickly as possible and closed the drawers before crossing the office toward the exit. That's when she looked out the window and froze once more, catching her reflection with those of the dead bodies on the floor behind her.

Dammit, she thought, sensing the trip down memory lane. Her face tingled as she fought the urge to cry. That quick glimpse of her reflection was all it took. It was the same reflection she had seen the day her family was killed.

That fateful day was only five years in the past, the pain nowhere near vanishing. She had joined her parents and brother for a day of Christmas shopping at the mall, having spent some time at home after graduating from the CIA. After the holidays, she was supposed to start her new life as an agent.

That never came to fruition after a gunman opened fire in the mall, killing dozens and wounding several more. The Lucila family had been caught in the wrong place at the absolutely wrong time. The gunman had barreled out of a clothing store, having used a dressing room to slip into tactical gear and load multiple magazines for his AR-15, and opened fire in every direction. The Lucila family had been across the aisle, waiting in line for a pretzel.

Arielle had stood in front of the line, and that was perhaps the only reason she survived. Her mother and father caught multiple rounds to their backs and collapsed to the ground instantly. Arielle's brother, Antonio, recognized what was un-folding and shoved Arielle from behind, sending her crashing into the pretzel stand counter. Blood had splattered across the walls and floor, Arielle slipping in it as she struggled to get back on her feet.

Antonio saw the shooter turn his attention in their direction, and he lunged toward Arielle, absorbing the bullets meant for her, in the most heroic action she had ever seen in her life—even to this day. She had been close to her brother, growing up only two years apart. As for their personalities, Antonio couldn't have been any more different from Arielle, the CIA agent. He preferred quiet nights in, and long weekends in the mountains where he'd take a handful of easels and paint the landscapes of the Rockies. She didn't even consider him brave; he being the older brother who ran out of the room if a spider was present, leaving his little sister to squash it.

Knowing him at his most intimate level only made Arielle wonder what had taken over his instincts to jump in front of a bullet. She might never know, but she swore to never waste another moment of her life. Doing so would be a dishonor to Antonio.

The gunman had fled the area and continued his rampage in a different part of the mall, and that was when Arielle had pulled herself onto her hands and knees, and saw her reflection in the clothing store's window, blood splattered across her visage, dead bodies on the floor all around her.

She hadn't realized in the heat of the moment, but that image would remain burned in her mind for the rest of her life. Only twenty-seven years old, she had a long road ahead of processing this tragedy over her remaining days. She could close her eyes and mentally go back to that moment, her jaw hanging, lungs filling with the unbearable stench of gunpowder, death clinging to her skin like leeches. Aside from the imagery, she could also recall the emotion she had felt that day, the instant numbness that filled her entire body once she finally stood and saw the three people she had loved her entire life lying dead on the floor. Perhaps it was survivor's guilt, but she had no problem picturing herself lying next to them, drifting off to whatever afterlife might await.

And now, as she stood in front of the window in El Guapo's office, it all came flooding back.

Chapter 2

Later that evening, Arielle arrived back in Denver, headquarters of the Road Runners under the leadership of Commander Martin Briar. The mission to kill El Guapo had been a rare one that didn't require any time travel to complete. Only the advance team had traveled back in time to scout their target and craft a plan for Arielle.

The Road Runners owned a fleet of private jets, and Arielle always had one at her disposal, a perk of being the top-rated Angel Runner. She had left Sinaloa within an hour after killing El Guapo, and now drove to the downtown Denver office to meet with the commander.

The Road Runners, a top-secret time-travel organization, had origins that dated back a handful of decades after they had branched off from a group called the New Age Revolution, who had been in the time travel business for centuries. The two groups had split in a schism over the differences of how they thought they should use their unique abilities.

The Revolution used time travel to manipulate governments and societies all around the world, implementing their own people to call the shots and create a world best suited for their selfish desires, leaving everyone else to fend for themselves.

The Road Runners wanted to do good, using knowledge from

the past and future to enhance lives in the present. They were a curious bunch, always investigating historical events, trying to stop future tragedies. But the Revolution, a group who vastly outnumbered them under the leadership of a lunatic, Chris Speidel, had always tampered with their goals.

After years of bloody war, Commander Briar was the one to finally get the job done and claim victory for the Road Runners only one year ago. The Revolution had since fizzled away, some members joining the Road Runners after a rigorous initiation process to confirm their loyalty. The Road Runners remained the lone organization within the time travel world, enjoying a peaceful transition under Commander Briar's leadership.

The Angel Runners—Angels, for short—were a subset of the organization that focused solely on missions, typically in the past, to prevent devastating crimes and tragedies from happening. They kept a live ranking of all Angels based on missions completed among other factors, and Arielle had risen to the top spot after five years with the organization. Being the top Angel afforded several perks, like access to private vehicles and jets, and scheduling flexibility.

And of course, one-on-one meetings with the commander. Arielle reflected on their past as she walked up the steps to their downtown office building, a street-level unit in the Ballpark District that appeared as a marketing agency. The main level, though employed by time travelers, *did* serve as a marketing agency for businesses in the Denver area. They operated at a slight loss, but it didn't matter, as the Road Runners had access to virtually unlimited funds.

Below the marketing offices, through a back door in the manager's office that led to the basement, was where the serious business took place. Arielle entered the building and strolled to the back room, nodding and smiling to her colleagues who ran the marketing front as she passed.

The stairwell had always been a strange sort of purgatory between the worlds, engulfed in sheer silence thanks to its concrete walls. She reached the bottom and pulled open the door, stepping into the Road Runners' bustling headquarters. Large monitors lined the walls, dozens of Road Runners sitting behind their desks in the office's bullpen. Some spoke on phones, others clattered away on their keyboards, and someone was always glaring at the monitors.

The monitors displayed live maps of different areas of the continent, small blips moving around that showed Road Runners' current locations.

The Road Runners in the office preferred to assist from behind the scenes. There was no shortage of needs for the organization, and people were always willing to jump into whatever role to help the team. Winning the war had brought a fresh sense of unity and purpose for nearly every member. Now that they no longer had obstacles to making the world a better place—plus no longer fearing for their lives—the Road Runners had jumped into their new era with vigor and motivation.

Arielle scanned the office that stretched fifty yards to the back wall, looking for familiar faces, but finding none that weren't already tied up with work. Her stomach growled, and she debated going all the way to that back wall where their kitchen housed plenty of food, but she stopped by the commander's office first.

The door was closed, so she gave a sturdy knock on the frosted glass window.

"Come in!" a man called from the other side, and she pushed

it open.

Commander Briar sat behind his desk, scribbling on a stack of papers before looking up. A grin took over his face. "Arielle! Always a treat. Congratulations on your most recent mission. Did you really kill twenty-one cartel members by yourself?"

Arielle smiled. "I did."

The commander rounded his desk and gave Arielle a quick hug before leaning against the wall and crossing his arms. He shook his head. "I see these reports about your missions, and I swear, they sound made up. How on Earth does one person kill twenty-one of the most dangerous men in Mexico?"

"Twenty-two, once you count El Guapo."

Commander Briar chuckled. He was a middle-aged man showing more gray hair each time Arielle stopped in. Early wrinkles appeared around his eyes and mouth, and Arielle assumed the conclusion of their war had aged the man at least a decade—he had a much more youthful appearance beforehand. "Yes, of course, can't forget about him. I actually spoke with Darius—remember, he was hiding around the mansion's rear just in case—and he said it was an absolute treat to watch you take all of those thugs down. I guess he was perched up in a tree and watched the entire show through his binoculars. Left quite the impression on him."

Arielle nodded, upset that she was just now finding out Darius had been her backup. The two had a long past in the Road Runners, starting together in the same training class and rising through the ranks together. It would have been nice to see her old friend, and maybe even grab dinner with him. "Well, I'm glad he could help out."

"Have you thought more about the offer I made to you before this mission?" Commander Briar asked.

Arielle knew the question was coming and still wasn't sure how she felt about the proposition. "I don't know, Commander. I've never had an issue going into these missions on my own. I've done how many now? Like 400 or something—I've lost count. I just don't see why we have to change things all the sudden."

She knew he would consider her opinion, but the commander ultimately made the final decisions. He had suggested Arielle work directly with a small team on future missions. Teams that prepared for a mission already assisted her, but Commander Briar's proposal was to send this team into the field with her, getting their feet on the ground for more comprehensive research.

"It's not your experience I'm worried about—you're clearly at the top of your game. We are in a time of peace, and with that, my primary focus is minimizing risk. You made it through this mission, just as you always have, but at some point you're going to meet your match. Your missions are dangerous, and involve some of the most violent human beings to walk the planet. I just don't want anything bad to happen to you."

"What would this team honestly bring to the table that I can't already do myself?"

"It's not about ability—it's about lightening your workload. Lapses in judgment stem from a lack of concentration. Our thought process behind this is to allow you more time to worry about what you're actually going to do on your missions, then execute it. Imagine arriving at your next destination and all the preliminary work is done. Or say you get there and find something isn't right. Instead of having to make adjustments on the fly, you can delegate that work to your team."

Arielle nodded. "And who would be on this team? I hope it

12

would be permanent, and not a constant rotation like it has been."

"It would absolutely be a permanent team. We want you to develop chemistry and cohesiveness. We want them to anticipate your needs before they arise. That can only happen by dedicating their time to nothing else. We have a couple of names in mind: Felix Francisco and Selena Nicole. Are you familiar with them?"

"Yes. I've worked on some missions with Felix—he seemed to know his stuff. And Selena is that actress, right?"

"That she is. We stole her from Hollywood right before she attracted major attention. We took a peek into her future. Had we left her alone, she had an incredible career ahead, like on Meryl Streep's level. We paid a ton of money to get her to leave Hollywood and join the Road Runners, but she'll be worth every penny. She can act any role, and under pressure."

"Okay, I don't see the harm in trying it for the next mission. Have you found anything for me yet?"

"How many days are you looking to take off?"

Angels could take as much time off as they needed in between missions. Most opted for seven to ten days. Arielle usually took three.

"Two days—I get bored too fast."

Commander Briar chuckled and shook his head. "Of course. I'll have to get back to you in the morning to see what we have—I haven't looked yet myself. Been busy."

"Oh? Are things finally in motion with the laboratory?"

"They are. Construction began a week ago, and they estimate a month for completion. It's brought a lot of work and moving parts—I have to hire a whole new team to run the lab."

"Exciting. Congratulations, Commander. I know this has

been one of your biggest goals."

After the war had ended and Chris Speidel was split into multiple parts and buried around the world, the Road Runners recovered perhaps the grandest secret that belonged to their foes: The Book of Time.

Its writings dated back centuries and outlined the origins of all aspects of time, including time travel. Initially, to join the world of time travelers, one would need to get a special Juice from the Keeper of Time, which had been Chris Speidel. The Road Runners had worked hard in trying to reverse-engineer the liquid to create their own, but they could never quite get it correct. The Book of Time contained the recipe, and Commander Briar moved forward by creating a laboratory to mass produce the Juice, ensuring they could always recruit new members to their organization, and provide unlimited Juice for their existing members. Not only did they have the recipe, but they discovered Chris had been creating a limited version of the liquid. One intended to hinder certain aspects of time travel.

"Thank you. We've come a long way since that night in the woods. Sometimes I think back and can't believe everything that's happened."

"I know—it's been quite the ride. At least we have the future to look forward to. I want to hear more about what you've found in the Book of Time. Maybe before my next assignment? It's been such a game changer not having to fall asleep and worry about my body being left behind in the present. This new method is much more efficient. And safe."

"Of course. There is some good stuff in that book. Time portals all around the world that we never knew of. We're trying to figure out how to best use them."

A steel safe sat on the bookshelf behind Commander Briar's desk, and Arielle nodded toward it. "You still let him keep you company?"

The commander grinned. "I know it might be a little morbid to keep the head of our greatest enemy in such plain sight. But did we not earn this? I enjoy having the reminder of how bad things can get. Helps me keep perspective."

Arielle thought back to the night in the woods when Commander Briar had successfully murdered Chris Speidel. She had driven him to the mission and was the first to meet him at the scene after time had been frozen for two hours. It had been the highlight of her career, getting to be part of the most important mission in the organization's history. After that, her career skyrocketed.

"I suppose that's true. I should go now. I'll be back in two days, if that works for you?"

"Definitely, enjoy your time off."

"Thank you, Commander. Give the lieutenant my best."

Arielle let herself out of the office and escaped the headquarters before anyone stopped her. She had become quite the celebrity within the Road Runners—a common occurrence for any Angel who cracked the top three in their ranking system.

Chapter 3

The next morning, Felix Francisco entered the Road Runners' headquarters at eight o'clock sharp for a meeting with the commander and another colleague about a new role. He ran fingers through his sandy hair, assuring it was properly slicked to the side. Felix rarely worried about his appearance, but made it a point to spruce himself up when visiting HQ. He still felt lanky, despite recent efforts to bulk up at the gym. And he always struggled with self-consciousness, thinking his skin was too pale and his hair too light. He knew this insecurity stemmed from his Hispanic heritage, and being teased by other kids throughout his childhood for not being "brown" enough. Those ghosts of playground bullies past still haunted him today.

Felix dealt with all things technology for the Angel Runners when preparing for their missions. After a scout had deemed which areas and times of day were safest at the mission's location, Felix worked on setting up surveillance and bugging any phone lines and homes for the subjects in question. His tasks were some of the first steps to ensure a smooth mission, and if done correctly, could lead to their targets walking straight into a trap. He made the Angels look good while getting little of the credit, and that was fine in his eyes. Felix didn't need the spotlight and preferred to excel behind the scenes.

Since his work contributed to the Angel Runners, he had a spot on their sacred rankings, but would never break the top 100 Angels, since he never worked in the field and captured the bad guys himself. He was, however, the highest-ranking Angel in his role. He had counterparts all around the continent, and most would call Felix for advice. He didn't mind, and was happy to share his knowledge.

He stood outside of Commander Briar's office, informed that he was finishing a call before their meeting. He stood on one side of the doorway, while a woman stood opposite, scrolling and tapping away on her cell phone.

She looked familiar, but he couldn't pin down her name. With Felix standing six feet tall, he figured to have at least six inches over the young, athletic woman. She looked up for a moment and batted her brown eyes at him, brushing back her long, wavy brown hair with a slender finger. Felix guessed she lived near a beach, judging by her dark, sun-kissed skin.

He looked around the office for any familiar faces, but didn't find anyone he recognized. He used to work in the Denver office regularly, but had shifted to working from home one year ago after buying a new house and transforming the basement into a state-of-the-art office.

The organization didn't mind. Felix could get more work done if he felt the urge in the middle of the night—something that occurred more often than not. He had been both blessed and cursed with an overly active mind, earning a Firestone Medal from Stanford University, while also fighting insomnia most of his life.

The office door swung open and Commander Briar strolled

17

out, his signature wide grin lighting up the room. "Felix, so good to see you!" He turned to the woman. "Selena, welcome. Are you both ready?"

Felix had no idea the meeting participants included the famous Selena Nicole. She was a rising star within the organization, earning a reputation as one of their best field scouts. She was also known as a loose cannon, enjoying lively celebrations after missions. For someone like Felix, driven by data and logic, Selena was too much of a wild card.

"Good morning, Commander," Selena said. "Can't say I'm much of a morning person, but happy to be here." She grinned at Felix before they both followed the commander into his office.

"Please take a seat, you two," Commander Briar said as he closed the door and shuffled around to sit behind his desk. "Can I get anyone a drink? Or even some breakfast?"

"I'm okay," Felix said.

"Do you have mimosas?" Selena asked, brushing her light brown hair behind her ears as she crossed her legs to get comfortable.

The request caught Commander Briar off guard, but he smiled and nodded. "One mimosa coming up." He typed a quick message on his computer before leaning back in his seat. "Have you two met before?"

Selena shook her head. "Not that I recall."

"Felix meet Selena. Selena meet Felix." The two looked at each other and exchanged awkward nods. "You may not know this, but you two are actually some of our first members recruited for your skills. Before, we only recruited relatives of existing Road Runners, or people who had their lives ruined by tragedy, as has been the norm for years. Commander Strike believed we had the potential to strengthen the organization by recruiting top talent. Felix, you were top of your class at Stanford. Selena, you were very much ahead of your time at Juilliard. We took gambles, not knowing how it would play out pulling regular citizens off the street to join our group. But you two have performed so well. I'm expanding our recruiting efforts to bring in more members like you."

"Why thank you, Commander," Selena said with a wide smile. "Are we getting some sort of award? I'm not entirely sure why this meeting was called."

The door knocked and opened. Commander Briar's assistant, Rolando, entered with a mimosa and placed it on the desk before leaving without a word.

"No award," the commander said, gesturing for Selena to take her drink. "I wanted to talk to you both about an opportunity. The Angel Runners have been running so smoothly since we've restarted them after the war, but we feel we can do even more. Having the Angels broken into set teams is the best way to improve our efficiency. As is, we have so many moving parts: different area scouts, different advance teams. And while everyone is fantastic at their job, no one does it all the same way. If we had a dedicated team working with a specific field agent on each mission, the consistency will yield even better results."

"So you want *us* to work on the same team?" Selena asked, nodding to Felix.

"Exactly."

"And what if we don't have the chemistry you hope for? Are we able to move to different teams until we find the best fit?"

"We will evaluate those scenarios on a case-by-case basis. We're going to align our teams based on talent and trust that all

19

Road Runners can work together. You two are the best at what you do, and that's why you'll be together as a new advance team for Arielle Lucila."

"Arielle Lucila?!" Selena jumped from her seat and gasped.

"That is correct. You two have earned it. What do you think, Felix?"

"I'd be honored," Felix said, beaming in a rare show of emotion. "I've done a few missions for her in the past, and all ran smoothly."

Felix rarely fawned over celebrities, but Arielle Lucila was one person he couldn't help but admire. She seemed to have superhuman abilities, having the same technological knowledge as him, combined with a plethora of other skills. He had worked with her on missions before, but had done little directly with the top Angel, instead focusing on the preliminary work. This new opportunity would change his life now that he'd have a front-row seat to watch the organization's phenom carry out her missions.

"I want to be up front with you both," Commander Briar said. "I know the chance to work with Arielle is a high honor, but understand she is a person of great intensity. She is prompt, strict, and monitors every detail. I've had more than my fair share of complaints from other advance teams about how demanding she can be. It can take a toll on your mental health if you're not prepared. But I think you can handle it. Who knows—she may even lighten up once she has her own dedicated team for each mission."

"I'm not concerned about it," Felix said.

"It takes a lot to upset me," Selena added.

"That settles it then," Commander Briar said. "I'm still working on finding the next mission for Arielle, and expect to meet with her tomorrow to discuss it. I'd like for you both to come to that meeting and get to know her a little better. Does that work?"

"Yes, sir," Felix said, overcome with glee. "Should I not worry about the mission they assigned me last night?"

"Toss it. We'll shuffle things around tomorrow. For today, enjoy the time off—it's supposed to be a sunny day. Maybe you two can take some time to get to know each other better."

Felix looked at Selena as she took a sip from her mimosa. "Sounds good," she said. "You like breweries or rooftop bars better?" she asked Felix.

"There's actually a Rockies game this afternoon. Do you like baseball?"

"I hate baseball. Gotta be the stupidest sport. But Coors Field has both a brewery *and* a rooftop bar, so I think we can make that work."

Felix grew antsy thinking about spending the afternoon with Selena. She was already planning the rest of her day drinking before even finishing the mimosa. He wondered if she was an alcoholic, or just a young adult enjoying her life. Her reputation spoke for itself, and he couldn't argue that he was now working with one of the best, no matter how off-the-walls her methods were.

"Sounds like you two have it settled," Commander Briar said. "If you wouldn't mind, I have a ton of work this morning. Glad we could get together for a moment. So good to see you both."

He stood up and extended his arm across the desk, shaking Felix's hand while Selena chugged the rest of her drink to free up her hands. "Thank you for this opportunity, Commander," Selena said. "We won't let you down."

Chapter 4

Five hours later, Selena and Felix enjoyed a drink together at the Coors Field rooftop bar. Felix had babbled for the last thirty minutes about baseball stats and standings, and why the team needed new ownership if they ever wanted to win a World Series.

Selena quickly grew bored with the conversation and dreaded if this is what the rest of her career with the Road Runners would consist of. She needed to change the subject to avoid the urge to jump off the rooftop deck. Felix was a nice guy, but had a glaring lack of social skills. She knew the type, having worked with plenty of his counterparts on other missions. The tech team came off introverted, rarely accepting invites to celebrate successful missions with Selena.

"Tell me about yourself, Felix. How old are you? Do you have a girlfriend? How did you end up with the Road Runners?"

His passion for discussing baseball immediately waned now that he had to talk about himself. The gentle grin that had remained while he rambled about home runs and batting averages turned into a slight frown.

"Uh, okay," he said. "I'm twenty-four and single. Had a serious girlfriend in college, but we broke it off before graduation."

"Oh no, I'm sorry to hear that."

"It's okay. She went off to Europe. She invited me, but I wasn't interested in living out of a backpack for three months. I guess we realized then how we didn't quite agree on what life should be like after college."

"I suppose those things happen."

"I don't know. It kind of came out of nowhere. So that's my love life, or lack thereof." Felix giggled, taking another sip from his rum and Coke. "Anyway, as far as me joining the Road Runners, they approached me at Stanford. It was literally the day after graduation. I had been applying to all kinds of jobs and had interviews lined up all summer. They used their marketing firm in Denver as a front to get me to interview."

Selena nodded, her story not much different.

"From the beginning," Felix continued. "I thought it was all a prank. I had applied for a software engineering job with them, and after speaking on the phone and learning the salary, it felt like a scam. I researched the company and found they had been around for a while, so not some start-up in over their heads. Then they sent me my flight tickets and hotel reservations. I still had my doubts, but it was a free trip for a broke college graduate."

"Did they take you back in time at your interview?"

Felix nodded. "I'm very focused on facts, so they needed to persuade me. I was about to walk out of that building, then they showed me the basement, gave me a sip of Juice, and took me back to when I was in elementary school. Just a kid playing at recess with his friends. But it was me."

"And have you been doing the same work since joining?"

"Pretty much. I've bounced around to work on different projects and have expanded to some other fields, but technol-

23

ogy is always at the core. Research and preparation, too. I find the currency for the year we're traveling to and make sure we have enough to last the mission. I bug the phones and hack into computers, but also get all the weapons and wardrobe ready for the missions."

"Wardrobe?" Selena asked, expecting that to be the last thing Felix would handle.

He chuckled. "Yeah. My mom is a fashion designer in San Fran, so they figured that somehow qualified me to handle the wardrobe for missions."

Selena looked Felix up and down, wondering how the technology genius dressed in faded jeans and a Star Wars t-shirt was qualified to handle fashion for some of the world's greatest assassins.

"I know, I know," Felix said. "Why don't I dress nicer? I just want to be comfortable. Honestly, the wardrobe part of my job is just research. How did people dress in the particular era and locations? Does that change based on their class or job? That's all I do . . . but I have an eye for it. Guess that *was* passed down from my mom."

"And she still does fashion design?"

"Sure does. My parents didn't have it easy. They came here from Colombia after they got married. Worked together for a cleaning company that served businesses all around San Fran. One of the stores was a clothing boutique. It took my mom over a year to work up the courage to just tell the owner that she loved the clothes and had always had an interest in fashion. After that, the owner started giving my mom scrap materials, then eventually full materials to let her create new things. It all sort of grew from there. Now my mom is the top designer in NorCal, and my dad helps her run the shop."

"Such a beautiful story," Selena said. "I love hearing things like that." She placed a hand over her heart.

"What about you? What led you to becoming such a legendary actress? How old are you? Like twelve?"

Selena didn't expect a joke from Felix, and her jaw dropped in surprise. "Very funny," she said, slapping Felix on the arm. "I'm only a year younger than you. My childhood was . . . interesting. Parents divorced when I was eight. I had grown up in Florida, but after the divorce, my dad moved back to France and my mom moved to New York."

"You're French?"

"French and Spanish. I'm fluent, too. I spent the summers in France with my dad, and the school year in New York with my mom. I watched a ton of movies on those seven hour flights. I could never sleep on planes—still can't. But that's when I fell in love with the work of Julia Roberts and Hillary Swank. From that point I knew the only thing I wanted to do was act. Here I was, an eight-year-old girl not even aware of what a pain in the ass it was to fly across the world to see my parents. But I didn't notice—I was too busy practicing accents and pretending to be someone I wasn't. Looking back, I think that's how I dealt with the pain. If I didn't have to be myself, then it was like my parents were never divorced. I just lived in my own world, even more when I stayed with my mom—she worked two jobs and I rarely saw her."

"I'm sorry, that sounds so hectic. I can't imagine."

Selena shrugged. "It's like anything, I suppose. You get used to it, and it becomes your normal. It wasn't until I was older that I realized my mom was working that extra job to save money for college. By then, I had acted in high school theater and kept inching toward a career in acting. I ended up going to Juilliard, earned my Master's, and moved to Hollywood. And that is where the Road Runners found me. Made me an offer I couldn't turn down." Selena paused and shook her head. "I still wonder if it was worth giving up my dream of winning an Oscar. But that's the thing about Hollywood—your background and education don't guarantee a thing. I could have spent the next twenty years chasing something that might have never happened. That made it hard to pass up the money the Road Runners offered. I mean, my God, I've already made more than Meryl Streep in the past three years. I'll have to settle for thanking my mom by putting her in a mansion."

"Can't argue with that."

"I know. It just feels like I sold out for money. The worst part is the fire still rages within me. I want to win an Oscar—I don't think that desire will ever leave me."

"And maybe you will one day. You're already climbing the ranks. The Angels at the top get to do whatever they want. Maybe you'll make a connection in Hollywood *because* you're a Road Runner. Don't give up on your dreams."

"Oh? And what are *your* dreams?"

Felix tossed his hands in the air. "To become a billionaire." He laughed. "I know that sounds silly, but I see these guys who create websites or apps and become billionaires. And I'm so much smarter than them. And I want to do it the hard way, not by cheating with my time travel abilities. Obviously, I could have a billion dollars tomorrow if I really wanted, but it's the journey I want—the challenge."

"A billionaire? Wow, that's definitely ambitious. And do you know what you would do with all that money?"

Felix shrugged. "Donate it. I don't need it. I'd probably start some scholarship programs and open better schools in low-

26

income areas. My parents did everything they could to make sure I had the best education—sounds like they had a lot in common with your mom. The hardest part about all of this has been keeping my life a secret. We're a close family and know everything about each other, but I know my parents just won't understand the Road Runners or time travel. So I tell them I work as a software engineer for Google. When they ask about work, I just speak technical jargon until they lose interest."

Selena laughed. "Well played. I've just told my parents that I'm struggling in Hollywood. They think I'm waiting tables at night and doing auditions all day. I guess at some point I'll have to change my story to explain why I drive a Lamborghini. But until then, I'll let the good times fly. Another round?"

Felix examined his cup as if he had forgotten about it. "Okay, sure."

Selena grinned, oblivious to the baseball game happening in the background, and slapped her hand on Felix's shoulder. "I'm glad to be on your team," she said. "It should be interesting to see what Arielle thinks about working with us, but I get the sense that neither of us really gives a shit."

Felix laughed. "I'm just here to do my job."

"I'll be right back with our drinks," Selena said, turning away and pushing through the crowd toward the bar. She already felt better about Felix after having cracked his hard exterior. Her father had once told her that if you wanted to know a person's true self, give them a couple of drinks. She'd yet to see that plan fail, and with it, looked forward to working with her new teammate.

27

Chapter 5

Commander Briar called for a meeting in his office the next morning, inviting the new super-team to gather in the same room for the first time. Arielle arrived first, eager to learn what her next mission would be, curious how things would work with a permanent team in place. For all of her career with the Road Runners, she never had to worry about developing chemistry with those working on missions with her. She rarely had to mingle with the advance team and never had to consider others when diving headfirst into a mission.

"Excited?" Commander Briar asked from behind his desk, his eyes drawn to the computer screen in front of him.

"I don't know why I feel a little nervous," Arielle replied from the wall she was leaning against.

"I know why. Ever since you lost your family, you've done a good job of closing yourself off to others. This new structure is forcing people into your circle, and I apologize for that. But understand that we are doing this in the best interest of our members and the entire organization. Our top talent was too widespread, either physically or logistically. This is more about refining our ways."

"No need to apologize, Commander. I understand, and I know I'll be fine. It's just a big change."

"I'm sure there will be kinks to work out in the beginning, but in the long run, I think we'll all look back and won't believe it took us so long to do things this way."

A knock came from the door.

"Come on in!" Commander Briar shouted, and the door swung open to reveal Selena and Felix. "Have a seat, you two." The commander waited for them to take their places, Felix dropping a briefcase on the floor. "I can't believe this is finally happening. Arielle, meet your new team, Felix and Selena."

Arielle stepped forward and shook their hands. "Good to see you, Felix. Selena, I've heard so much about your work—looking forward to teaming up with you."

"Likewise," Selena replied with a soft smile.

"Alright," Commander Briar said. "Before we jump into the details of your first mission together, does anyone have questions?"

"Not a question, Commander," Arielle said. "But I want to say something to the team. I want you to know that I have been riding solo for a long time. I've gotten used to doing things a certain way, but please don't think I'm closed-minded. I'm always open to feedback and new ideas. Don't be intimidated by my status as top Angel—if you think we can do something a better way, then just say it. This goes for our work and for me as a person. I'm not interested in drama or tension, and just want a solid relationship where we can all work in harmony."

Felix and Selena didn't reply, but only gave quick nods, and Arielle immediately worried that she had come off as too aggressive.

Commander Briar recognized the awkwardness in the room. "I think what Arielle is trying to say is just talk to her. Open communication is key. I've had plenty of discussions with all three of you, and it's clear this whole thing is going to have a learning curve. You're going to figure out how to work together, but it takes time. You might each have to make sacrifices based on the way you've done things before, but as long as you arrive at solutions as a team, I don't foresee any problems."

Arielle leaned back on the wall, feeling like the first day of school when she had to make new friends. How was anyone supposed to know, upon first impressions, if they were making the right choice? Could personal friendships blossom in forced professional relationships? It had certainly happened in the past, but so had shoddy relationships and rivalries. If they were going to all work together for the foreseeable future, then Arielle wanted personal relationships. True chemistry came from a deeper understanding of one another. What made these people tick? What did they like, or hate?

"Understood," Felix said.

"I'm not intimidated by anything," Selena said. "So you don't have to worry about me. I'll call you out if needed."

"Well then," Commander Briar said. "Let's talk about the mission, shall we?" He closed his laptop screen and reached into his desk drawer to retrieve a file, dropping it on top of the desk. He flipped it open and splayed out three different pictures of a chubby middle-age man with pale skin, a receding hairline, and stubble peppered across his jaw. "This is Mason Gregory. In 1988, this man was found shot to death in his car in the middle of nowhere. He left no paper trail, but the murder makes us believe he was killed for a reason. That's where we come in. Our primary focus is to save his life. His family fell into a tailspin afterward. Kids grew up to be drug addicts, wife suffered from lifelong depression. The murder really rippled through Mason's community."

"Sorry, Commander, you haven't mentioned where this is," Arielle said.

"Apologies. This is somewhat local. Pueblo, Colorado."

"So this is it?" Selena asked. "Just stopping a murder for this random guy? Was he even important?"

"Sorry to burst your bubble, Ms. Nicole, but not every mission is going to be high-profile. Mason worked for a credit card processing company in Pueblo to take care of his wife and two kids. A family man, from what we've gathered. A *regular* man."

"So, why does this warrant our attention?" Selena asked. "Even if missions aren't high profile, I've at least always worked on ones that have a widespread impact."

"I don't appreciate you undermining the work we are doing. The range of impact for a particular mission should make no difference to you. And this murder affected the entire town. Back then, they were a much more tight-knit community. Mrs. Gregory and the police department had made some false accusations that caused others around town to attack innocent people over rumors they heard. They never found the actual killer. That information is *not* our priority, but naturally something you'll figure out if you successfully stop this murder from happening. Think of this mission as a practice run for you as a new team. We aren't going to just thrust you into something magnificent on your first go-round. Learn how each of you works. Learn your strengths and weaknesses, both individually and as a team. If you don't like it, Ms. Nicole, then we can put you on the next flight to Hollywood to figure out your life from there."

Commander Briar leaned back and crossed his arms, his lips

pursed tightly. Selena said nothing and allowed the room to hang in awkward silence before Arielle spoke up.

"When do we start?" she asked.

Commander Briar broke his stare-down with Selena and looked at his top agent. "Whenever you'd like. That's probably up to Felix to decide how much time he needs to get weapons and other matters in place."

"I have fast access to weapons in pretty much any year," Felix said. "I have a guy in the Springs—not too far from Pueblo. We can stop on the way and load up."

"We're driving together?" Selena asked, disgust buried beneath her appalled tone.

"Why wouldn't we?" Felix asked. "We're working as a team now. It's up to Arielle how far back we should start."

"I like doing two weeks prior to the murder," Arielle replied. "In my experience, that is plenty of time to figure out what is going on and stop it."

Felix pulled out a notepad from his briefcase and started writing.

"If we can have the file, Commander, we can grab a conference room and start planning out the mission," Arielle said.

"Eager as always," the commander said. "But not so fast. I want to make sure you three are all aware of your specific roles. Felix, you will get the weapons, clothing, and handle any bugging of necessary properties. Selena, you will immerse yourself in Pueblo for those two weeks and learn everything you can about Mason through his wife, Lindsay. And Arielle, you handle the items on the down-low—scout suspects, follow leads, whatever it takes. Are we clear?"

"Understood, sir," Arielle said.

Commander Briar shifted his glare to Selena, who only

responded with a nod.

"Perfect," the commander said, closing the file and sliding it across the desk. "The mission is all yours."

Chapter 6

Arielle marched down the hallway with her new teammates by her side, all heads in the office's bullpen following them, as they had never seen such a group of high-profile Angel Runners together at once.

The main conference room was still occupied by the Council, a group of seven Road Runners who served as a sort of Supreme Court for the organization. The Revolution had destroyed their original offices in New York toward the end of the war, and their new location in eastern Washington State was still under construction. Arielle chose the conference room next door to the Council, a smaller space with a lone table, six surrounding chairs, and a 70-inch flat-screen TV hanging on the wall.

They entered, and she closed the door, giving them complete privacy within the frosted glass windows that served as walls. She dropped the file on the table and leaned back into a seat across from Felix. Selena had taken her place at the end of the oval table.

"Before we jump into the mission details," Arielle started. "I think we should talk about how we like to do our work. Let's get an understanding of each other's styles."

"What's there to understand?" Selena asked. "We're all the best at what we do. Let's do our thing and kill bad guys."

"It's not that straightforward," Arielle replied, stuffing her hand into her pocket to pull out a pack of gum, quickly popping two pieces into her mouth. She liked to chew gum when she wasn't in a peaceful state of mind, and Selena seemed set on pushing her buttons at every opportunity. "Felix, you do all the prep work. Are the two weeks enough time for you, honestly?"

"They are. When missions get dumped on my calendar, I typically work with one week before they set the agent to jump in. Two weeks is perfect."

"And you, Selena?"

"I can make it work."

"Okay," Arielle said. "Let's plan for an arrival two weeks before the murder. After we're done, we can evaluate and see what we liked and didn't like, and make adjustments from there. We don't have to set anything in stone. Obviously, for these smaller missions, two weeks should suffice, but at some point we're going to get a big one, and that can require anywhere from six months to a year."

"You've spent a year on a mission?!" Felix asked, shaking his head. "I can't even comprehend working on one mission for that long. What was it?"

"Two snipers in D.C. killed ten people over three weeks. In 2002, I believe."

"And you needed a whole *year*?"

"Well, keep in mind, the bigger the event, the more resis-tance I get from the past. I have to literally tiptoe around the event and the suspects before making a move. It's never as simple as finding the suspect and shooting them dead. The past doesn't allow that. See, we don't just fight the bad guys, we are fighting the past trying to preserve itself."

"The past is the hardest puzzle to crack," Felix said, staring blankly at the wall.

"The point is—this is a long, dangerous process. That's why it's important to not tinker with anything in the past. We all need to gather the materials and information we need, and I have to figure out how to best use it without the past trying to throw at us every roadblock it can."

"You know," Selena said. "We can help. Well, I can't speak for Felix, but I am comfortable helping you. My role required I go through the same field training as you."

"Good to know," Arielle said. "Hopefully it doesn't come to that, but I'll keep it in mind."

"And I'm just fine staying behind the scenes," Felix said.

"Let's talk about Mason Gregory then," Arielle said, opening the file to a picture of the heavyset man standing in front of a grill loaded with burgers and hot dogs while he smiled over his shoulder with a spatula in hand.

"What a horrendous name," Selena said, more to herself, scrunching her face as if she had just tasted something sour.

Arielle glanced up, but paid her no attention. "Mr. Gregory had two kids with his wife. Amanda, aged six. David, aged three. He lived in Pueblo and worked at CreditConnect, a credit card processing firm. This job was also in Pueblo, so we believe he spent nearly all of his time in town. However, authorities found him dead in eastern Pueblo, nowhere near his house or office. Police reports contained interviews with the wife, and she had no idea why her husband would have been in that area."

"An affair?" Felix asked.

"The wife says not likely, but isn't that the point? We'll investigate an affair, but I also want us to keep our eyes open for drugs. Whether that was him using or involved in some sort of dealing ring."

"I don't know," Selena said. "Seems there can be all kinds of possibilities. Sounds just far enough for privacy, but not far enough to arouse any suspicions at home. He could make it home in a hurry if needed."

"Could he have been living a double life?" Felix asked. "I know that seems absurd to us today, but think back before social media and cell phones—it would have been much easier to get away with that sort of thing."

Arielle shrugged. "These are all excellent suggestions, and hopefully we'll be able to figure it out after a couple of days of tailing this guy. I'm thinking we find a place to stay together. Probably a hotel with adjoining rooms, or even a house, if we can find something that works—the Road Runners have no problems with buying properties in the past and flipping them in the future."

"You tell me," Felix said. "I've handled plenty of real estate transactions for the Road Runners."

Arielle rubbed her chin as she thought. "Let's plan for it. We can stay in a hotel while you and Selena pretend to be a couple looking for a new home."

"I don't really think that's necessary," Felix said. "I can get a home on my own, no problem. And within a day."

"Well, you're quite the Eighties man," Selena said. "Can do it all yourself."

Felix chuckled. "It's not like that. I'm just saying, we have unlimited resources. It's not like I need a co-signer or something to buy a house. If you want to buy the house, go for it."

"Unfortunately, Selena makes a valid point," Arielle said. "It's the Eighties, and if a woman tries to buy a house on her own, it will draw suspicion. Keep in mind, this won't even be two decades after women were *allowed* to get a mortgage without a male co-signer. Even though it's legal in 1988, there was still discrimination."

"So we're just going to roleplay and pretend to be some strange family who lives together?" Selena asked, crossing her arms.

"Exactly."

Selena rolled her eyes as she looked to the ceiling, remaining silent. It had quickly become apparent that Selena kept people on their toes, and left many wondering what exactly was happening inside her head. Arielle supposed that was simply the nature of a talented actress.

"I think we should do a house," Arielle said. "Hotels don't make it easy to mingle with the locals, and we're too many for an apartment. Felix, think you can have a house purchased within three days?"

Felix snorted. "With a duffel bag of cash, I can have a house in three hours."

"That won't be necessary. I still want you to take your time and find something that works for what we need. We need to be within a fifteen-minute drive of our target's home and work. We shouldn't face any major streets or highways. And we need as few neighbors as possible, preferably none if we can swing it."

Felix nodded as he jotted this information down. "I'll see what I can find. May take me longer than a couple of hours—they didn't exactly have Zillow back then, so I need to drive around or speak with a local realtor, if that's okay?"

"I'm fine if you work with a realtor who isn't popular. Well-known realtors know everyone in town—we can't have that.

Find someone new and inexperienced—you just need them to find out what houses are available for sale. And come up with a backstory for why you are buying. Something that keeps suspicions low."

Felix parted his lips, but remained silent as all color flushed from his face.

"Is something wrong?" Arielle asked.

"I-I just don't know how to do all that. I normally tell them I moved to town for a new job, and that's it. Never had to worry about so many rules, let alone a backstory."

"I'll help you," Selena said. "That's literally the first part of my job—creating a massive backstory for who I am and why I'm in town."

"Perfect," Arielle said. "Do you two want to work on that now? I need to head home to pack some things before we start this mission."

"We can do that," Felix said. "And I'll head into the past this afternoon to start the home search. Let's tentatively plan for two days from now to start the mission."

"Friday it is. I'll text you both my phone number—if anything comes up or you have questions, just let me know."

"Thanks, Arielle," Felix said, watching her pack the papers back into the file and sliding it across the table to him.

"You hold on to that file. We'll review it more once we're in 1988 Pueblo, but I think we're at a good starting point for now. Talk to you guys soon."

Chapter 7

Arielle stormed out of the headquarters with her head down to avoid conversation with anyone who might want to strike up a chat with the organization's top agent. She had kept her composure in the conference room, something she had no problem doing, but deep inside, her stomach churned. And once she stepped outside, her arms immediately trembled.

The meeting felt forced, unnatural. Too much talent had been gathered in the same room, and Selena had an ego that Arielle simply couldn't dismiss. They were bound to clash.

She debated calling Commander Briar to express her concerns, but already knew his response. They hadn't even started the mission yet, hadn't given it a fair shot working together as a super team. He wouldn't budge on this new experiment for the Angels, and she was stuck figuring out how to best make it work.

"It's just part of the job," she muttered under her breath as she started down the sidewalk toward Sixteenth Street Mall to grab lunch. She had gained so much freedom and flexibility in her role that she often forgot she was indeed working a job, no matter how unconventional it may be. She still had to report to someone and take orders without question. It was more like the military than a corporate job.

"Just one mission," she whispered to herself as she tore down the sidewalk, still fighting to get her arms under control. Few things bothered Arielle as much as unnecessary change. Everything had been working up to this point in her career as an Angel, so why the sudden decision to throw a wrench into their system? Her new team had no natural chemistry, and while it could develop over time, she had a hard time imagining it. It reminded her of the times in middle school when a teacher would assign groups for a project, and everyone came together and pushed through as quickly as possible. All to return to their usual bubbles and not having to mingle with others.

Arielle had already walked two of the four blocks between the office and the mall, increasing her pace with each step while the whirlwind of thoughts and doubts swirled in her mind like a hurricane.

A shriek echoed down the alley on her left, freezing her mid-step as she snapped out of her trance and spun around. At the far end of the alley, about fifty yards away, a woman ran from a man wearing raggedy clothes. The woman tripped and fell, the man promptly lunging toward her, flailing for the woman's purse slung around her shoulder.

Without a second thought, Arielle broke into a sprint toward the mugging, the brick exterior of the surrounding buildings passing by her vision in a blurry reddish-brown. "Hey!" she screamed, closing the distance in a hurry. "Get off her!"

Once Arielle was within fifteen feet, the man moved into a crouched position and looked over his shoulder, his eyes immediately widening as Arielle leapt into the air, rearing one foot back and thrusting it crisply into the man's forehead.

His head jerked sideways as the strength in his body vanished, leaving him to tip over and collapse beside the woman.

"Oh, my God!" the woman cried, scrambling to her feet. "I was running late from lunch and thought I'd take a shortcut through the alley. This guy jumped out from behind a dumpster and started chasing me." She looked down at the man, bobbing his head from side to side, while he mumbled incoherently. "Guess that's the last time I'll be taking shortcuts. Who are you?"

"My name is Arielle, and I've taken plenty of self-defense classes. I suggest you do the same. The world seems to get a little more dangerous each day."

"You can say that again. I could hardly see you because he was over me. Did you come flying out of the sky? One minute, I thought I was about to die, the next he's on the ground and you're standing behind him."

Arielle studied the woman. Middle-aged, clearly dressed for work in a button-up blouse, knee-length skirt, and high heels. "Did you say die?" she asked, scanning the man for a weapon, spotting a switchblade clutched in his hand. "I don't think so."

Arielle stepped toward the man and kicked the knife out of his hand, followed by a stomp on his face that sent a stream of blood from his nose.

The woman gawked at Arielle, jaw hanging open as she stared back at the man on the ground. She clutched her purse a little tighter, clearly intimidated by Arielle. "Do we need to call an ambulance for him?"

Arielle let out a faint giggle, quickly realizing that didn't help ease the woman's worries. "No, he'll be fine. Hopefully, he learned his lesson and won't try to mug women in the middle of the afternoon!" She directed this last sentence toward the man, shouting it to ensure he heard her within his daze.

The man moaned as he continued to rock his head, eyes

42

barely open while he rubbed his face with one hand and his shoulder with the other.

"See. He's alive," Arielle said. "Nothing to see here. You can get back to work now. Sorry this asshole tried to ruin your day."

The woman turned and took one step away before stopping and spinning back around to face her heroine. "I don't know who you are—or if you're even real—but thank you."

Arielle couldn't help but let a laugh slip out. "You think I'm part of your imagination?"

"No. I see you standing right in front of me. Maybe you're a guardian angel or something. You look way too sweet to kill grown men with your bare hands."

"Well, I can assure you I'm a just a regular person. Happy I could help."

The woman gave a tight-lipped grin before returning to work. Arielle remained standing over the moaning man.

"Are you homeless?" Arielle asked him, her shadow covering his face as he opened his eyes and allowed them a moment to focus. She already knew the answer, judging by the man's tattered pants and scattered holes across his shoes. His eyes had welled with tears that he promptly blinked away.

"Yes," he said. "I'm sorry."

Arielle offered her hand to the man. He stared at it for at least twenty seconds, looking from it to her face, trying to gauge his next move. He eventually gave in and grabbed it, Arielle pulling him up to his feet.

"You don't need to apologize to me, but you should have to that poor woman. You may have just changed her life forever. Now she'll always walk around looking over her shoulder, paranoid that she's going to be attacked. For the rest of her life. Can you believe that? *You* did that." She jabbed a stern finger into the man's chest, a move that caused him to flinch.

"I'm sorry, lady. I just wanted to take my girlfriend out for a nice date night. Dinner and a movie."

"And you felt this was the best way to go about it? Robbing an innocent woman on her way to work? What were you going to do with that knife?"

He shook his head, avoiding eye contact with Arielle as he gazed at the ground, licking his dried and cracked lips. "I've never hurt no one. Just use it to scare people."

She studied the man, sensing genuine guilt and regret for what had just unfolded. She had spent enough time in downtown Denver to understand there were a wide range of causes behind the growing homeless population. For many, it was a choice. Those who chose this lifestyle rarely caused a stir. The man in front of her, however, radiated desperation and shame.

"Look at me," Arielle demanded. The man lifted his head until their eyes met. Behind the fear and struggle, she saw a broken man. Everyone faced some demons in their life, and some people let those demons get the best of them. "You've already proven today you can change a life. You have that capability. Put that same energy into yourself, and I know you'll be able to turn your life around. It's never too late."

The man's eyes welled again, prompting Arielle to shake her head.

"Stop crying. I'm sure you've had plenty of time to feel bad for yourself."

The man sniffled and watched cautiously as Arielle reached into her pocket. She pulled out a small wallet and opened it up, flipping through a thin wad of cash.

Arielle whipped out a bill and held it in front of the man's face, showing a clear look at Benjamin Franklin. "Go have your date night. Take your girlfriend to see a movie, then go to dinner somewhere you can sit down. I want you two to talk about the next steps you're going to take to get your life back. I know you weren't always in this position, but you can get back. Fight for your life while you're still on Earth. Are we clear?"

"Yes, ma'am," he said, studying the hundred-dollar bill before Arielle forced it into his hands. "Thank you."

"I never want to see you again. Good luck."

The man gulped before he spun around and ran off, limping every other step until he disappeared from the alley and returned to the bustle of downtown Denver. Arielle watched him the whole way, arms crossed and head shaking, thinking about an ex-boyfriend from years long gone.

Chapter 8

"You're telling me you've never wanted to pretend to be someone else?" Selena asked Felix. They had remained in the same conference room to hash out details for the upcoming mission.

"I guess not. Don't see why I would pretend to be something I'm not."

"But you've gone on these missions before. And you just tell them you want to buy a house? Don't they ask you questions?"

"Sure, and I tell them the truth. I'm in town for an indefinite amount of time. I'm from Denver and need a place to live. Not interested in paying rent. And that's always been enough."

Selena shook her head in amazement at how long Felix Francisco had survived taking dangerous trips into the past. Amazed at how any human on the planet could simply go about life and everyday interactions as the happy-go-lucky guy he seemed to be.

Since acting had been flowing through her veins at a young age, perhaps Selena couldn't relate to others who lacked the same passion. She, too, knew herself and was comfortable in her own skin, but she had an obsession with acting. Trying to figure out the best way to portray a character and bring them to life required patience and precision. Most of all, it gave her a rush each time. She was always herself around family and friends, but meeting new people always presented an opportunity to test out her skills.

"You've never even gone to a bar, met a girl, and told her a little white lie to get her interested?" Selena asked.

Felix shrugged. "I rarely go to bars. And why would I want to start off a relationship with a lie?"

Selena clenched her fists. "Acting isn't lying. It's an *art*. No different from a painter, writer, or musician trying to capture a moment in life."

"I get that, but if you go around pretending to be someone else, how is anyone supposed to get close if they don't know who you really are?"

Felix always spoke in such a calm tone, regardless of the topic. It drove Selena mad how he could sit there so nonchalantly, while her emotions boiled within.

"Whatever. Let's talk about your backstory."

"Fine with me."

Selena scoffed. "The purpose of creating a backstory is to make you seem three-dimensional. You've probably been going around on your trips like a pretty generic person."

"Isn't that what I want, though? To be forgettable so they never think about me again?"

"It depends who you're dealing with. Another aspect of acting is to feed off your surroundings, and that includes the people you encounter. People remember others who are just like them. In your line of work, yes, it is important to be forgotten, and that will be easier to achieve if you understand your backstory. Say you played sports growing up. If you find yourself in a conversation with someone in the past and that comes up, avoid discussing it to make yourself more forgettable. Compared to meeting someone who was focused on theater in high school, there's no harm in you mentioning that you played sports."

Felix nodded. "Okay. Makes sense. So what should I use in my backstory?"

"Since you can likely get away with being the same 'character' each time you make a trip into the past, you're honestly fine using your personal history as your backstory. That way you don't have to keep track of details that aren't true of yourself. Your biggest focus should be on knowing when to chime in with something, and when not to."

"So I just have to be myself? And this is all you did to become the best scout in the organization?"

Selena offered a crooked grin. "It's a lot more complex for me, mind you. I interact with a variety of people on each mission. I need to fit in with groups of people who are nothing like me. I need to be accepted by them if I want any chance of learning valuable information they would otherwise keep secret from strangers. I've portrayed bartenders, churchgoers, strippers, book club members, engineers. Hell, anything you can think of from all sorts of eras in time. I have hundreds of backstories that I've used, all while juggling how to best use my character to get what we need from locals."

"Can't lie—I'm impressed. Never realized how much thought went into what you do. All my work can get so technical, I guess I never imagined that anyone else had to think so much to make these missions work."

"My work may not require the level of technical education like yours, but there is plenty that goes into it. More than meets the eye. I suppose it's like anything else. Those who have mastered their craft can make it seem easy to do. In reality, it's just years of practice to reach that point."

Felix nodded. "I've learned a lot already from this conversation. Excited to put it to use."

"Oh, good! When do you think you'll head to 1988?"

"Later today. Need to tend to a couple of matters for the mission before jumping back. Probably need to circle back with Arielle one more time."

"Ahh, yes. Queen Arielle. What do you think of her?"

Felix let out a nearly inaudible laugh. "I've worked with her before. This isn't something new for me."

"Then humor me. Tell me what it's like."

"You don't like her. You make it obvious."

"I like her just fine. I'm just not a person who automatically bows down and gives respect to someone based on their title. Respect should always be earned, especially by people with as much power as Arielle Lucila."

"And you're not going to tell her this?"

"I don't have to tell her anything. A true leader exposes their character to you, not the other way around. So we'll get to see soon if she's the real deal or not. I suspect she is, but I want the proof."

"Well, I've worked with her, and I can vouch she *is* the real deal. She has a rare combination of confidence and humility. Strength and intelligence. It's kind of intimidating to be around someone who can change the direction of your life."

"Felix, darling, there is no need to ever be intimidated by another human being. Regardless of the person they might seem on the surface, they are regular people like you and I. Everyone has skills, flaws, passions, and fears. Even Arielle. I'm sure within the next month we'll all get to learn those about each other. And that's the beauty of life, isn't it? Celebrating one another despite our flaws and differences."

She caught Felix with a distant gaze as he calculated a response. Selena had spent plenty of time around other brainiacs, and while she admired their self-control during conversation, she rarely lost an argument. They were too busy thinking, talking themselves out of each response until they found the perfect one.

"Look," she said. "I've followed Arielle's career. She's incredible. She sets the bar for the rest of us. Professionally, she's everything we strive to be. But with these new permanent teams, our relationships are going to become more than professional. It's about to get very personal, so I hope you're ready to open up. I know that's a traumatic thought for you, but I'm just warning—it's coming."

"I would never. Work is work and life is life. The two never have to intertwine."

"You keep thinking that. But it's going to be weeks of *living* together. At some point, the conversation around the mission is going to run out and we'll start talking about life. How we got here. Where we want to go. Our childhoods and hometowns. It's natural for people who spend a lot of time together to discuss these things. You already started telling me about yourself at that awful baseball game. I know your type."

Felix snorted. "You know nothing about me."

"There are only a few personalities in the world, Felix. Let me guess. You're a closed box who never tells anyone about your feelings. You can probably count your friends on one hand. And there's nothing wrong with that, because your friends are likely high-quality—always there when you need them. Your family and friends are the only ones who know the real you. Only they don't. Because the way you think of yourself is so much bigger than anything they could imagine. You're not just good at your job—you're the best. Yet, you don't have to proclaim it—you just show up and work every day. Your actions speak on your behalf. You want someone to share your life with beyond the holidays and random nights out with friends. You want someone there all the time to share your incredible success with."

Selena paused and stared at Felix, his jaw hanging open. "I . . . uh."

"You don't have to say anything. I know I'm right. See, part of acting is understanding the personalities of the world. Not just how to portray them, but how to interact with them. That's something I've understood from a very young age and a reason I had the success I did as an actress. I started studying the psychology of personalities in middle school and analyzed everyone I met—still do."

"People aren't that simple. Humans are more complex than that."

"They are, but also, they aren't. There are only so many combinations of personalities that exist. And humans will often have a bit of each within them, pulling out different ones in unique situations. But we always return to our home base. We can't run from ourselves."

Felix scratched his head. "What you say makes sense, but you can't reduce me to something you read in a book."

"I'm not reducing you to anything. I just understand what makes you tick. I know your buttons, if you will. There is more to you than everything I just mentioned. But I also know once you trust me and Arielle, you're going to open up and tell us everything about yourself. That could take months or years, but it will happen. You know it, and I know it."

Felix pursed his lips and nodded. "Okay. I don't want to talk about this anymore. I need to get ready for this mission and buy this house. But I'm sure you knew I was going to say that."

Selena giggled. "I'm not a psychic, but thanks for the flattery. I'm sorry if it disturbed you, but now you know a little about me."

"Sure do. I know I'm not gonna say a damn thing around you that isn't work-related. You and Arielle can do as you please, but I still plan on keeping my life to myself."

"Okay then," Selena said, crossing the room to the door and opening it. "I'll just get out of your way, Mr. Francisco, and let you do your work. See you when the mission starts."

Selena stepped out and slammed the door shut behind her, knowing that simple act would cause Felix's mind to stir in a frenzy.

Chapter 9

A knock on the door startled Felix after his mind wandered for the last five minutes. Selena had left in a rage, and he couldn't figure out what exactly he had done to spark it.

"Come in," he said, hoping it was Selena returning to apologize. Instead, he saw Commander Briar and immediately jumped out of his chair, circling the table to meet him at the door. "Is everything okay, Commander?"

Their leader rose a calming hand. "Nothing to worry about. May we come in?"

Felix craned his neck for a look and saw a short man hiding behind the commander. He was young, college-aged, with spiked black hair.

A new recruit, Felix thought.

"I saw Selena leave, and figured you were getting ready to start the mission," Commander Briar said. "Was hoping to catch you before you jump back in time. This is Eddie Alvarado. We just recruited him from Nicaragua, and he's spending the next month shadowing our team here at headquarters."

"Nice to meet you, Eddie," Felix said, extending a hand. "My family is originally from Colombia, so we're not too far from you."

"Beautiful," Eddie replied, his accent strong but clear. "My family used to vacation in Santa Marta every summer when I was a kid. We took a cruise from Nicaragua across the Caribbean. One of my fondest memories from childhood."

"Oh, how cool!"

"Sounds look you two will hit it off just fine," Commander Briar interjected. "Felix, I've brought Eddie to spend just the initial part of this mission with you. I want him to see how the setup process works upon our arrival into a new era."

Felix felt his palms become slick with sweat. "Wait, so he's going to be by my side while I buy the house?"

"Yes, is that a problem?"

"No, sir. Just making sure I'm clear on the instruction."

Everything was changing since the war had ended. Commander Briar's top priority was to increase recruitment efforts, and that meant more training. Now Felix had to adjust his plans to factor in having someone by his side.

Another backstory.

"Perfect," the commander said. "Once you buy the house, send Eddie back here and he will shadow elsewhere."

"Understood."

"I'll leave you to it," Commander Briar said, patting Felix on the shoulder before leaving the conference room.

"Let's head out," Felix said, starting down the hall. "We have to drive to Pueblo."

Eddie stayed by Felix's side as they stepped outside and walked down the block to Felix's car.

"Whoa," Eddie said, stopping as Felix unlocked the car. "This is what you drive?"

Eddie whistled as he squatted to admire an all-black 2020 Mustang Shelby GT500.

"Was my dream car for the longest time," Felix said. "She's

my baby. But it's not what we're driving today. We're traveling to 1988 and need to blend in. Can't exactly roll down the street in this thing." Felix reached in and pulled out his backpack, slinging it over his shoulder before locking the car again. "We're taking that one." Felix nodded to a silver car parked two spaces in front of the Mustang. "A 1985 Acura Integra."

Eddie threw his head back and laughed. "Well, that's a bummer, but it makes sense."

They got into the Acura and Felix fired it up, giving a minute for the engine to warm up. "So what kind of role are you looking for with the Road Runners?" They pulled onto Blake Street.

"I was actually a driver and a realtor in Nicaragua before getting recruited. Commander Briar wants me to handle real estate for select parts of Central America and the Caribbean. I volunteered my driving services, but he said there isn't much of a need for that."

"Interesting," Felix said. "Sounds like we're becoming a lot more business-focused. Did he mention what sort of real estate?"

Eddie shrugged. "I'm not sure. I've gone through the basic training and orientation, and now he wants me to shadow multiple teams across the continent to see if my skills might plug into other areas as well. He was adamant about me joining you on this part of your mission, since you'll be buying a house."

Felix pulled the car onto the freeway and floored the accelerator as they started their trip to Pueblo. "That's funny, because I don't consider myself an expert on real estate by any means."

"Well, how many transactions have you done?"

"Somewhere around twenty."

"And you never work with a realtor?"

"Only the selling agent."

"Mr. Francisco, my friend, you're an expert, even if you don't know it. No one makes that many real estate transactions without knowing what they're doing."

"I've never thought of it that way. I'm not exactly negotiating—we have unlimited funds, so I just pay whatever the asking value is."

Eddie nodded. "The commander mentioned that. He's wanting to do more with our real estate. Says there's a lot of unused property. So I think he's more interested in selling."

After the war, the organization outlined plans to generate more funds aside from playing the stock market in the past. Having a team of in-house realtors would make that easier. The organization was growing, and that meant more exorbitant signing bonuses for people to leave their regular lives behind and dedicate to a life of secrecy.

"Do you have your Juice?" Felix asked.

Eddie stuck his hand into his pocket and pulled out a bottle no bigger than the miniature shooters you could buy at the liquor store. A light purple liquid swirled around inside.

"That tiny bottle is all they give you?" Felix asked with a chuckle.

Eddie grinned. "Oh, no. I have my big one at home. They required us to travel with the smaller one and leave the big one behind. Something about an incident where a lady dumped her Juice and vanished into the future."

"Wow. I didn't realize there was a new rule about that. Must only apply to new bottles of Juice, because I haven't heard of that."

"So you know the story behind it?"

"It's a long one. We'll have to chat about it another time."

"I haven't time traveled in quite a while. All of our training was physical and educational—nothing with time travel itself."

Felix furrowed his brow. "You haven't taken a sip on your own? You don't need permission to time travel, only to do missions."

"I understand. But I haven't done it since the day I got my Juice."

Felix thought back to his days of training. Depending on the type of work a recruit wanted, the training program could take anywhere from four months to two years. Even if Eddie was on the lower end of that scale, it seemed absurd for someone new to the world of time travel to have no interest in visiting different eras. "Why not?" he asked, not sure what else to say.

Eddie shook his head. "It's odd. Going through the transition, or whatever it is. Arriving in a new world—an *old* world—and breathing in the air. For the life of me, I can't wrap my head around it. Part of me thinks I've died. And there are too many rules—I'm scared to mess anything up. The last time I went back to 1954, I saw my grandmother as a teenager. She spoke to me, and we talked for ten minutes. The experience was . . . life-changing. But it scared me. I can't process it."

"Look, Eddie, I think any Road Runner you meet has gone through similar thoughts. It all seems like something out of a cheap film, but it's real. You need to be careful if you go into the past and interact with your family. The simplest thing can lead to you not existing. Say that conversation you had with your grandmother prevented her from crossing paths with your grandfather. Just like that, you could stop existing. That's why you'll hear most people don't even take the risk. And if they do, they keep a safe distance to avoid interaction."

"What happens if you prevent your own existence?"

"You die. See, the past is sensitive. Your life exists in the past and has branched into several possibilities for your future. The time we're in right now, we call it Original Time—some refer to it as Real Time. If you die in the past, you die in your Original Time. That's why it's important to prepare for these missions to ensure maximum safety. One slip on these missions can end it all for you."

Eddie nodded. "And that's what scares me. I'm comfortable in my Original Time. I know this world and the safe places—and dangerous places. Staying in the present is low-risk. Once I venture into the past, I'm basically a tourist in a foreign country."

"Then travel to a safe time. We know history—pick an event and check it out. Be a spectator. You don't have to speak to anyone or do anything. Just check out the world and come right back."

"I've thought about that, but it seems like a waste of Juice."

Felix shook his head. "You can't waste Juice. When you run out, they just get you a fresh bottle. We have the Book of Time, thanks to winning the war, and can now produce all the Juice we want. In fact, I'm surprised that wasn't the first team Commander Briar started with. He had mentioned dedicating a new location to strictly produce Juice."

"Maybe he needs the real estate first," Eddie said with a crooked grin.

"Very good." Eddie was growing on Felix. He rarely enjoyed meeting new people, and especially dreaded being forced to mingle with a stranger. But Eddie had a natural calm about him, a welcoming aura. "Do you have questions on the basics before we hop back in time?"

Eddie squirmed in his seat and fiddled with his fingers. "Honestly, Mr. Francisco, I need a refresher on *everything*. There are so many rules—I don't know how you all keep track of them so easily. You make sure every piece of the plan is in place before the other team members get there—weapons, passports, finances... there's so much to learn. I suppose it doesn't help that I haven't time traveled in so long."

"First off, just call me Felix. Please. As for the rules, it's best to learn them as you go. There are rules you may never encounter based on the type of work you do. The two biggest to keep in mind, however, are to never encounter your past—or future—self. And never stay beyond the point of your Original Time."

"So if I were to travel back to yesterday, I'd need to return before the day ends?"

"Exactly."

"Okay. And what happens if you don't?"

"Look, time travel is all fun and games as long as you respect the rules of time. We're dealing with multiple dimensions here. If you stay past your Original Time, you'll remain trapped forever. And that means there will be two of you existing in the same world at the same time. Remember, only ten minutes pass in our Original Time, regardless of how long you spend in the past or future. That means there is no reason you should ever allow it to become a close call. If you have business to tend to from the prior day, make multiple trips back and forth. It's just not worth it to get stuck. We've studied the Book of Time and this rule is confirmed—there's no way around it."

"And if I encounter myself?"

Felix twirled a finger beside his head. "You'll lose your mind.

59

A mental implosion is the best way to describe it. There have been a wide range of reports to what exactly happens. Some people turn violent and go postal. Others completely separate from reality and their life free falls out of control. Again, you're dealing with multiple dimensions, and the rules of time just can't allow one's past self to encounter their present self. Sadly, most of these time travelers who fall victim end up on the streets, walking in circles all day, talking to themselves about nonsense. The encounter completely damages their mental circuit board, if you will."

Eddie shuddered at the thought. "Say no more—I'm convinced. Last question before we jump back, what exactly are we able to change in the past?"

"You can *try* to change whatever you want. The bigger the event, or the more people an event had affected, will cause the past to resist your changes. History likes to preserve itself, especially the major moments. If I go back in time and change the color of the car I bought, not much is going to happen. But if I go back and try to change, say, a presidential election, my very life will be at risk. The past has no limits on what it will do to stay the same. That's why our missions are so thoroughly researched—we have to be ready for anything."

"And buying a house in the past is pretty straightforward?"

"Usually. As long as the house doesn't have some sort of historical significance, it's not considered a major event in world history."

Eddie nodded. "Okay, I think I'm ready."

Chapter 10

Arielle finally returned home after the excitement downtown. She had given up on lunch, losing her appetite after pounding the homeless man within an inch of his life. She had always tried to avoid the homeless population when strolling through downtown, not out of fear or elitism, but to avoid the emotions that accompanied witnessing someone living on the streets.

The drive home was a blank spot in her memory, her thoughts too consumed with her ex-boyfriend, Kevin Fletcher. Some moments in life were impossible to close the door on, and the chapter with Kevin had proven the most difficult for Arielle.

She parked her car in the garage of her tri-level home in the suburb of Thornton, Colorado. Arielle lived in a gated community with neighbors ranging from surgeons to attorneys to business executives. It was a quiet, upscale neighborhood, with plenty of luxury vehicles parked in the driveways, her BMW not out of place.

She slipped inside and kicked off her shoes, racing down the hallway toward her living room, where she dove onto the couch, trying to shake the ghost of Kevin.

He was still alive, as far as she knew, having lived on the streets for the past two years after getting kicked out of rehab for an opioid addiction. Their relationship had been strong and full of love before Kevin suffered a torn ACL while playing a club soccer game on campus.

As Arielle had learned, the addiction was not something that happened overnight. Everything had been fine through Kevin's surgery and recovery in physical therapy, which spanned eight months after the operation. He took two pain pills in the morning with breakfast, and two in the evening with his dinner, to allow for total comfort while fighting his way back to full strength. Kevin had been an athlete, playing multiple club sports, so no one expected a struggle in his recovery.

What Arielle didn't know—nor did anyone—was the increasing tolerance Kevin developed against the drugs. This led to him taking more than prescribed, and it started out innocently enough. Arielle had been by his side throughout most of the recovery, tending to him in his off-campus apartment after long days of classes. He'd complain of increasing pain and would pop an extra pill with dinner, sometimes before bed. She should have seen the signs, but by the time Kevin started taking ten pills each day, it was too late.

Arielle often beat herself up, still to this day, for not putting a stop to it. It had been the only regret in her young life, and she wondered at least once a week what her life would look like today had she put her foot down.

A tear streamed down her face, prompting her to jump off the couch and run up the stairs to her bedroom, barreling toward her closet as she swung the doors open and dropped to her knees, rummaging through a pile of shoes until finding an old tattered box against the back wall.

The box wasn't much bigger than a typical shoe box, and she pulled off the lid to find the remaining memories of her past relationship. She sifted through the photos of her and Kevin on various vacations they had taken during their four years together. Some showed them posing in front of major landmarks. The photo on top had the happy couple grinning in front of the Eiffel Tower.

Under the portraits were a couple of handwritten notes Kevin had penned during their college years, slipping them under her dorm room door in the middle of the night so she could wake up to a romantic greeting. He had written about a dozen notes like this, but only two had survived long enough to make it into the box.

She kept all the jewelry he had gifted her—necklaces, earrings, bracelets. He had always talked about finding the most special engagement ring when the time came.

The emotions had become too strong, so Arielle pulled out her cell phone and scrolled through her list of contacts, partly dreading, partly wanting to make a call she had done roughly once every three months. She found Riann Fletcher and tapped the name to dial while she stood to pace the room, waiting for an answer.

It rang four times. "Hello?" a tired voice answered, prompting Arielle to check the time, forgetting California was an hour behind. She often lost track of the date and time during her life as a time traveler.

"Hi, Riann. It's Arielle. . . how are you doing?"

"Arielle!" the voice immediately brightened up. "I'm doing okay. Always great to hear your voice. How are you?"

Even though she knew this phone call would stir up more emotions, Arielle felt instant relief at hearing Riann's optimism shine through the phone.

"I've been alright, drowning myself in work. Having an off

day, though. Passed by a homeless man, and it's made me think about *him*."

"Of course," Riann said, her voice softening. "Happens to me often, too."

"Have you heard from him lately?"

Kevin would randomly reach out to his mother, speaking with her two or three times a year for a few minutes. Sometimes from jail, other times from a stranger's cell phone. But only during the rare times he sobered up enough to think of calling.

"Heard from him a couple of months ago, actually. We talked for three minutes. He was at a park. Sounded okay, but I could tell he was still so far from himself. Still in San Francisco. Said the only other place he'd go live is San Diego, but that he was fine with things the way they are for now. I guess he made a friend with someone who runs one of the shelters and they guarantee him a bed at least three days a week."

The pain never stopped upon hearing the love of her life suffering in the world. Kevin went to school for marketing, and even dragged himself to the finish line of graduation. That summer, with internships and interviews lined up with seemingly every tech company in Silicon Valley, was when everything spiraled out of control.

"Well, that's good," Arielle said, glad to hear Kevin was still alive.

"I suppose. You know, they say the worst pain a parent can feel is having to bury their child. But let me tell you, I think this is much worse. My son is such a danger to himself and others that I can't even let him into my house. And because of that, I have to fall asleep every night knowing he's sleeping on a park bench where anything could happen. He could die at any moment, and I might never find out. Each time I hang up

64

the phone, I accept it may be the last time. I just don't know."

Riann's voice wavered, causing Arielle to break into fresh tears.

"I miss him," Arielle said, sniffling. "I miss what we had together. How he loved me and made me feel like the most important person in the world. We had our whole life planned out together."

Riann sighed. "If only we could go back in time and change it all."

Riann had no idea about the secret world of time travel. Arielle hadn't told anyone, not even her grandmother, who still lived in New Mexico. Kevin's injury happened shortly before Arielle had lost her entire family, and only a few weeks before the Road Runners had initially approached her.

She could have jumped back in time right after the injury happened and prevented it. In that moment, the change would have been minuscule, the past likely offering no fight since no one's life had been severely altered yet. But they didn't know what would come down the road, and once it did, it was too late. Arielle could count the number of mistakes she had made as a Road Runner on one hand, and trying to prevent Kevin's injury had been the biggest. She experienced firsthand what happened when you tried to change the past without a plan, and that made her never overlook another detail again.

"That would be nice," Arielle said, her leg bouncing out of control. "I guess all we can do now is hope for the best. There's always a chance he cleans himself up and gets back on his feet. It wouldn't be the first time something like that has happened."

"You're so positive, dear. I used to be, but it's hard for me to keep the hope. My son is gone, my husband is dead. I guess

I'm supposed to be alone in this world, and that's okay."

Arielle had no response. Riann had been alone ever since Kevin wound up on the streets. She couldn't make recurring visits to her once future mother-in-law, especially as she climbed the ranks within the Angels. The thought had crossed her mind on plenty of occasions of recruiting Riann to the Road Runners, but she brushed it away. Even with a beneficial background as a nurse, Riann would certainly spend all of her time trying to tinker with her past. Trying to bring back her husband and son would certainly kill her.

"I should get going, Riann. Thank you for talking with me—I needed to vent to someone who understands how I'm feeling. I'll call again soon."

"Of course, sweetie. Don't work too hard, and I'll look forward to our next chat. As always, you have a place to stay if you're in the area."

They hung up. Arielle stuffed the box of painful memories back into her closet, and collapsed onto her bed.

Chapter 11

Felix and Eddie sat in the parking lot of an abandoned gas station in Pueblo.

"I still don't understand," Eddie said. "We're about to go back in time to buy a house. It doesn't reset when we return to today?"

"Nothing ever resets," Felix explained. "We can go back in time and change things, and they will remain. Even when we jump back forward to our present day, the past will have caught up by the time we arrive. For example, say we went back in time and stopped Lincoln's assassination. That change will remain, and the history books will reflect it by the time we're back. It's perhaps one of the most fascinating parts of our work—changing things and coming back to learn how it affected the world we live in today. Commander Briar actually has an interesting story of when he went back to 1996 and stopped the Columbine shootings from happening."

"Columbine shootings?"

"My point exactly. How old are you, twenty-one?"

"I will be, later this year."

"I didn't know about it, either. I was a baby when the shooting would have happened in my Original Time. But the commander had gone back and stopped it, so it never occurred.

Now people like you and I grew up never learning about it. Instead, we know the story of when Columbine caught fire and burned to the ground."

"I was wondering if you were referring to that Columbine," Eddie said, shaking his head. "Didn't like 200 people die in that fire?"

"Precisely. See, the past still corrected its course. It seems as if that school was destined for tragedy. Commander Briar stopped one from happening, but the past still made sure it took its victims. Now, we haven't found this to be a universal occurrence. In fact, it is the exception to the rule. But it is something we urge our members to keep in mind when they tamper with the past—there will always be consequences when you return."

Eddie stared out the windshield, studying a crow that had landed atop one of the old gas pumps. "What about us? We know the past, but Road Runners are changing it every day, right? How are we supposed to keep track of everything that has changed?"

"You don't. Our knowledge of events is fluid, so when something changes in the past, our memories will reflect those changes. Road Runners never watch the news because there is no point—it's *going* to change, most likely, at some point. Honestly, though, the missions we work on nowadays aren't well-known enough. Say we stop this murder in Pueblo from happening. It's only going to change the lives of those close to it. The victim's family, the suspect and their family, and perhaps a few members of the area. But beyond that, no one outside of Pueblo has even heard of Mason Gregory. It's not often we take on a major mission, like say, the Lincoln assassination, but when we do, everyone in the organization is notified and ready for what might happen."

"What has happened?"

Felix shook his head. "Afraid we don't have time to go into all that right now. We have to get back to 1988 and buy this house."

"Okay, my bad, sorry for all the questions."

Felix cracked a small grin. "Check your vocabulary. People didn't say 'my bad' in 1988—keep that in mind. I avoid slang unless I'm comfortable with a particular era. Otherwise, I'll speak as neutrally as I can."

"Understood."

"You ready to go?"

Eddie nodded, holding his gaze to the crow. Felix wondered what he was thinking about, remembering how anxious he used to get in his early time travel days. Every trip, no matter how well planned, had always felt like crash-landing in a foreign country. And in many ways, that's exactly what it was. Many new members treated time travel more like a vacation. Few understood the elevated levels of risk they were stepping into. Time travel and the past had rules accompanying them, and there had been plenty of stories of new Road Runners who never came back from their first trip.

"Let's do it," Felix said, reaching over to open the glove compartment and pull out his flask of Juice, spinning the cap off. "We're going to February 11, 1988. Be sure to touch part of the car with your hand to make sure we go together."

Eddie remained silent as he pulled out his small bottle and twisted the cap off. Felix noticed the liquid shaking within the man's trembling fingers.

"Hey," Felix said, placing a hand on Eddie's shoulder. "Nothing to be nervous about. Quick, easy trip."

69

"Thanks," Eddie said, his voice distant and occupied.

"Cheers," Felix said, raising his flask and taking a quick swig. Eddie followed suit, and they both replaced their caps and leaned back in their seats. "Give it a minute and we'll be on our way. Slight rumble, but that's just us passing through."

They sat in the car, both men staring forward while they remained undisturbed in the abandoned gas station. Within a minute, they felt the rumble, and the world turned black.

* * *

Seconds later, they arrived in 1988.

Eddie shot forward, rubbing his head and eyes. "I don't remember it being so fast."

"You were probably just nervous last time. That can make the simplest of tasks feel like forever. But see, quick and painless. Now we're here—let's get to work."

"Were you able to research who we should speak with?"

"I tried," Felix said, opening his car door and sticking a leg out. "But I couldn't find anything. No databases of realtors from 1988 were available, so we'll have to do it the way people used to, and find a phone book."

Eddie scanned the area, finding the gas station active and with customers strolling in and out of the store's front door. "This is the same place we just left?"

"Yes," Felix said in a hurry, stepping all the way out of the car. "Let's go."

Eddie followed, Felix already near the entrance after hustling across the parking lot.

"You always end up in the exact place you left," Felix said over his shoulder. "The landscape will obviously change depending on what year you go to. Go back another two hundred years and this area is probably swarming with Native Americans."

Felix opened the gas station's door, poked his head inside, and closed it back shut. "This way," he said, strolling down the sidewalk and rounding the building's corner. On the backside were bathroom doors, but more importantly, two payphones, each with two thick cords dangling from the bottom, metal cases connected to the other end.

"Wow," Eddie said. "I don't think I've ever seen an active payphone before. I've seen some that were old and out of service—just chunks of metal—but never one I could pick up and make a call."

"It is fascinating to look back and see how far we've advanced. Just think, this giant phone book was essentially Google." Felix raised the steel box and dropped it on the base of the payphone's booth. "Almost five inches thick."

He flipped open the Yellow Pages and searched for the section starting with the letter R, slowing when he reached it, running a finger up and down the pages until finding the section labeled with "Realtors".

The two splayed open pages contained nothing but lists of realtors and their phone numbers.

"Goodness," Eddie said. "How do we pick? That guy has twenty years of experience." He pointed to a paid advertisement of a grinning man with slicked back hair, calling for all home buyers and sellers to call him for their real estate needs.

"Nope. Twenty years of working in this area means he's connected and knows everyone. We don't need our realtor telling everyone in town about us. Look at this one." His finger slid down the page and stopped on the name of Joseph Graham. "This is our kind of guy. Says he has three years' experience. That means he knows the area well enough, isn't entirely new to remember us as early clients in his career, and just maybe we can push him around to get us a better deal on his commission."

Felix picked up the phone, dropped coins into the slot, and dialed the number.

"Thank you for calling the office of Joe Graham. How can I help you?" a woman answered.

"Hello, I was hoping to schedule a time to meet with Mr. Graham today. Looking to buy a property in Pueblo and would love some guidance."

"Let me check. Mr. Graham is out at a showing right now, but it looks like he has an opening this afternoon. Three o'clock, if that works for you."

Instinctively, Felix pulled out his cell phone to find it showing a time of 00:00, and hurriedly stuffed it back into his pocket. "I'm sorry, ma'am, what time is it right now?"

"12:30, sir."

"Okay, perfect. I'll be there at three."

They hung up and Felix copied down the address from the phone book before closing it and returning it to its proper place.

"Forget your cell phone doesn't work?" Eddie asked.

Felix nodded. "Gotta remember the little details. It can get confusing because some technologies exist in different eras. The thing is, the technology itself has to exist in the year you're visiting. There *are* cell phones in 1988, but they're not too common yet, and the technology is vastly different for my phone from 2022. You'll notice we rely on two-way radios during any missions after 1940. It's an old technology that has remained consistent throughout time—therefore, it's highly reliable for us."

"So we have some time to kill before we meet with this realtor?" Eddie asked.

"Yep. It's twelve-thirty right now. I see you have a watch—that's another important thing to bring on any trip, so you don't look like a fool pulling out a device from the future like I just did."

Eddie checked his watch and promptly adjusted the time. "I never leave the house without a watch, so I guess I'm good there."

"Let's drive around and find somewhere for lunch. We can eat and get to know each other more. I'm sure you have more questions about our . . . business."

Chapter 12

After two hours at a local diner where they munched on burgers and fries, Felix and Eddie returned to their car and headed for the realty office of Joseph Graham. They had asked their server for directions, and were delighted to find the office a quick seven-minute drive away.

They pulled into the parking lot of a two-level building surrounded by nothing but open fields. An entire business park would develop in the coming years, but for now, the solo building housed realtors, insurance agents, and accountants. It had a brick exterior with blackout windows, and couldn't look any more vanilla if it tried.

Felix found a spot in the front row, and the two men made their way inside. They entered a lobby with a front desk impeding their path to the elevators, an older gentleman nodding off in his chair behind the desk.

Hank, according to the name tag clipped to his shirt, startled back to consciousness upon seeing them enter. "Good afternoon. How can I help you?" Hank had dark skin with contrasting white hair and a goatee.

"Hello," Felix said. "We have an appointment with Joseph Graham."

Hank cracked a grin. "Joey is a good man. Suite 206—take

the elevators up if you like."

"Thank you."

Felix strolled around the desk, Eddie following two steps behind. They rode the elevator up one level and found themselves in a new hallway, filled with a dozen doors and plenty of silence.

"Do you ever wonder if we encounter other time travelers?" Eddie whispered.

"We certainly do. Even with only one percent of the world's population having access to the ability, that means there are a little over three million time travelers in the United States alone. It's highly likely you have crossed paths with a fellow time traveler."

They moved down the hallway, Felix grumbling once he realized their destination waited at the furthest end, a frosted glass door with bold lettering that read: *Joseph Graham Realty.*

"Just follow my lead," Felix muttered.

He opened the door and stepped into the office, a young red-headed woman greeting them with a wide smile from behind a reception desk.

"Good afternoon, you two. Are you Mr. Francisco?" she asked, pushing a pair of horn-rimmed glasses up the bridge of her nose.

"Yes, ma'am," Felix said, approaching the desk.

"Perfect. Mr. Graham had a last-minute cancellation and is ready for you a few minutes early. Please, follow me."

She stood, and the two men gazed at the curves outlining her slender figure before following her down a short hall where an office awaited with its door open.

"Mr. Graham, your three o'clock is here."

A man not much older than Felix, stood from behind a

massive desk that nearly took the entire office space. He wore a metallic suit, had a gaudy gold watch on his wrist, and smelled of cheap cologne.

"Mr. Graham," Felix said, extending a hand to shake. "My name is Felix, and this is my associate, Eddie."

"Pleasure," the realtor replied. "Just call me Joe. Now, how can I help you gentlemen today?"

Joe sat back down on his throne and gestured for Felix and Eddie to do the same.

"Well, Joe," Felix said. "We have cash and are looking to buy a house in the area. Hoping we might get something this week, if possible."

Joe leaned back, his hands clasped in front of his mouth as he stuck out his index finger to his lips. "You one of those rich gay couples moving here from Denver?"

Felix laughed, while Eddie remained silent and confused.

"No, definitely not us. Is that a thing?"

"Goodness, yes. The gay community has been making its way down here to Pueblo. Can't blame them—it's one of the few areas outside the big city with a more accepting community. Though, if you ask me, I don't think folks down here are as much accepting as they are disinterested. Most just mind their own business and don't worry about what others are doing."

This statement was fantastic news for Felix, and precisely what they needed to set up shop for a mission. "Interesting," he said. "I'm curious. How long have you been doing real estate?"

"I've been doing it in Pueblo for the last year, but started in Denver a couple of years ago."

"What brought you down this way?"

Joe shrugged. "Less competition. The Denver market can be absolute cutthroat. You get into some of those up-and-coming neighborhoods, forget about it. The suburbs are still growing, but Pueblo is exploding. It's a gold mine down here for real estate—both residential and commercial."

Felix nodded, as if accepting this explanation. While it wasn't his field of concentration, he had picked up plenty of skills in negotiation for times just like this. He had every intent on securing a property and only paying four percent commission to Joseph Graham. "Well, that sounds great. Me and Eddie are business partners, and we're looking to expand our operations here in Pueblo."

Joe shot forward. "So, you're looking for a house *and* an office?"

Felix had to fight from bursting into laughter. Joe's conclusion left him looking like a dog desperate for its owner to throw a ball in a game of fetch. "Just a house. We conduct our business right from home."

"Oh," Joe said, deflating and leaning back into his comfortable position. "Well, I don't see why we can't find a suitable home for you. What kind of space do you need?"

"Preferably two levels, plus a basement."

Joe leaned forward again, though not as aggressively. "For just you two?"

Felix hadn't encountered such a nosy realtor in his previous housing transactions, and wondered if Joe might not be the best choice after all. Was he the guy to show up at random to check on his clients?

"We'll both have some family stopping by from time to time. Would like to have guest rooms for them."

Joe nodded. "And what kind of budget are we looking at?"

77

"You tell me. We have the cash."

Joe's eyes lit up like a child unwrapping the first present on Christmas morning. "What you're looking for is definitely on the higher end for Pueblo. Probably somewhere around two hundred thousand."

"And your commission?"

Joe looked up, calculating how much money he could massage out of Felix's wallet. "Eight percent."

Felix immediately scoffed, all part of his act. "Mr. Graham, don't insult me. Maybe I should have clarified. We're expanding our business. We're looking for a realtor to handle repeat business. I suggest you don't swing for the fences on this one purchase and think of the big picture."

Joe nodded and leaned forward, planting his elbows on the desk. "My apologies—I really wasn't under that impression."

"And you thought high-balling me was wise, anyway? I know the average commission is between six and seven percent."

Joe shook his head. "I'm sorry. Don't hold that against me. I'll do six percent."

"Three."

Now it was Joe's turn to scoff, and he leaned back as he tossed his hands in the air. "Three percent? Have you lost your mind? The absolute lowest I'd consider is five."

"Very well," Felix said, standing from his seat.

Eddie looked up at him, confusion smacked on his face until he remembered he needed to follow whatever Felix did. Felix was already halfway to the door when Eddie rose, and Joe shouted, "Wait! Don't leave."

Felix paused with his hand outstretched toward the doorknob for added dramatics.

"Four percent," Joe said, nearly muttering it under his breath. "And I can't go any lower."

Felix pivoted around and returned to his seat. "Deal."

The men shook hands.

Joe reached into a desk drawer and pulled out a binder. "Let's look at some properties."

For the next hour, they flipped through dozens of pages of properties from around the Pueblo area. Joe had access to everything currently on the market, along with some expected to be listed soon. Felix and Eddie consulted on each property until whittling a list down to their top three. Joe assured them if they truly had cash to spend, they could expect no competition for any property they desired.

Within minutes of choosing their favorites, all three men were on the road, Felix and Eddie following behind Joe's Toyota hatchback as they set out to tour the three homes. Fortunately, during their two hours together that evening, Joe didn't once ask what kind of business his new clients were running.

Felix found this suspicious, wondering why the nosy man omitted this simple question after prodding about nearly everything else. Perhaps he felt intimidated after Felix turned the tables on him in his office.

Regardless, Felix was glad it was one less lie he'd have to tell and keep track of. By the end of the night, Eddie had returned home to 2022, satisfied with learning enough of the real estate process Felix had taken him through. Felix called Joe to let him know which house to place an offer on the next morning.

It was the exact house he had sought. Three floors with bathrooms on each level, a fully finished basement, and a quick ten-minute drive from Mason Gregory's home. Since the house was in an upscale, spread-out neighborhood, the nearest neighbor was an entire quarter mile away. They'd enjoy complete privacy while working on their mission to solve—and hopefully, prevent—the murder that would soon turn the community upside down.

Chapter 13

The next morning, Felix had traveled back to 2022 to call Arielle and let her know the address and details of the new house he secured for their mission.

She had been awake since six o'clock, reviewing the electronic mission files and getting in the right mind frame to start within the next couple of days. When Felix had called at eight, Arielle was deep into Mason's work history, mapping out all the areas he had worked since his first job scooping ice cream at the local parlor as a sixteen-year-old boy. The Angels had members dedicated to doing this tedious work, but Arielle always wanted to absorb as much information as she could about her subject. Some argued it was unnecessary, while others said that was what made her the best. She simply viewed it as another weapon in her never ending arsenal. Anyone could master firearms, sword fighting, or hand-to-hand combat, but for Arielle Lucila, knowledge trumped everything.

She took the new address and added a sticker on its location in their travel atlas. Felix planned to meet them back in 1988 once Arielle and Selena arrived in Pueblo. Right when Felix hung up, she dialed Selena.

"Hello?" Selena answered, voice groggy.

"Are you still sleeping?" Arielle asked, trying to soften her voice to not sound like a scolding mother.

"Yeah . . . what time is it?" Selena mumbled in response.

"Eight."

"Ugh! I just fell asleep four hours ago. Why are you calling so early?"

"Are you hungover?"

"Hungover? No. I might still be a little drunk."

"Jesus Christ, Selena, we are about to start a mission. You can't be doing this stuff."

"'This stuff'? Get off your high horse. We all have our ways of blowing off steam. No need to crucify me for being twenty-three. Maybe you should try it sometime. Let me guess, you spent last night working. You were probably up as late as I was."

"I did some work, yes. But I also got eight hours of sleep, especially on the eve of a new mission."

"You're such a grandma."

Arielle paused and pursed her lips. No one within the Road Runners organization had ever spoken her to like that before. "We're arguing about nothing. As long as you're ready to work, it doesn't matter what you do in your free time."

"Thank you, that's all I ask. So why are you calling me so early?"

"Felix found a house for us. Great location, tons of privacy. We should all be able to move in over the next few days, but I thought you might want a head start to scout the area."

"So leaving today? I can make that work in the afternoon. Have a couple of matters to tie up here first."

Like sobering up, Arielle thought, but didn't cave to the temptation of shooting back cheap insults. "Okay, great. Today is Thursday, so if all goes well, I should be there either tomorrow night or first thing on Saturday morning."

"And we have our own rooms in this house, I take it?"

"Yes, it's huge—lots of space for all three of us."

"Good. Okay, anything else?"

Arielle sensed the shortness in Selena's voice and fought away more snarky comments. "No, that was all. Have a good morning, and I'll see you soon."

Arielle returned to her home office to gather her notes and files, stuffing them back into the bulky binder that housed all information for the mission. She had done enough research for the day and needed to clear her head. She found herself in the awkward phase before the start of a mission where all preliminary work was complete, and most of what remained would have to wait until she arrived in the new city and year.

She left her office and moved down the hallway to her bedroom, passing the portraits of her family on the wall, avoiding eye contact with them, as she needed to maintain her intense level of focus.

Once in her bedroom, she rummaged a stick of gum from her nightstand drawer and popped it into her mouth while turning on the TV. Arielle rarely had time to watch TV, so she didn't bother keeping up with new shows. They came and went while she worked, rising in popularity around the world while she couldn't pick one out of a lineup.

Instead, she used her 70-inch television to play music, finding her favorite channel that played pop and hip-hop music from the early 2010s. fun.'s "We Are Young" came on, mentally taking her back to her senior year of high school when it had first released and exploded up the charts.

Her college days were typically the memories she reminisced, perhaps because high school seemed like another lifetime.

Always a popular student since day one in high school, they had voted Arielle the most likely to become famous. And while no one in regular society had ever heard of her, she had indeed become a living legend among the Road Runners, all before her twenty-seventh birthday.

Arielle crossed her bedroom and stood at the window, looking out to the vast landscape that stretched miles into the distance, the Rocky Mountains glowing under the early morning sun. She wondered where her life had gone. Deep down, part of her wanted to quit the Road Runners and run off with her accumulated fortune. She could live anywhere in the world, and spend her days drawing pictures, binge watching TV, and cooking world-class meals for dinner. She supposed these desires stemmed from her old life when she used to find joy in doing such therapeutic activities. Even in CIA training, she had time to watch a couple of episodes at night before falling asleep. She used to read a book each week, and now couldn't remember the last time she had even seen a set of bound pages.

The most frustrating part was considering how much time she spent on private jets, providing plenty of time to enjoy leisurely activities. But all she could ever do was sleep. Even with a consistent routine of eight hours each night, her time awake was so involved and active, by the time she reclined in the luxury of the Road Runners' private jets, a nap was all she wanted.

Her life had gone under constant transformation since surviving the mall shooting, yet she only realized it when she had down time between missions to reflect. And it never hit her all at once, but in bits and pieces. Sometimes she would realize how losing her family left her alone. Other times revolved around losing her soulmate.

Today, however, she couldn't help but dwell on how she had become a Road Runner. It was something she rarely considered, but now, staring down yet another mission from her massive empty house, she wondered if it was all worth it.

Her father had always preached the importance of not letting a job consume one's entire life. And he backed it up, always home in time for dinner, and never missing his children's extracurricular activities. *Family isn't everything—it is the only thing.* She thought of the words he used to say at least once a week.

The phrase rang true, but Arielle found it impossible to keep living up to it when she had no family nearby. She never felt guilty about essentially marrying her job after she lost everyone of importance. It had been a gradual process as she found herself back at the CIA, her evenings left to either sulk and mourn, or hit the books and learn everything she could. She always chose the latter and never looked back.

When the Road Runners reached out to her, days after she had returned to the CIA, she dismissed the encounter as nonsense, perhaps a scammer trying to get a cut of her family's life insurance. But once she returned and had some time to clear her head, she thought back to meeting the man who offered no name and had spewed a bunch of random facts about her life that no one had any way of knowing. It felt sleazy at first, but after further consideration, seemed more legitimate considering what the man had known.

She had called him back on the phone number listed on the plain business card he left for her. They spoke for an hour, the man identifying himself as Brendan Costner, a recruiter for the Road Runners. He explained the work his organization focused on trying to make the world a better place, and didn't explain the bit about time travel until the very end, once Arielle had expressed an interest in joining.

She thought back to the precise moment, one that she supposed would have been laughed off under normal circum-stances. But she had grown so vulnerable during that time of mourning, and slept on the matter. The next day, after hours of research into the science from those who believed time travel was at least a possibility, she called Brendan back and agreed to meet with him in person.

Within a week, she met him at the Denver office and enjoyed her first taste of time travel. She had traveled back to the year 2000, and stopped by her fifth birthday party at a park, keeping a safe distance with Brendan by her side, explaining the rules and restrictions that came with the territory.

Seeing her family, much younger, and herself, was all the proof she needed. Of course, her initial thought was that she had been killed and had fallen into a strange purgatory. But when they returned to the present time, and all was the same, she ran out of ways to explain it away.

Life had knocked her down, but just as quickly yanked her back up, flinging her into a whole new world. Her only regret was not getting to say farewell to her previous life.

Chapter 14

By the evening, Arielle had grown antsy after packing her bags for the mission. She went down her checklist five different times to ensure not a single item had been missed, zipping her suitcase closed and sitting on the foot of the bed as she racked her mind for any last tasks to handle before jumping back. Only ten minutes would pass in 2022 while she spent a couple of weeks in 1988, but she didn't want to return home to a long to-do list.

After enough stalling, she retrieved her bottle of Juice from her nightstand drawer, took a sip, and lay on the bed while focusing on the date of June 24, 1988. The night of the murder of Mason Gregory.

Arielle preferred to jump into the past before traveling to the location. A two-hour drive was more than reasonable, and once she experienced the rumbling of the world, shifting through the dimensions of time, she arrived in 1988, in the middle of a dirt lot, her suitcase by her side as she had kept contact with it through the time travel.

Jumping through time always left her head cloudy, but the sensation typically wore off within five minutes. Arielle lived at the top of a hill, having done thorough research to find the prime location for her chaotic lifestyle. She had few neighbors in the immediate vicinity. No matter when she had to travel to the past, she could guarantee the location would either be her house or the dirt lot.

From there, she had a one-mile walk to a Hertz car rental location that had opened in 1978. If she traveled to a time before that, it was only an extra half-mile to the nearest gas station that had a payphone to call a taxi to either take her to the airport or a different car rental agency in downtown Denver.

She didn't mind the walk, even though she had to lug a 50-pound suitcase through the dirt—and sometimes mud. It gave her just enough additional time to mentally prepare. Because once she arrived at either the airport or a car rental agency, all other matters in her life took a backseat to the mission.

Arielle climbed to her feet, slightly off balance, as she hadn't completely shaken the fog from her brain, and drew in a deep breath of the crisp 1988 summer air. The Denver metro area had yet to see its boom in population, so she always enjoyed traveling back to the days of less pollution and crowds. Being near the foothills of the Rocky Mountains also put her back in touch with mother nature, grounding her, and reminding her how insignificant a speck she was in the universe.

"Here we are," she whispered to herself, grabbing her suitcase and starting her trip down the hill. She had to take careful steps. One false move could send her tumbling to the bottom. Rocks and dirt decorated the ground, the occasional weed tickling her ankles.

It only took five minutes for her to reach the bottom, at which point she turned and looked back to the top of the hill, her mind filling in the blanks of where her house would one day stand on this magnificent landscape. As much as she dwelled on her past life, she never let a moment pass without feeling some gratitude for the lifestyle she currently enjoyed, no matter how lonely it was.

From the bottom of the hill, the nearest road waited another quarter mile away, where she would find flat ground and the sidewalk leading to the strip mall that hosted the Hertz rental agency. Arielle hurried to it, thankful no rain had fallen to turn the ground muddy. Her calves and thighs burned, and she cursed herself for having skipped her workout routine the past two days.

Arielle took great pride in her twelve percent body fat, adhering to a strict diet and exercise routine. The only time she strayed was in between missions, often eating a pint of ice cream and enjoying a glass of wine. Sometimes on the missions, she had no choice but to eat junk food, depending on when and where she traveled to. She required her temporary residences to have full kitchens so she could cook a healthy meal in the evenings.

Her stomach growled, and she wondered if she was actually hungry or if the past was already trying to slow her down. She expected as much resistance from the past, but also couldn't recall what time she had eaten last.

The most important rule of time travel, and perhaps the most difficult aspect to understand and adapt to, was the past refusing to be changed. No mission was as simple as barging into a room and shooting a future murderer years before they had the chance to commit heinous crimes. No matter how dark it might be, the past was only interested in preserving itself.

Arielle remembered how they explained the past in her early days of training with the Road Runners. Her instructor, the third-ranked Angel Runner at the time, likened the past to the

Pando, a tree colony comprising over 40,000 individual aspen trees, yet still considered a singular living organism.

The thousands of trees all intertwined within the same root system. If a person were to go underground and cut just one root, it could lead to the death of hundreds, or possibly thousands, of trees. Tampering with the past was to be treated with the same caution.

While stopping an isolated murder seemed the right thing to do, on the surface, the Road Runners always had to consider the consequences of such an action. A dedicated team always studied the ripple effect—or butterfly effect—but they only had access to so much information. The rest of the work had to be carried out by the Angels in the field once they gained a true understanding of all the moving parts within the mission.

On top of uncovering where all these potential roots led, another factor that weighed on the team's mind was how wide of a reach the particular event had in the past. The wider the reach, the more they could expect the past to protect itself.

It was the main reason their missions focused on fixing more small-town tragedies, instead of things like trying to prevent Hitler's rise to power. The bigger the event, and the more lives affected, only opened doors to chaos if they tried to tamper with it.

The past understood what lay within one's heart and soul. It understood when Arielle had traveled back to significant moments in American history—the Battle of Gettysburg and the moon landing—to gather more information. Not to change anything.

"The past is our ultimate ruler," Arielle muttered under her breath as she reached the sidewalk and increased her pace, grateful for the flat concrete. Respecting the past was the only way to understand all the nuances of time travel. The past held no prejudices, and would stop anyone trying to alter it using any means necessary.

The Angels had learned after enough failures what sort of things to expect. Arielle already expected events like flat tires, gas running out, random explosions, and outsiders to serve as roadblocks in her mission to save the life of Mason Gregory. Every mission had thousands of little details to consider, and Arielle looked over nearly all of them, despite having dozens of fellow Road Runners with jobs dedicated to doing just that.

A sign hung over the side of the road showing the names of all the businesses within the strip mall. It wasn't quite the evening yet, so its lights hadn't been turned on, instead catching an orange glow from the sun starting its descent behind the mountains.

Arielle's stomach fluttered—she always got a small amount of jitters before starting a new mission. This one had a few more than usual, now that she had a dedicated team working with her. She didn't have total control over every aspect of the mission, as she had become accustomed to. Felix and Selena were already at their shared home, hopefully hours into research and planning. As of right now, Arielle was the missing puzzle piece to the mission.

She stepped into the Hertz office, eager to begin.

Chapter 15

The drive to Pueblo took the two hours as planned, but Arielle faced a delay at the Hertz office. When she arrived, she found no one from the staff for fifteen minutes. They had apparently taken a break to swing by the neighboring ice cream shop.

A man and woman eventually returned and apologized profusely, citing it as their slowest time of day when customers never came in. After filling out all the paperwork, Arielle didn't hit the road until a few minutes before six o'clock, and she had to speed to make up for lost time, since the murder took place between nine-thirty and ten.

The first part of any mission was a brief observation of the tragedy to ensure it actually happened. Unlike detectives looking for a missing body, the Road Runners had the advantage of going back in time to confirm the incident was a murder and not a case of someone running away or being kidnapped.

Since Mason Gregory's body had been discovered hours after the murder, this initial observation was more to confirm they had the correct time and location. From there, Arielle and her team would work backwards to find the best opportunities to prevent the crime from happening.

Arielle arrived in Pueblo just after eight o'clock. Everything had been marked out on her map, which she studied under the bright lights of a gas station where she had parked to figure out the next several hours. The site of the murder had a circle drawn around it, and less than a block away was another circle where she would park, the location confirmed to be in the shadows where the murderer would never see her.

Her stomach growled, and she couldn't put off eating any longer, especially since she wanted to be at the site no later than nine o'clock. It was a Friday night, and the restaurants she had passed looked jam-packed with the weekend crowds and families. She wouldn't have time to sit down and order, dread settling over her now that she'd have no choice but to eat fast food.

"First day of the mission and already stuck eating a burger," she said, shaking her head as she studied the map. Arielle pulled out of the gas station and turned back onto North Main Street, where the bars and restaurants lined both sides of the road. She passed a Wendy's and Taco Bell before seeing the bright yellow sign of a Subway, and immediately swerved over a lane to turn into the sandwich shop's parking lot.

She always chose the sandwich chain when possible—there weren't many other options for non-greasy fast food when traveling into the past, and she counted her blessings every time she found one, since they still hadn't become as widespread as many of their greasy competitors.

Arielle ran in and took five minutes getting her sandwich, deciding to drive to the murder scene and eat from there. She returned to Main Street, driving away from the center of town, toward the outskirts.

She got onto Highway 50 and headed east, into the darkness of the night. It took five minutes until she escaped the neighborhoods and businesses of Pueblo; the landscape turning into open fields as far as she could see. After ten more minutes, she exited the highway after passing a group of industrial warehouses. She turned onto a frontage road that connected all the warehouses and turned off her headlights once she found the one with a tattered sign that read *Big Z Home Office.*

The lot had two parking lots, one on the north and south sides of the building. The murder would occur in the north lot, which was already abandoned, two dim lights casting a weak glow over the empty parking spaces. Arielle's hiding spot was between the two lots where a row of roughly twenty trucks stood with trailers backed up to the warehouse. She parked next to the first trailer, engulfed in darkness, as this area had no lighting. A small courtyard, only thirty yards long, separated Arielle from the northern parking lot. She had a clear view of the lot, and with her binoculars, shouldn't have any problems witnessing the murder, even in the night.

They had informed her the warehouse closed at eight o'clock, and that appeared true, as she had yet to see a single person walk from the building. It was already 8:45 once she killed her engine and unwrapped her sandwich to eat. She rolled down her window to keep an ear out for anyone passing by, but had already fallen lost in her dinner.

Shortly after nine, a pair of headlights appeared from the south, startling Arielle into crumbling up her empty wrapper and tossing it aside on the passenger seat. She reached under her seat where she had stashed her pistol and pulled it out, just in case.

The car moved at a snail's pace as it crawled along the road in front of her. Her stomach tightened once she had a clear visual of the vehicle, a 1982 Honda Civic.

It's him, she thought, already knowing what Mason Gregory

drove. The show seemed to start early, and she was glad to have arrived on time. The car continued past Arielle and finally turned into the north lot, parking right under the lone lamp.

She could only see the silhouette of the car, and immediately doubted her position was good enough.

The car's door swung open, and out stepped a heavyset man she knew was Mason. His silhouette stood in front of the car before taking a seat on the hood. His arms fumbled in his pockets for a moment before she saw the flicker of a lighter. Mason remained in the dark, sitting on his hood, a lone orange ember from the tip of his cigarette standing out strong through Arielle's binoculars.

Doesn't have the look of a man who thinks he might die within the hour.

She mentally ran through a checklist of possibilities that she always considered when investigating a murder. Did the victim seem startled in the moments leading up to it? In this case, no, Mason seemed completely fine, from what she could tell. Someone afraid wouldn't have stepped outside of the car. This suggested he was meeting someone he knew, and that always helped narrow the pool of potential suspects. The location opened the door to many more questions. Why would a family man like Mason be out? Granted, it wasn't *too* late, especially for a Friday. The deserted warehouse suggested a potential drug deal, perhaps an off chance he was indulging in a romantic affair—though something nefarious was seeming more and more likely.

Arielle braced to witness a crime of passion, perhaps an escalation of events that left Mason dead in his car. The file mentioned that they had found him dead with a bullet wound to the head, slumped forward over his steering wheel. He was a large man, so it wasn't likely the suspect took the time to lug him back into the vehicle—someone definitely shot him while behind the wheel.

She watched Mason through the binoculars, the soon-to-be dead man still minding his business, puffing a cigarette without a care in the world. A motor roared from the opposite end of the property, prompting Arielle to spin around and drop her binoculars. She found the new set of headlights and followed them as they crept toward the north lot.

"Jackpot," Arielle said, recognizing the vehicle as an older muscle car. Even though it was too dark to make out the exact make and model, just knowing it was older would drastically help narrow down the suspect in this affair.

She regained her focus and watched as the car pulled up and stopped right in front of Mason's car; the headlights turning off to leave them in darkness. A man stepped out of the vehicle and circled around, shaking hands with Mason and leaning on the hood to face him. The two chatted, heads nodding, and it appeared nothing more than a couple of friends catching up.

They carried on like this for twenty minutes, Arielle growing somewhat bored as she watched the entire muted conversation through the binoculars. At one point, Mason accepted another cigarette from his acquaintance, the two appearing to laugh multiple times. For a moment, she wondered if she had possibly stumbled across the wrong suspicious meeting in the middle of the night, and doubted the second man who had arrived was the actual killer.

That was, until their conversation ended and Mason returned to his car. The other man paced back toward his vehicle, but hesitated as he walked in a circle in front of his door before returning to Mason's car.

Mason rolled down his window, and the two exchanged more words for another minute. The man reached behind his shirt and whipped out a pistol from his waistband, promptly stuffing it through the open window and blasting a slug into Mason's head. Arielle couldn't make out the gory details, but there was no mistaking the flash and bang that accompanied the lone shot.

The man stuffed his gun back into his waistband and hurried to his car, hopping behind the wheel and speeding away, sending smoke into the air from his screeching tires. Arielle followed the vehicle through the binoculars and noticed it was missing a license plate. She instantly knew she was dealing with a professional criminal, possibly even a hit man. The body of the car could have been a Camaro, but she still couldn't get a clear enough look. It didn't help that a lot of the older muscle cars had fairly similar body types.

"Shit," she muttered, shaking her head. Arielle had hoped for a simple mission, but should have known better. The Road Runners didn't give the top Angel simple missions—those were for newbies still cutting their teeth on this new life. For Arielle, her missions would forever be complex and take at least multiple weeks to resolve.

She turned her attention back to Mason, able to see his silhouette slouched over the steering wheel, not a single movement coming from his vehicle. That was how the warehouse morning crew would arrive to find him, and how he would remain for the rest of the day while the police and a team of detectives investigated.

And that's where Arielle, and her team, had to step in and fill the gaps.

Chapter 16

After witnessing the horrific scene, Arielle took a swig of her Juice to jump back to June 10, 1988, the same day her teammates had arrived in the past.

Arielle reached her home for the next two weeks at 10:15 and already had hundreds of thoughts running through her mind on the way over. There were always unanswered questions in any murder case. But she braced for even more than usual on this mission, since all the information they had on Mason Gregory didn't portray a man who should have even been in the empty parking after hours.

She lugged her suitcase up the walkway, unable to see the yard in the night, as the light on the front porch only illuminated the three steps that led up to the entryway. All the lights on the main level were on, and she saw the movement of shadows through the windows as she reached to open the oak door.

It opened before she could touch the doorknob, Felix greeting her with a wide grin. "Welcome home!" he said, stepping aside and opening the door all the way.

Arielle stepped in and scanned the area. To her left was a living room, fully furnished with a light gold sofa and two love seats, all centered around a wooden coffee table. An obnoxious chandelier hung from above, lighting up the room that only had a fireplace to look at. She saw the adjoining kitchen where all the blondewood cabinets complemented the matching kitchen table. Flowery wallpaper decorated the top perimeter of the room.

"My goodness, we really are in 1988," Arielle commented. "I've seen old pictures of my grandma's house, and this place looks a lot like it."

Felix chuckled. "And to think this house used to belong to a home decorator. This is just how the times were."

"The place came with all of this?"

Felix nodded. "I guess the last owner had a sudden family emergency and had to move to Georgia. Only the closets are empty. Even the basement is full of stuff they left behind. I figured we might as well hire someone to come clear it out, since we'll be holding on to this property to resell down the road."

"Fine with me. Where's Selena?"

"In the other living room, watching TV."

Arielle continued through the kitchen, into the dining room where a long table with eight seats sat in the middle, fake plants standing tall in each corner. A tall china cabinet stood against the wall, displaying vintage plates, mugs, and teakettles.

From here, she saw Selena sitting on a couch with a glass of wine in hand, watching videos on the old MTV channel—one that used to base its existence on music.

"Hey, Selena."

"Evening, Arielle," Selena replied, standing up and crossing the room to give Arielle a quick hug. "How did it go tonight? Did you see the murder happen?"

"She just got here," Felix interjected. "Give her a second to settle in."

"It's fine," Arielle said. "I need to talk about it."

No matter how much death she witnessed in her line of work, murder never lost its shock factor. And it always disturbed her old memories of the day in the mall.

Selena returned to the couch and turned off the television, patting at the open space beside her. Arielle obliged and sat, Felix getting cozy in a love seat to their side.

"I'm not sure what we're dealing with," Arielle said. "I think a professional killed him."

"Well, shit, that complicates things."

Arielle nodded. "It's nothing we haven't dealt with before. We've handled the mob, the cartels, plenty of hitmen. Sure, it makes things a *bit* more complicated, but we'll be okay."

Felix nodded, the wheels clearly turning in his mind.

"So, how do you propose we spend the day tomorrow?" Selena asked.

"We need to learn Mason's routine. Let's tail him for three days. Figure out what time he leaves the house in the morning. When he comes back home. And what he does in between. He's definitely involved in something that I don't suppose his wife knows about. Once we figure that out, we'll be able to track down the killer. Also, the killer was driving an old American muscle car. I couldn't make out any details, but it was a dark color, and could be a Camaro. Just keep an eye out for any vehicles in that range while you're out and about. I'll tail Mason—Selena, will you be trying to get close to his wife?"

She took a sip of wine and nodded. "That's my plan. I'll be waiting for her to go *anywhere,* at which point I'll follow her and accidentally bump into her. She'll have no choice but to become my friend. I'll find out as much as I can."

"Do you ever do things like get invited over for dinner?" Felix asked.

"Quite often. It's not a guarantee like I want it to be—maybe fifty percent of the time someone is comfortable enough to invite me over. Not bad, considering I'm dealing with people I've just met. Would you invite a stranger over to your house after meeting them a few days earlier?"

Felix laughed. "I invite no one over. For any reason."

"Challenge accepted," Selena said with a smirk. "Arielle, I'm going to get us a dinner invite to Felix's house in 2022 by the time this mission ends."

"I'm sure you will," Arielle said. "And what do you have planned for tomorrow, Felix?"

"A visit to the weapons warehouse in Colorado Springs. Any special requests for either of you?"

"I'll take a tommy gun," Selena said with a chuckle.

"Very funny. Seriously, what do you need?"

"Just a small Glock to keep in my purse," Selena said. "I rarely need anything else."

"I'll make the same request for each mission," Arielle said. "A nine millimeter, an AR-15, a lightweight butterfly knife, throwing knives, and some liquid poisons."

"Damn, girl," Selena said, taking another swig of wine. "You're crazy! What are you going to do with poison?"

"You never know. You think you can get all that for me?"

Felix had opened a notepad to jot down his weapons list, and nodded as he slapped it shut. "Shouldn't be a problem. And if either of you think of anything else, just let me know. I won't be leaving until nine o'clock tomorrow morning. I'll also stop to get clothing, just in case you need to blend in more around town."

"Thank you, Felix," Arielle said. "Your attention to detail is always appreciated."

Selena tipped her wine glass all the way back to finish the remains. "Anyone want to play some cards?"

"It's almost eleven—we need to get to bed."

"Ah, that's right," Selena said. "The queen needs her beauty rest. Felix?"

"It's been a long day," he replied. "Count me in tomorrow night—I'm running on fumes right now."

"Wow," Selena said. "Okay. You two enjoy your sleep. I'll be up for another couple of hours if you change your mind."

"Good night," Arielle said, returning to the foyer to grab her suitcase and haul it up the stairs. She would be asleep within fifteen minutes of settling into the master suite, replaying the image of Mason Gregory getting shot in the head.

Chapter 17

The next morning found Felix at the kitchen table, a pot of coffee brewing, its irresistible aromas filling the house. He was ready for the day, and just wanted to enjoy a cup on their back patio, an elevated space with breathtaking views of the Rocky Mountains to the west.

Selena came downstairs, a robe tied around her body, her hair rolled up into a messy bun. "Good morning," she said. "You make enough for me to have a cup?"

"I made enough for all of us," Felix said, standing from the table and going to the counter where the pot was just about ready. He rummaged through the cupboards and pulled out three mugs, aligning them next to the coffee machine.

"You're my savior."

"You stay up late like you said?"

"Of course. I'm a night owl. The only time I'm in bed before midnight is when I catch a cold. Even still, I'll stretch it until eleven. There's just something about unwinding from the day that gives me a new boost of energy—no matter how busy I was during the day."

"Well, today should be a busy one. Was Arielle awake up there yet?"

"Her door was closed, but it sounded like she was moving

103

around. She's probably been up since four o'clock, plotting the day."

"We all have our methods. I suppose there is a reason she has been the top Angel for so long."

"If that's what it takes, then I guess it'll never be me."

"That's what you don't get, Selena." Felix's tone shifted. "*We* don't have to reach that high. We're Angels, sure, but we're role players. I know you don't follow sports that much, but every successful team has role players to support the superstar. They know they'll never be the star of the team, but they are the best at their specialties. Combine all of that around a superstar like Arielle, who also has leadership qualities, and there is no stopping that kind of team. *We* can be a super team. Even if Arielle gets all the credit and recognition, we'll know that we're the ones who made it possible. And as long as we accept that as our role, all the other fluff and rankings won't matter anymore."

Selena joined Felix at the counter as he poured coffee into the mugs. "That makes sense. We are highly regarded in our own ways."

"Exactly. You're the best at what you do. And I'm the best at what I do. Just because we don't have as wide a range of abilities as Arielle doesn't make us any less. People come to us for advice and direction."

"I'm honored to be working with you two," Arielle said, her voice startling them as they spun around to find her standing in the kitchen's entryway. "Felix, I'm impressed. Never heard you open up like that. You're quite the team player."

Felix's face flushed with embarrassment. "I . . . sorry, Arielle."

"No. There is nothing to apologize for. We need more of that.

We *are* a team and will only succeed if everyone is carrying their weight. I'm sorry if I've ever seemed too solo. It's not you guys—I've just always had a certain way I like to do things. This is a change for me—for all of us. I have faith that we'll have this all figured out by the end of the mission. And if I ever stray, just reel me back in. I can't stress it enough to you two—always tell me what's on your mind."

"Coffee?" Felix asked, nodding to the steaming pot sitting on the counter.

"I'd love some."

For the next twenty minutes, they all sat on the patio chairs outside, enjoying their morning brew and mountain view. Arielle ran through her plans for the day and asked for the same of Felix and Selena.

Felix hadn't grown any less intimidated since Arielle's arrival, still ready to jump at any request she had, but their morning meeting started softening his perspective toward the top-ranked Angel. He saw her more as a human than the superhero others around the organization often portrayed.

Arielle slurped her coffee and smacked her lips after each sip. Felix always caught these sorts of details with everyone he met, and was relieved Arielle had such subtle nuances.

"I need to get going," Felix said, standing from his seat and soaking in one more view of the mountains. "I can arrange dinner plans for this evening if we think we'll all be back in time."

"You're a chef, too?" Selena asked.

"Well, yes, I am an excellent cook, but I rarely cook during missions—not enough time to grocery shop and all that. I can make us reservations somewhere, or find takeout to eat here."

"It's impossible for me to know where the day will take me,"

Arielle said. "When will you be able to set up surveillance on the Gregory property?"

"I scouted the area—well, I drove by it when I first got here. Looks like entry should be easy enough. As far as bugging the inside and tapping the phone line, that's more up to Selena finding out the safest time for me to enter the home when it's empty. I need at least thirty minutes of guaranteed alone time in that house."

"If you can have it set up today, I can plan to join you for dinner. If not, I'll have to stay near the property. I need to know all of his movements."

"I should be able to do that. That's part of what I'm picking up at the weapons warehouse—they store all of our spy gear, too."

"Sounds like you're on top of it," Arielle said. "My apologies—again, I'm not used to having a fully functioning team like this."

"I'm all for double-checking things to make sure nothing is missed. But I really need to leave now—don't want to be late."

Arielle waved her hands to hurry Felix back inside the house, and he left with a quick nod to both women on the patio. He patted his pockets while crossing the house toward the front door, confirming he had his wallet and keys.

Satisfied with everything, Felix stepped outside and ran down the steps to his car.

* * *

Felix arrived at an abandoned office building in Colorado

Springs and killed the engine. The Road Runners loved using commercial buildings for their own, whether abandoned or active. For the active ones, they operated similar to the mafia, using the main level of an office as a business front for the public, while operating their secret existence in the depths of the basement.

This location in Colorado Springs was an abandoned one, an older building falling apart. The windows had webbed cracks, chunks of the wooden exterior hanging on for dear life. Even the "For Lease" sign hung crooked. The colors and wording faded after years of the sun beating on it. This part of town had been abandoned after being run down by crime. It was the only part of Colorado Springs where few people dared visit—making it a perfect hideout for the Road Runners.

Felix only had to pass through the rough neighborhood, and doing so in the early morning proved non-threatening. Once he arrived, he couldn't see another soul in sight. The front of the building faced open plains, tall yellow grass ruffling in the morning breeze.

He stepped out of the car, the ground crunching beneath his shoes as he checked around the area once more to ensure he was alone. Felix climbed up the three steps and pulled open the door, the hinges screaming loud enough to draw attention. He hurried inside and closed the door shut behind him.

"Hello?" he called out down a long hallway, his voice bouncing and echoing back. "Anyone in here?"

Felix didn't expect a response, knowing the weapons warehouse was underground, but he made a habit out of declaring his presence whenever entering one of these buildings. On a prior mission, a homeless man who had been hiding out in a similar building had startled Felix when he burst into the place without a care in the world. The man had pulled a knife, and Felix had to react with the combat skills he hadn't used since his early days of training. His line of work rarely put him in danger, and that's why he took a more proactive approach now.

No one responded, so he continued down the hallway, its wallpaper a faded yellow tint after years of suffering water leaks that likely went unrepaired. Heavy wooden doors lined the hall, portals into the former office spaces that once were. In his early days on the job, Felix liked to explore what lay behind the doors. He had an itch to catch a glimpse of the life that once was, but after going through so many and rarely finding anything of interest, he now pressed through toward his destination, a man on a mission.

He reached the end of the hall, where the stairwell waited under an exit sign. The stairwell fit in with the rest of the place, but as he descended, the surroundings started to morph. The walls had fresh paint, even though they were black, and a functioning light fixture hung above the door at the bottom landing, also painted black.

"Like I'm entering a house of death," Felix muttered under his breath before knocking. It made a hollow thud that echoed all the way back up the stairs. He braced himself for the fellow Road Runner he was about to meet, since the people in this position were hit-or-miss in terms of their social skills and general awkwardness.

The door swung open, the first one in the building that did so without a loud creak. A man appeared in the doorway, nearly filling its entirety. Felix found himself eye level with the man's bulging chest and had to raise his head to meet the eyes of the behemoth. He had a bald head and a thick, black beard connecting one ear to the other.

"Felix?" the man asked, his voice slightly softer than a grumble.

"Yes, sir," Felix replied, unsure why he felt nervous all of a sudden. "And you are Lou, is that correct?"

The man nodded, revealing his teeth through the jungle of his beard as he cracked a friendly grin. "The one and only Lou Garrison at your service." He stuck out a meaty hand to Felix, revealing an arm covered in tattoos.

Felix grabbed it and shook, offering a smile in return. "Nice to meet you, Lou. Did you ever receive our list of requests for this mission?"

"I didn't. Those bastards at headquarters like to forget to send over the important messages. . . like the ones I need to do my job. Fucking bureaucrats."

One similarity that was pretty much universal across the spectrum of all weapons warehouse operators was their disdain for the organization. It's not that they hated the Road Runners. They simply saw the governing body as too powerful, and never wasted a moment to throw dirt on their names. Commander Briar was the first commander to not receive as much hate, thanks to winning the war, but they didn't love the man, either.

"Never to worry, though," Lou continued. "I've been at this job long enough to know I can't ever rely on getting the information I need. So, I reached out to them this morning. Told them I need weapons ready for the next century's top-ranked agent, and that they better get their shit together. And what do you know? I got a list faxed over within fifteen minutes. Bunch of sorry chumps—no offense if any of them are your friends."

"I'm sure some of them are, but I have no way of knowing who works on these specific requests. That team has hundreds of people."

"Well, you'd think they'd do a better job with so many of them. Enough about that, though. I got everything you need. I've heard some stories about this Angel you're working with in the future. Is she as good as I've heard?"

Even though the weapons warehouse workers were Road Runners and had full access to time travel, few of them exercised that rare gift, and opted to stay in their present time, living a standard, linear life. These weren't people interested in participating in missions themselves, but they still served a critical role in all the mission work carried out by the organization.

"Arielle Lucila? Yeah, she's the real deal. I know it's too early to say, but she could very well go down in our history as one of the best Angels ever. She has that sort of drive about her. All she thinks about is missions and how to complete them. When you talk to her, it's like her mind is elsewhere, even though she's still engaged in your conversation."

"I know the type. I've met enough Angels to understand. Some of them are like robots. Killing machines. I love that about 'em."

Felix studied the tattoos on Lou's arms, most of them tribal designs that led all the way into his sleeves, but he caught the words *Semper Fi* entangled within the design. "You were a Marine?"

Lou let out a soft chuckle. "It's never *were*. We are *always* Marines. I was a young kid out of high school when I fought in Korea."

"I had an uncle in the Marines, so it's always nice to meet

you guys."

Lou nodded in appreciation and uncrossed his arms. "Likewise. Let's have a look at your equipment, shall we?"

He pivoted around and led them deeper into the warehouse. Shelves lined the perimeter, reaching as high as the ten-foot ceiling, filled with hundreds of guns of all shapes and sizes. Six rows of tables ran from the front to the back in the middle of the room, and those contained a wider variety of items. Lou took them down a row toward his desk in the back corner, and Felix caught sight of boxes of ammunition, hand grenades, security system parts, and even a table full of swords and machetes.

They reached the desk in the back, where scattered papers covered every inch of its surface. A long, black duffel bag rested on top, and Lou unzipped it, reaching in and pulling out every item on Felix's list.

"Got a nine, AR, butterfly knife, throwing knives, poisons, and the cameras and mics for bugging," Lou said as he studied the objects now splayed atop his paperwork. "And ammo for the guns. Everything look good?"

Felix nodded as he looked up and down at the equipment. "This should do. Can I get a couple of extra pistols? Just something small and easy to conceal."

"Not a problem." Lou shuffled away from his desk and crouched to reach the bottom shelf ten feet away, grunting as he stretched to grab two more guns. "Two extra nines—that way you can use the same ammo. Anything else you can think of?" Lou asked, dropping the firearms into the duffel bag.

Felix shook his head. "I think this is everything. We're staying in Pueblo, so it's not much trouble if I need to come back for more."

"Don't be a stranger. I'm here for you guys and whatever

you need. Just call me if anything comes up." Lou reached over his desk and pulled a business card from a stack, handing it to Felix. It had a handwritten name and phone number for Lou.

"I appreciate your help so much," Felix said, sticking out a hand to shake.

"Let's get you packed up," Lou said. "I know there is never a second to waste on your missions. You guys trying to stop another murder?"

"We sure are."

"Well, Godspeed to you all. Good luck out there."

Chapter 18

Selena was the only one without a car, and debated between renting one for herself, waiting for Felix to come back, or figuring out how to get to Mason Gregory's neighborhood on her own. She may have gone through her regular life with the simplicity of punching in an address into her cell phone, but she had also put in the time to study living in different eras, taking retreats of living at least one year in different decades to get a feel for life and how to function like a basic human.

She despised the complexity of such a menial task in 1988, wishing she could open Uber and call for a ride that way. Without knowing how long Felix would be, she had no choice but to head into the wild world of 1988 Pueblo. The Gregory house wasn't too far, but it wasn't a quick stroll through the neighborhood, either.

They had brought an atlas of Colorado and she found it on top of the kitchen table, the book hailing itself for its detailed topographic maps and extensive update through the year of 1987. "Where the hell do we find this shit?" she asked, picking it up and studying it like an ancient relic. She put it back on the table and flipped it open to the table of contents, finding Pueblo, and flipping to the page.

Someone had already highlighted and circled all the important locations for the mission, and made it a simple task for Selena to find the exact route from their house to her destination. "I can walk if I absolutely must," she said, but figured a bus ran up and down the main road outside of the neighborhood. Even catching that would save her twenty minutes. If she arrived five minutes too late and missed Mrs. Gregory leaving the house for whatever reason, it could cause an entirely wasted day. Their missions had virtually no room for error or wasted time.

She memorized the route and wrote the address on a small slip of paper to carry in her pocket. "Time to go," she said, and left the house.

* * *

After a three-minute walk to Buffalo Road, a bustling street with small businesses and evenly-spaced bus stops, Selena only had to wait another five minutes before a bus arrived, headed northbound. She inserted three quarters into the farebox and was on her way, arriving within six minutes to her stop.

All the homes looked similar as she passed them: ranch-style houses with chain-link fences and short driveways that led to the back door. Garages were not common in the area; neither were manicured lawns. Many yards boasted tall weeds or long grass sticking through the fences.

She rounded a corner and turned onto Brush Street, the Gregory residence only two houses down. She walked on the opposite side of the street to avoid being caught snooping.

The Gregory house had an off-white paint job with light green trim. From across the street, Selena saw the front door and two windows on each side. On the left-hand side was the kitchen, a figure moving around freely within, and on the other appeared a living room, as she could see TV antennas standing tall, and a small bookshelf further in the background. The yard was in slightly better shape than most of the ones she had passed, although it had plenty of dirt patches beneath the scattering of children's toys and two plastic cars the little ones surely pedaled around in. A bush in desperate need of trimming sprawled out below the living room window.

Perfect hiding spot, Selena thought, never afraid to hide in shrubbery in the middle of the night. And in front of the living room, she'd have no trouble spying through the window to see what Gregory family life looked like in the evenings.

She had fallen too deep into her thoughts to realize the figure had stopped parading around the kitchen and now stood on the front porch.

"Lindsay," Selena whispered to herself, moving her feet again, seeking a tree to hide behind. According to the mission report, Lindsay Gregory had been married to Mason for seventeen years, in which the couple had one daughter and one son, aged six and three in 1988.

Lindsay stood on the porch, hands on her hips as she studied the lawn, shaking her head before shuffling around to pick up the toys, placing them in a wide plastic chest tucked alongside the house. She was slowly gaining weight these days. That would snowball later with the depression and binge eating following Mason's death. Her long, dirty blond hair, trailed as she whipped around the lawn, tidying it up within a couple of minutes.

She never saw Selena slip behind a van parked on the side-walk, peering around the back bumper as she crouched. Selena watched as Lindsay finished cleaning and strolled to the side of the house and sat down in her car.

"Fuck!" Selena muttered, standing up while Lindsay backed out of her driveway and took off in the opposite direction. She pulled out the notepad she kept in her back pocket and jotted down that Lindsay drove a maroon Geo Metro, its paint fading, both hubcaps missing from the driver's side of the vehicle. "Dammit!" she cried, frustrated she had no way of keeping up, potentially losing an entire day of spying on the soon-to-be widow.

Where are the kids? she wondered. It was definitely summer break, and the kids weren't of age to be left alone. Maybe Lindsay had just left to pick them up from a summer camp or daycare. Selena had spent plenty of time as a youth in such places, seeing as both her parents were always consumed with work. These were the details left out of mission reports—the holes she had to fill in.

It was almost ten o'clock, so the timing seemed strange if she had left to pick up the kids. Selena would plan to arrive earlier tomorrow, likely before the sun rose, and would certainly rent a car today to avoid any more issues.

A black car crept silently down the street, and Selena's first instinct was to hide behind the van again. She watched as it stopped in front of the Gregory property and sat there for two minutes.

"Felix?" she whispered. She had been too flustered to register the car in front of her, and couldn't help but laugh as she stood up and crossed the street.

Felix had to reach over the empty passenger seat to roll down the window. "Selena?" he asked. "What are you doing? She just left."

"No shit, Sherlock," Selena snapped. "I didn't think I was going to have to follow her already. The reports said she was a stay-at-home mom, so I figured she'd be here most of the time."

"I'm sure she'll be back soon enough. Since you're here, want to stand lookout for me? I can work much faster knowing I'm covered in case she returns."

Selena shrugged, nothing better to do since her target had disappeared. "Alright. You're early, aren't you?"

"I always try to get this part of the work done as soon as possible. I never know how many opportunities I'll get to set up my surveillance."

Selena saw the duffel bag resting on the passenger seat. "Got a gun in there for me?"

"Slow your roll. Yes, I do, but we don't need all that right now. I'm going to park across the street. You can sit in the driver's seat and just watch both directions for Mrs. Gregory. If you see her coming back, honk three times really fast and I'll be out of there."

"Easy enough."

Felix nodded before turning the car around and parking it behind the van where Selena had just hidden. He grabbed the duffel bag and sprinted to the Gregory house without another word.

Chapter 19

Felix didn't waste a second once he stepped foot on the property, bolting around the house, scaling a wobbly wooden fence, and landing in the backyard that had seen even more neglect than the front. He rushed to the back door, relieved the fence was just tall enough to prevent the neighbors from seeing him about to break and enter.

The duffel bag, strapped over his shoulder, clanged against his back while he rummaged through his pants pockets for a lock pick.

"Wait," he whispered to himself, reaching out and turning the doorknob, stomach tightening as the door creaked open into the kitchen. The smaller the town, he had found, the more likely people were to leave their back doors unlocked, especially ones that were fenced off. Even though this was Felix's field of expertise, breaking into homes always made him feel like a criminal.

His heart thrummed, adrenaline flowing through all his limbs as he took his first step inside the house. He had done this same routine at least two hundred times in his young career, but always feared the possibility of the homeowners returning before he finished. He had yet to encounter that scenario, and had no clue how he would react. He didn't carry a weapon when entering a private residence, not wanting a situation to escalate out of control and result in further complications. The lock pick was perhaps the closest thing he had to a weapon, the object nothing more than a dull-tipped screwdriver.

The house was a cramped mess. Piles of mail and bills were stacked on top of the counter next to him. They left pots and pans on the stovetop, the smell of bacon lingering in the air, something guaranteed to make Felix's mouth water, no matter the situation. The family didn't appear to have a dining room, as the table in the kitchen was far too big for the space, allowing little room to navigate around the area. It had six seats, two of which were full with more stacks of papers, these looking like drawings and homework assignments from the kids.

Felix had cameras in his bag, but rarely installed them inside of a target's home. They were twice the size of the miniature microphones he used to bug for sound. He saved the cameras for outside, where they used the views to help learn the schedule of their subjects.

He dashed toward the kitchen sink, finding an elevated cupboard beside it and reaching under to feel for any metal brackets. It had none, so he raised himself up on the sink, flailing for the small domed light fixture above.

"Jackpot," he whispered after feeling the cool touch of metal. He was equipped to plant the bugs on any surface, but using the attached magnets made his life much easier. The bug made a faint clapping sound as it attached to the light, and Felix eased himself down, spinning around to head for the living room.

A raggedy couch and rocking chair were next to each other, facing the old box TV on a small stand across the room. The coffee table in the middle had an ashtray with two cigarette butts left in it, and circular stains scattered across the surface.

The living room had plenty of areas for him to plant the bug: the TV, two lamps on either side of the furniture, under the coffee table. He preferred higher elevation, so he decided the lamps would do.

Figuring a majority of the conversations between Mason and Lindsay would come from the living room and bedroom, he planted a bug on both lamps to ensure complete coverage of the space.

An opening from the living room connected to a short hallway, where Felix found two bedrooms and a bathroom. He entered the first bedroom, finding it had two beds on opposite walls. One wall was covered with dinosaur pictures, while the other had princesses and unicorns. A toy chest stood in the middle of the room, its lid open as costumes and toys poured out of it.

Felix expected little useful conversation from the children's room, so he planted one bug on the lamp that stood next to the doorway. He did the same in the bathroom, having to stretch above the sink to secure it to the light fixture.

He continued to the bedroom at the end of the hall, finding it only slightly bigger than the kids' room. The bed had been made, but the comforter showed the ruffled imprint of a body having laid on it earlier. A dresser stood opposite the bed, clothes piled high on it, with more on the floor. They had left the closet doors open, a bottom rack covered in both men's and women's shoes. Suits and dresses hung from the rod, and winter outfits piled on the top shelf, touching the ceiling.

"This family definitely needs some more space," Felix said, and a sick feeling crept into his stomach as he realized they *would* have more space in two weeks. Once Mason was dead. He shook his head and resumed his search for the best spot to plant a bug.

The dresser left a small gap along the bottom just big enough to slip a hand into. Felix dropped to his knees, and that's when a horn started blaring outside.

"Shit," he gasped, all the blood in his body rushing to his head. He already had the bug in hand, but had no time to stick it since it would need glue or tape. He jammed it into the corner, stuffing it behind one of the dresser's legs, ensuring it was out of sight, before jumping to his feet and slinging the duffel bag over his shoulder.

Felix's vision pulsed in sync with each heartbeat. He dashed out of the bedroom and returned to the back door, stepping out- side and spinning in a quick circle to gather his surroundings. A dog barked—a horrendous *yap! yap! yap!* from a chihuahua in the yard that backed up to the Gregory residence.

"Shut the fuck up!" Felix hissed toward the fence, to no avail. The world spun in slow motion. He tried to focus on the sounds coming from the front yard, but couldn't hear a damn thing. How he wished he could punt the chihuahua across a football field right now.

He shuffled to the fence, legs tense and ready to sprint, and pressed his face against the coarse wood, fighting for a visual through the thin slots between pickets. The Geo Metro had just turned into the driveway, stopping less than three feet away from where Felix stood.

The rattling engine turned off and the driver's door swung open, prompting Felix to jump backwards, praying his sil- houette hadn't been visible through the fence. Lindsay was speaking, and the sound of her voice made Felix's heart stop cold in his chest.

He pivoted around and debated running to the other side

of the house. Instead, Lindsay continued speaking, in the distance. And in no ways suspicious. Cell phones were still rare in 1988, so he leaned forward to listen more closely.

"Mommy, I want a peanut butter and jelly sandwich," a little girl's voice said.

"I think we can make that work," Lindsay said, and the sound of their footsteps moved further away as they went to the front door.

Felix froze, calculating the distance from the car to the front door, and also how long it would take him to hop over the fence and dash off the property.

Just go, dammit, he thought, and lunged toward the fence, jumping as high as he could until his fingers grasped the top of it. No one was in sight as he fell down on the other side, landing square on his back, the duffel bag tangled around his arms and neck. Felix hurried to his feet, staying in a crouched position, as the kitchen window faced out the side of the house. If Lindsay went straight to the kitchen sink, she'd spot him.

She didn't, and the moment he heard the front door slam shut, Felix sprinted away from the house.

He reached the sidewalk and never looked back, rushing to Selena in the car around the corner, leaning on the hood to catch his breath.

Selena stepped out. "Well, that was exciting for you," she said with a light chuckle.

Felix shook his head, still panting like a dog. "That was . . . the closest call I've had."

"How much were you able to get done?"

"Bugged all the rooms. Still need to set up the receiver, and tap the phone line. That's all stuff that can be done from outside the house—much less risky. I'm going to have to stay here today, though. I need to at least find a spot in the area to hide the receiver. Within 300 yards of the house."

"How big is it?"

Felix patted the duffel bag where he kept it. "About the size of a shoe box."

"I'll help you look. I'll even drive. We should leave the area for a bit. Got an older woman six houses down working in her front yard. She hasn't looked this way, but might as well play it safe." Selena nodded in the direction, and Felix saw the lady standing near the sidewalk with a water hose in hand.

"Good call. Let's head out."

Chapter 20

While Felix and Selena spent the rest of their day driving around the Gregory neighborhood searching for a hiding spot for the radio receiver (an overgrown bush that separated the neighborhood from an adjoining park that clearly hadn't been attended to in the past year), Arielle fought off the most unbearable waves of boredom she had ever endured.

Boredom was certainly part of the job, especially during the current phase of staking out and following a target, but Arielle typically used that downtime to work on other aspects of the mission—matters that now fell into the hands of Felix and Selena. For the first time during a mission, Arielle had nothing to do but wait for her target to step out of the building he had entered nine hours ago. At one point, she even considered running to a bookstore and returning with a stack of new reads. Her lifestyle had put restraints on her longtime favorite hobby, but if her days looked like this, she just might have a chance to jump back into the imaginative world of books.

The building she had followed Mason to, and remained parked outside of since nine in the morning, stood two stories tall and had CreditConnect posted in big block letters across the top windows. She already knew Mason had worked for the company for the last two years, manning the phones in an account manager role for the credit card processing company. Just as she already knew—or could at least take a highly educated guess—which route he would drive home. You couldn't enter a stakeout without already knowing ninety percent of the information needed. It was the other ten she had set out for, and with that came the waiting game.

After sitting in her car for the entirety of Mason's workday, she shot up in her seat when he finally stepped out of the building at six minutes past five. He walked with a small group of two other women and a man, and Arielle was quick to study any signs of suggestive body language between Mason and the others. He showed none and shuffled to his car after a quick wave to his co-workers, who had split their own ways. A majority of affairs occurred in the workplace, or at least *with* co-workers, and this first outing suggested nothing of the sorts.

"It's never simple," she whispered as she twisted the key in the ignition. She had parked two rows behind Mason, providing a direct line of sight to his car, and also the opportunity to pull out easily and follow him.

She did exactly that as Mason steered his old Civic out of the parking lot and pulled onto the road. Tailing someone in a car was second nature for Arielle, and she did so with the expectation of finding nothing of significance.

For the next fifteen minutes, Arielle followed Mason on the exact route she expected him to take home. He made no stops and followed all traffic laws. When they pulled into his neighborhood, Arielle hung back at least one hundred feet since she lost the concealment of traffic on the main roads. She pulled aside and waited for Mason to coast into the driveway.

It was a hot June evening, and the sun wouldn't quit for

another three hours, so Arielle rolled up her windows and blasted the air conditioning, something she couldn't have done all day, as cars from the 1980s were even less fuel-efficient than those from her Original Time. But she couldn't take it anymore, and as she parked across the street from the Gregory residence, her heart froze when she saw Felix in his car a few feet in front of her.

There was no issue with Felix being there, but she expected little overlap with her new teammates while working on missions, especially in the middle of the day. They were to all work during the day, and convene at night, if plausible. He stared at her from his rear-view mirror, and she promptly hopped out of the car and hurried into his passenger seat.

"What are you still doing here?" she asked. "Isn't everything supposed to be in place?"

"Ran into some issues. Almost got caught inside the house. I didn't get the chance to set up the receiver until recently. I wanted to hang out to make sure everything is running smoothly."

Felix raised his left hand that had been tucked along the side of his leg, and revealed a handheld radio receiver. A wire ran from it to his left ear, connecting to a small earphone.

"I see."

In the past, Arielle had been used to just showing up to a mission and having these kinks worked out. She knew how to retrieve the memory chip from a receiver, insert a new one, and take it back to her computer to listen to the footage. While she understood that more went into the process, she had never experienced it firsthand.

Felix pulled the cord out of the headphone jack, allowing the receiver's built-in speaker to flood the car with the voices of Mason and Lindsay. He recoiled at how loud it was, and promptly turned down the volume dial.

"Busy day at work?" Lindsay asked.

Arielle stared at the receiver, not realizing Felix watched her.

"Pretty busy, yeah," Mason said, the first time either had heard their target's voice. He spoke with a slight slur, like he might have a toothpick in his mouth. "How were things around here today?"

"Good. Picked up around the house, got things ready for Amanda's ballet recital Friday night. You told the guys you won't be able to make it to poker night, right?"

"Yes. They actually rescheduled for Saturday night, that way I can go."

Arielle whipped out her notepad to jot down the information about Saturday night. She had an obligation to follow Mason's every single movement if he left the house by himself. A poker game could serve as a cover for lots of things, allowing him privacy for at least three hours at a time. Her face prickled with heat at the thought of getting closer to solving, and hopefully preventing, his murder.

"Oh, good," Lindsay replied. "Amanda is so excited to dance on the big stage."

Mason chuckled. "She's too cute. Just like you."

Lindsay giggled. "Oh, Mase, stop it."

"Just speaking from the heart. What's for dinner tonight? It smells delicious in here."

"Made your favorite: meatloaf with steamed carrots and mashed potatoes."

"You never stop amazing me. How did I get so lucky?"

Arielle and Felix listened for ten more minutes before Felix lowered the volume once the Gregory family all sat down for dinner. He looked at Arielle as she gazed into the distance.

"They sound like a happy, normal family," he said.

Arielle nodded. "That they do. Which only makes his murder more mysterious. He's clearly a good man. A family man who loves his wife and kids. Who would want him dead? *Why?*"

Arielle knew better than to jump to conclusions. She'd seen plenty of instances where the first impressions of her subjects weren't always what they seemed.

"They moved a poker game from Friday to Saturday," she said, and flipped to the front of her notepad where she kept the calendar for June 1988. "That means if the poker game is weekly and returns to its regular schedule, it will fall on the night he's murdered next week. We need to find out where this game is and who plays in it. Then we need to see if we can get Selena a seat at the table. This upcoming Saturday night game is now our top priority."

Chapter 21

By Thursday, June 16, the team was in a groove. All plans centered on the Saturday night poker game where they hoped to find something of substance to aid the mission. On Monday night, the three Angels had met for a late dinner where they discussed their first few days working on the mission. Felix confirmed he had set up the audio and its receiver, and he would drive to the neighborhood to pull the data for them to listen to each night.

Selena rented a car and tailed Lindsay, finding she stopped at a park in the mornings, after dropping off the kids at a summer camp, for a leisurely walk. She was now ready to make her move.

Arielle had two more boring days of sitting in the parking lot of CreditConnect, using the downtime to outline requests for more information like contacts at the company and the summer camp that they could research. She placed a nightly call to the Road Runners headquarters in 1988 to request the assistance.

While Arielle spent Thursday once more outside the office building, and Felix listened to the prior evening's recording from the Gregory residence, Selena sat on a bench in Ranchero Park, five minutes east of the Gregory house.

It had only taken two days of following Lindsay to learn her daily routine, so Selena could only trust nothing would change by the third day. She dressed in jogging shorts and a tank-top, a water bottle clutched in her grip as she looked both ways at the trail in front of the bench. The trail circled a playground and open fields where kids kicked a soccer ball around, geese waddling around as they picked at the grass.

After fifteen minutes, Lindsay finally appeared in the distance. Selena had watched her enough during the past three days to know exactly what she looked like from afar. Lindsay jogged, still three hundred feet away from where Selena sat on the bench.

Selena scanned the area and saw no potential spectators, so she stood up and started stretching. She always got the slightest of jitters before her initial encounter with a new target. The past had never thrown major roadblocks in her way, but that didn't guarantee it would always be the case.

Her role was strictly grounded in research. Selena was never to tamper directly with the past, but would only unearth the information needed for Arielle to decide what was worth pursuing. She had mastered the art of adapting to her target's personality, needing to develop trust within minutes.

With Lindsay approaching, about fifty feet now, Selena started jogging toward her, the water bottle intentionally loose in her grip. She was within immediate range of Lindsay in a matter of seconds.

Lindsay paid no attention to the woman jogging in her direction, her ponytail bouncing side to side while she kept her head high and eyes focused ahead. Once they were within ten feet of each other, Selena let out a gasp, tossed her water bottle on the trail directly in front of Lindsay's path, and tumbled to the side where she lay on her back in the grass, hands clutched around her ankle as she pretended to writhe in pain.

Selena watched as Lindsay's eyes widened, jaw dropping as her sneakers screeched against the pavement to a sudden stop. "My Lord!" Lindsay cried, rushing to Selena's side. "Are you okay, sweetie?" She crouched down, eyes running up and down Selena's body.

Selena grunted as she sat up, still rubbing her ankle. "I think I rolled my ankle." She clenched her teeth and drew in a sharp breath to sell the faux pain. "I can't believe this happened to me—I used to run track. Now I can't even jog through a park. This is *so* embarrassing." Selena looked down to avoid eye contact, getting lost in her role and the story she was creating.

"What's your name, hon?" Lindsay asked, placing a gentle hand on Selena's back.

"Selena."

"Nice to meet you Selena. My name is Lindsay. Everything will be fine—I promise. Worst-case scenario, you'll need to take it easy for the next couple of days. If it's mild, you'll be fine by tonight."

Selena shook her head, mentally returning to the days of her parents' vicious divorce to let tears well up in her eyes. "I don't think I can stand up."

"It's just your ankle that's hurt, right?" Lindsay asked, her voice softening into a natural, motherly tone while her hand continued running up and down Selena's spine.

"Yes, but it hurts so bad."

"Okay, let me help you up. Then we'll be able to tell how serious this is."

Selena nodded as Lindsay took a step back and extended her hand. She grimaced as she reached up to grab it and put all her weight on her supposed good foot.

Lindsay kept her eyes focused on Selena's feet. "You need to put some weight on it—just to see."

Selena nodded, keeping her lips pursed as she gradually shifted her body's weight from her good foot toward the other. She winced, but continued, pleased to have every ounce of Lindsay's concentration. "Okay. I'm on it," she said. "I don't know if I can walk yet."

"That's good," Lindsay said, a smile touching the corners of her mouth. "If you can stand on your own, then it's not too severe. Maybe sit on that bench for a few minutes." Lindsay pointed to the same bench Selena had just left moments earlier. "I'll help you over there."

"Thank you. You really didn't need to do all this."

"Oh, it's nothing. I have two little ones, and they're always getting hurt. This is practically a part of my daily routine." Lindsay giggled at herself, and Selena couldn't help but grin at the joyous sound.

Selena had to work fast in figuring out Lindsay's personality, competency, and overall state of mind. She had studied advanced psychological techniques to pinpoint these traits when meeting new people, but relied more on her instincts and experience after having traveled all over the world since a young age and meeting a wide-range of people. From what she could gather, Lindsay loved life and had a motherly instinct. She cared for others, which meant she saw the good in people, no matter the situation. Lindsay radiated kindness, and it frustrated Selena to think someone would harm such a gentle soul's husband and family life.

Lindsay wrapped an arm around Selena's waist and served as a crutch while they limped toward the bench. "How old are your kids?"

"I have a six-year-old girl, and a three-year-old boy. They are the sweetest kids."

Selena wanted to ask where the boy was the other day while Felix had been bugging their house. "I love kids. Used to babysit in high school. I don't suppose you need a sitter? I'm looking to make some extra money."

"Do you go to college here?"

"No—I graduated last year. Been bouncing around from job to job ever since. Seems like I made more money playing poker games in the dorms than in the real world. So if you know anyone who needs babysitting services or runs a poker game, I'm all ears."

"I wish I could help you, sweetie, but I don't work and have no need for babysitting. If you give me your number, I'll definitely call you if anything comes up on the weekends. My husband and I don't go out too often, but you never know."

"What does your husband do?" Selena asked.

"He works in finance."

They reached the bench, and Lindsay helped Selena sit down, taking a place next to her.

"Thank you for your help. I'm not sure what I would have done if you weren't here."

"Do you not have any friends or family in town?"

"I'm afraid not. All the friends I made in school moved out of Pueblo after graduation. My mom lives in New York. My dad lives in France. No siblings. No grandparents. No cousins."

Lindsay frowned, and Selena knew she had struck an emotional chord. "If you don't mind me asking, what made you want to stay in Pueblo? Was there a boy?"

Selena shook her head, hair falling over her face, and Lindsay immediately reached out to brush it back. "No boy. I like it here. I grew up spending my time between New York City and Paris. I was in such a bubble, I hardly knew smaller towns like this existed."

"We're hardly a small town in Pueblo."

"No, but Pueblo is laid-back. No one worries about having the best fashion, cars, and things. I like living in town even more than on campus. My parents will send me money with a quick phone call, but I'm more interested in making a life on my own. Neither of them will approve of me staying here, so it's not a call I'm going to make."

Lindsay sat back, her folded hands resting atop crossed legs as she stared into the distance. Selena could see the thoughts swimming behind her eyes.

"It sounds like you've had quite the childhood. I can only dream about visiting Paris one day, and you've *lived* there. And now you want to live *here*. I always thought it would be the other way around."

Selena deflated. She needed to make one more push. "Paris is as wonderful as advertised. It is a magical place to visit. But living there is a different story. Same with New York. I guess it's hard for me to pass fair judgment because I was always alone. My parents were always at work—I had to explore the cities on my own or with a babysitter. Looks like I'll have the same experience here in Pueblo, but at least I'm used to it now."

That was as desperate as she could make herself sound without disgusting herself.

After an eternity of a pause, Lindsay finally said, "No, you won't."

"I won't what?" Selena replied, stretching her ankle to give the appearance that she was at least trying to nurse her fake injury.

"You won't have to have that same experience. I won't allow it. You're welcome to dinner any time at our house. If you want to spend time with a family over any of the holidays, just say the word. You're too sweet of a girl to sit by yourself all day."

"Really? You would do that for me?" Selena knew no matter what she said, Lindsay wouldn't back out on her offer. People kind enough to make such an offer in the first place were always true to their word.

"Life is short, sweetie. The older you get, the more you realize that. Once you have kids, forget about it. Time pretty much moves at a sprint once you spend all your time watching your kids grow up. It's important to make the most out of your life, and if I can help you in the slightest way by just providing a loving family you can interact with, then it's the least I can do."

"Lindsay . . . wow. I don't know what to say. This might be the nicest thing anyone has ever done for me. But I can't just impede on your family."

Impede? Selena thought. *I'm going to impede, infiltrate, and find out everything I can to save this woman's family from doom.*

"Not at all. The kids will love you. My husband won't mind. And it was all my idea. Maybe you can come over for dinner sometime soon and meet everyone?"

"I'll need to check my calendar and let you know. Can I call you later today?" Selena was done playing games. She received an invite to the Gregory home for dinner and would do nothing to jeopardize it. She didn't want to jump right into dinner tonight, unless Arielle thought it was a good idea. They still had eight more days until Mason would be found dead.

"Absolutely. Let me write down my phone number for you. If I don't answer, just leave a message and I'll get back."

Selena stood up, standing on her tiptoes. "I think my ankle is already feeling much better. I should be able to make it back to my car. Thank you so much for everything."

"Say no more. Call me, and we'll see each other real soon."

Lindsay reached out and hugged Selena before they parted ways. Selena returned to the trail and walked with her normal stride once Lindsay was out of sight. All she could think on this glorious summer morning was, *I'm in.*

Chapter 22

Arielle sat in her car outside of CreditConnect, nose buried in the newest Stephen King novel, *The Tommyknockers.* She fell into a routine rather quickly, thanks to a firm grasp of Mason's schedule. If he entered the building with his lunch pail in hand, he didn't step foot outside until his shift was over. It was boring, but it made her job simple until they made progress on other fronts.

This morning, she watched him enter with said lunch pail, and promptly reclined her seat to lie back and enjoy the alien horror novel. She left herself at an angle just high enough to see the entrance over the car's dashboard. Anytime the doors swung open, the movement would catch her attention, just in case.

It was 11:30 when her stomach rumbled, the turkey and ham sandwich she had brought weighing on her mind. She adjusted her seat to its upright position and reached into the backseat to grab her brown-bag lunch.

A car blazed into the parking lot; the tires making the faintest of screeches as it turned the corner into the row behind Arielle. It sped down the row, going at least thirty miles per hour, and this prompted Arielle to subconsciously reach under her seat where she kept her loaded pistol. Her fingers brushed the cool steel as she lost sight of the vehicle in the jungle of parked cars.

She debated stepping out for a better view, but decided it was too risky. One rule she followed was to never assume an action was meaningless. Sure, the speeding car was likely someone running late for their shift, but there was always the chance it had something to do with Mason Gregory.

Arielle rolled down her window to better hear outside.

Silence.

She figured the car had found a parking space, and shifted her focus to the office building's entrance, assuming whoever had parked would enter within seconds.

No one ever appeared, and when she heard the steady rhythm of footsteps approach from behind, she whipped out her pistol and raised it in front of her face. She glanced over her shoulder and saw the movement of someone walking down the row behind her car, and remained frozen in her seat, hoping the person would pass.

Instead, they turned into the space where Arielle had parked, prompting her to shove open the door and jump out, gun cocked and ready to blast. "Stop right there!" she shouted.

"What the fuck?!" Selena screamed, jumping back. "What the hell are you *doing*?"

"Selena? What are *you* doing?" Arielle lowered her gun and looked around to make sure no one had spotted their encounter. The coast was clear. "Get in the car. *Now*!"

Selena rolled her eyes and shuffled around Arielle's car, falling into the passenger seat and slamming the door.

"Seriously," Arielle said. "Why are you here?"

"Well, in case you've forgotten, we don't have any cell phones and I need to talk to you. Something major has happened." Selena stared out the windshield, head bobbing from side to side while she spoke.

"With Lindsay?"

Selena nodded. "I befriended her at the park today. She's already invited me over to their house for dinner, and gave me her phone number. I'm in, but I don't know the best day to ask to go over for a visit."

"Wow. You pulled this off after one encounter?"

"Don't act so surprised. You're not the only one who's good at their job."

Arielle bit her lip. Selena seemed to always want to pick a fight with her.

"It's not that I'm surprised you did it—I'm just shocked it happened so fast. A personal dinner invite to their house?"

Selena smirked, reveling in her success. "Yes, and I thought I'd check with our fearless leader how I should schedule this all out."

Condescending bitch, Arielle thought, returning a tight-lipped grin of her own. "Thank you for checking. Follow-up question. Do you think you can get into that poker game on the Friday he gets killed?"

Selena shifted in her seat, finally turning her head to lock eyes with Arielle. "I've been thinking about that on the way over. I think I can, but there are a few factors out of my control."

"Like?"

"For one, we don't know what kind of game this is. It's 1988. They might oppose a woman playing in their poker game. We also don't know who is hosting the game. I have a hunch Mason is involved with some shady people if he ends up murdered. This could be some sort of underground game that is invite-only. Aside from that, we're talking about the night of the murder. Going to that poker game could get some pushback from the past. My presence alone could change the trajectory of the night, so who knows what might come up?"

Arielle nodded in deep thought. Selena had looked at this from all angles, and had valid hesitations. "Okay. Plan the dinner as soon as you feel it's appropriate. You spoke with Lindsay, so I'll trust you to make that call. Let's plan to probe about the poker game, and possibly get an invitation. If we can at least find out where the game is taking place, and the timing of it all, that will help us a ton. Then on the night of, we'll have to make a judgment call if it's safe for you to enter the game, or hang back from the outside."

Selena nodded and looked back at the office building. "Okay. I'll see what I can get lined up."

"Sounds good. What do you have going on the rest of the day?"

"I'll go back home, call Lindsay, and schedule a dinner date. I have some reports to make, then will probably head to the mall. I need a new outfit for going out. Do you want me to wait for you?"

"I'll have to pass. I don't do malls."

"Don't do malls? What does that even mean?"

Arielle raised a hand. "Thank you for the invite."

Selena shrugged. "Suit yourself, but there isn't much to do in this boring town."

Arielle had enough of the attitude. "Look, not everywhere is New York, or Paris. Not everyone gets to live some jet-setting life between big cities. You've lived in Los Angeles, plus those two places. That is not how the rest of the world is. I would think you'd know that by now, after working on so many missions."

"Don't attack me for the life I've led," Selena snapped, her head whipping back as she turned to face Arielle. "I may have lived in some cool places, but my childhood was so fucked-up. Did you enjoy having both of your parents and a happy household growing up? Do you think it was fun being a teenager and having two different lives? School year in New York, and summers in Paris? It wasn't. It was impossible for me to make serious friends in either city, because I always had it in the back of my head that I would just be leaving. It was even harder to date. I tried having boyfriends, and it always completely blew up in my face." Arielle watched as the rage left Selena's face and gave way to pain. Tears streamed down her reddened cheeks. "I've just wanted a normal life, but I have no idea what that means."

Arielle shook her head. "I'm sorry."

"Like hell you are," Selena snarled, the rage apparently not completely vanished.

"No, I am. I'm sorry I've never taken the time to learn your story. I wish I could understand, but you're right. I had a mostly happy life growing up. Maybe I take that for granted."

"And I would think *you* would know how hard some people's lives have been. Everyone in the Road Runners has suffered tragedy, even if it doesn't seem like it on the surface. We all come here to escape our past lives."

"Is that why you joined?"

Selena shrugged. "Who knows? I had a dream life starting in Hollywood. I always think about what things would be like if I stayed. But that's part of life, isn't it? No matter which road you take, you'll always wonder what the other would have been like."

"I don't see it that way. I believe we're always right where

141

we're supposed to be."

"But you wouldn't be where you are without taking a certain path. And that's what drives me crazy about our time travel. We're not able to venture back and see how making a different choice might change our own futures."

Arielle nodded, reflecting. This was something she had thought over plenty of times. She might not have the power to go back and change her own life decisions, but she could very well travel back and stop the shooter from going on his rampage in the mall on that fateful day. Her life would indeed look different. "Maybe we're not supposed to know what life would be like had we made different choices. Maybe we have to trust things work out for the best—even when it doesn't seem like it. You may have not had the ideal childhood growing up, but look at you now. You're incredible at what you do."

Tears returned to Selena's eyes, pooling on the surface but remaining in place. "It's just hard for me to feel accomplished since I can't even share what I do with my parents. I wish I could tell them how well I'm doing without lying about the truth."

"We have to celebrate our successes among ourselves, un-fortunately. I know how you feel. I talk with my grandma after each mission and make up stories about the life she thinks I'm living. But that's what we signed up for."

Selena wiped her eyes. "You're right. I should head home. I have to plan out these next few days."

She leaned into her door and opened it before Arielle shot out a hand and grabbed her shoulder. "Hey," Arielle said. "I'm proud of you and all you've done."

Selena gave a tight-lipped grin before stepping out of the car.

Chapter 23

"So what did you get done today, Felix?" Arielle asked as they sat around the dinner table. Felix had prepared a dinner of homemade spaghetti and meatballs once he received word that all three of them would have a rare evening at home together.

"Well, there isn't anything new for me to do. Now my days consist of running over to the receiver, replacing the flash drive, and listening to last night's feed."

"Anything exciting?"

"Not in particular. They had dinner together as a family. Sounds like the girl is in a dance camp for the summer, and the boy goes to daycare at a friend's house. Lindsay left in the morning—for a run around the park, according to Selena. Then she came home, showered, cleaned the kitchen, then headed back out for another hour before returning home with the daughter. They spent a couple of hours together doing crafts, reading books, and watching TV, before she left again to pick up the son. From there, she prepared dinner, they ate, bathed the kids. Lindsay and Mason watched TV after putting the kids in bed and talked about their days. They had sex and called it a night."

Selena giggled. "Enjoy the show, Felix?"

Felix blushed. "No, pervert. It's just audio, and I fast-forward through it."

"You're *such* a professional," Selena teased, shoving a piece of garlic bread into her mouth.

"So, did you schedule a dinner?" Arielle asked, dismissing Selena's immaturity.

Selena nodded, chewing faster to swallow and reply. "Monday night."

"Four days before the murder," Arielle said, looking to the ceiling. "You don't think that's cutting it too close?"

Selena shrugged. "I didn't have much of a choice. That's the first date she offered. What was I supposed to say? 'Can I please come sooner so my friends and I can stop your husband's murder?'" She laughed as she twirled her fork in the pasta.

"Monday it is. Felix, would you be able to wait outside the house that night and listen to the live feed?"

"Why would he need to do that?" Selena asked. "You don't think I can handle it myself?"

"It's not that," Arielle said. "It will be the week of the murder. We'll all need to be ready for resistance from the past. And since we never have a clue what that might look like, I think it would be smart to have help close by, just in case. I might even stop by that night. It will be, at the time, the most important night of this mission. We need to get all the information we can about where Mason will be on the night of the twenty-fourth. Look for notes on their calendar and try to work it into conversation."

Selena nodded. "Of course. Won't be a problem. It's not like Mason knows he's supposed to die that night. Are you going to follow him this Saturday to see where the poker game is?"

"Absolutely. I'm assuming it's in the evening, so if either of you wants to join me, I wouldn't mind some company after sitting in my car alone all week. I don't think we'll have much else to do on a Saturday night."

They poked at their food, neither wanting to volunteer for such a dry task. "I'll go," Felix eventually said.

Arielle smiled in appreciation. "Do we have any thoughts about who might kill Mason? Felix, you've been in their house, and Selena you spent some time with Lindsay. I haven't learned a single thing sitting outside his office building. Maybe we should have gotten you a job there just to see."

Selena shook her head. "It's probably just a boring desk job. I doubt anything going on in there has any ties to his murder. If it had, it probably wouldn't be a cold case. I can say confidently that it is not his wife, either. She seems to love him, and they have a solid relationship. He hasn't stayed late at work so far, right?"

"Nope. The man is like clockwork heading out of that place."

"So, there's definitely not an affair. Eighty-five percent affairs begin at the workplace. If he was having one, he'd stay late, or at least not go straight home."

"Nothing I've heard on the tapes suggests anything is going on, either," Felix added. "The home life is solid. He's a family man. So we either have a completely random attack, or it's definitely tied to the poker game."

"It's not random," Arielle said. "He had to have been lured to such a remote location. He wouldn't have ended up there by simply driving around. I'm thinking drugs or prostitution were involved, and a deal went wrong."

"This poker game might be a front," Felix said. "Do we know if Lindsay has ever gone to one with him? Even just to hang out with other wives?"

They both looked at Selena, who only shrugged in response.

"I don't know if it's necessarily a front," Arielle said. "But there might be some shady characters who attend. You never know with underground gambling—it can attract all kinds of criminals."

"Yeah," Felix replied. "But those types of games are typically with wealthy people. Drug lords, pimps, that sort of stuff. Hell, professional gamblers. Mason Gregory doesn't exactly radiate that type of vibe. He seems like a guy who plays in friendly twenty-dollar games."

"True. That's why I think we need to all go this Saturday. I want to get the license plate numbers of all the cars in the parking lot, and we can start exploring who is attending this game."

Felix nodded. "We should be able to learn everything we need, short of who actually pulls the trigger."

Selena leaned back and crossed her arms, frowning.

"Something the matter?" Arielle asked.

"I agree we'll gain a lot, but don't you think it's dangerous for us to all be there at the same time? We don't know who we're dealing with. I'd hate for us to end up in a shootout."

Arielle thought back to single-handedly wiping out a dozen members of the Mexican cartel. "I think we can manage it. We've certainly had worse scenarios, and have always come out on top. And now we're a team. If you can find out where the game is played, maybe Felix can bug the place ahead of time."

Felix nodded. "Assuming it can be done, I'd love to."

"I really want as many eyeballs on the place as possible," Arielle continued. "You're right—we *don't* know who we're dealing with. Maybe one of us can keep watch while two of us explore the property. It will be nighttime, I assume, and I know I won't be able to notice everything on my own."

"We'll be there," Felix said, shooting a glance at Selena across the table.

"Yep," she said dismissively.

"Well, that settles it," Arielle said. "I look forward to it. Think we can all learn a lot from each other."

Selena had finished her meal and placed the silverware on top of the empty plate. "Well, if we're done chatting for tonight, I'm gonna head out." She stood and pushed in her chair before grabbing her plate to place in the sink.

"Going to check on Lindsay?" Arielle asked.

"No. Going to a bar."

"Excuse me? We're on a mission. We don't go out and party on missions. This is our work—the whole time."

Selena furrowed her brow. "Maybe *you* don't go out and have fun on missions. But *I* do."

"You can't!"

"Says who? Show me an official rule from the Road Runners that says I can't go to a bar and have a drink to unwind. Show me that and I'll stay."

Arielle clenched her fists under the table, nails digging into her palms. She knew nearly all the official rules the organization had, and there was no such thing preventing Selena from going out in a non-work fashion. "I'm running this mission, and I don't want you going out."

"Well, excuse you," Selena said, putting her hands on her hips, eyes bulging as they focused entirely on Arielle. "You're just the highest-ranking Angel. You don't have control over me. We all report to headquarters. Me and Felix don't work *for* you. If you really have a problem with this, then have Commander Briar call me about it. I was going to invite you, but clearly I forgot you hate fun."

Selena shot a wink at Arielle before pivoting and leaving them alone in the dining room. They listened as her footsteps stomped up the stairs and through the hallway as she entered her bedroom, slamming the door shut for added effect.

Arielle sat with her jaw hanging, Felix avoiding eye contact as he poked at what little food remained on his plate. "What the hell was that?!"

Felix looked up and shrugged.

"Am I in the wrong here?" Arielle asked.

"I'd rather not get involved."

"Just tell me—I need to know these things. I know I can't just command you guys, but am I making an unreasonable request?"

Felix stuffed the last bite of food into his mouth, and over time Arielle would come to realize he did this strategically to allow himself more time to process his thoughts and choose his words. After he swallowed, he said, "I've worked with lots of different Angels, and a lot of them go out during the evenings. It's not a big deal. Everyone is always responsible, and all the mission work still gets done. People have different ways of blowing off steam."

Arielle never partook in such activities like going out to bars. Restaurants were about the extent of her time spent in a social setting. She enjoyed going to the gym, taking hikes in the mountains, and traveling the world for pleasure between missions. She had no problem drinking a dozen piña coladas on the beach while on vacation, but wouldn't dare spend a night out drinking while on a mission. A glass of wine before bed was the most she had ever had while working.

"Do you think she does this often?"

"Selena likes to have a good time. She's also the best at what she does. I don't personally see a reason to argue with her over it. The work will get done at the highest quality you can get, and that's all that matters. Honestly, I think it's all part of her process. She likes going out to the local bars and getting a feel for the town. It helps her better understand how to relate to her targets."

"When did she tell you this?"

"After they assigned us this mission, her and I went to a Rockies game and had some drinks."

"So it's been there from the start. Good to know."

Felix shook his head. "It's not what you think. Selena likes to have fun—that's all there is to it. She doesn't do any hard drugs. Doesn't even get drunk."

"Why are you standing up for her so much?"

"Because no one ever has," Selena said from the entryway.

Felix spun around in his seat, face immediately turning red. "Wh—"

"Thank you," Selena said, a grin taking over her face. "Outside of my mom, I don't think anyone has ever stood up for me. Everyone writes me off as some party girl who can't be taken seriously. Even these fuckers in the Road Runners who rate me as the best actress in the organization don't truly take me serious. So thank you, Felix. Your words mean a lot to me."

"How long have you been standing there?" Arielle asked.

"What, am I not allowed to be stealthy like you? We all go through the same training."

Arielle didn't care if Selena had overheard the conversation, but Selena's ability to slither down the stairs without being heard had caught her off guard.

"I know. And I'm impressed."

"Oh? Well, thanks. I'm heading out now. Don't wait up for me, Mom."

Chapter 24

Selena ended up at the Paris Lounge, a far cry from her previous home. It was a hole-in-the-wall nightclub with cheap drinks, a mediocre DJ, and a sticky dance floor. She had driven over with a smile impossible to wipe away. Despite spending her whole life trying to prove doubters wrong, she often found herself to be her own worst critic. The luxury of her childhood had resulted in things being handed to her for most of her adolescent life, hampering her ability to stand up for herself. It wasn't until joining the Road Runners that she developed this skill, and telling off the great Arielle Lucila had her floating on a cloud.

She had plenty of respect for the Road Runners, and even Arielle, but took pride in knowing she could stand up to them. People would never understand her because she had no desire to live a cookie-cutter life. She had given up all the glory of a Hollywood career to track bad guys for unlimited income and resources. The way she saw it, she was playing with house money for the rest of her life. She had the skills the organization wanted, and therefore, the leverage for whatever pathetic argument might arise regarding her lifestyle.

She was on top of her world, and no one could stop her.

Selena stepped out of her car to find the parking lot jam-packed. She hadn't expected such a sizeable crowd for a Thursday night, but the sign taped to the glass doors at the entrance explained it all: *LADIES' NIGHT THURSDAY! LADIES DRINK FREE.*

She smirked upon reading it, mentally bracing herself for the type of men who were surely lurking inside. The cheapskates always came out to ladies' night, happy to pay the cover charge since they wouldn't have to gamble money on drinks for the women.

Selena's mother had taught her many lessons growing up as an adolescent in New York City, and one of the more important ones was to never let her attention be purchased by a man. "That's how your father landed me, and look where we are now," she'd say begrudgingly. She had heard plenty of stories about how her father picked up her mother with slick talk and expensive rounds of drinks. Charles Nicole had come from money and knew how to use it to get what he wanted, including luring attractive women to his VIP table, where bottle service continued well past two in the morning.

Fortunately, Selena never saw this side of her father. During her summers in Paris, if he wasn't at work, he was with her. They'd see movies, go to fancy dinners and art museums, and do touristy things like visiting the Eiffel Tower and the Louvre. She would see her father's eyes wander whenever they passed a beautiful woman, but he wouldn't so much as speak to one in her presence. Because of that, she always thought of her father as a gentleman, no matter what her mother had to say.

Regardless, her lessons rang loudly in her mind whenever she went out, and now, as she approached the entrance for the Paris Lounge.

The door handles were shaped like the Eiffel Tower and she

couldn't help but giggle as she pulled them open. The muffled booming of music became clear as she entered the building where a hostess stood behind a podium, smoking a cigarette. The young woman blew a puff of smoke into the air as Selena approached.

"Just you tonight, hon?" she asked.

"Just me."

"Let me check your ID."

Selena's heart sunk as she fumbled into her pocket. *Did I get a new ID for this mission?*

Other members of the Angels handled hundreds of little details before a mission. Matters like fake IDs, birth certifi- cates, social security cards, and time-appropriate currency were always taken care of. She simply couldn't recall getting those for this mission, but blew a sigh of relief when she pulled the ID out of her wallet and saw an older Colorado driver's license that listed her birth year as 1965.

The hostess checked the ID without a fuss and let Selena pass into the club. The dance floor was strategically placed on the opposite side, two bars along the side walls where crowded lines had already formed, with plenty of women waiting for their free drinks. Tables of men filled the space between the entrance and the dance floor, all eyes scanning the room for their evening's prey.

Selena immediately noticed a couple of men checking her out as she made her way into the mob. She refused to give Arielle the satisfaction of knowing her one rule while on missions: no men. At most, she would flirt for free drinks, but didn't have to worry about that after tumbling into this ladies' night. If things went her way, she'd strike up a conversation with another woman and get a feel for the locals. She loved to dance,

153

and would share one with a man as long as he didn't get too touchy. Otherwise, her plan was always to get a solid buzz to ride out for a couple of hours before sobering up enough to drive home safely.

A man wearing glow sticks as a necklace danced toward Selena as she stood at the back of the line, and started thrusting his hips in her direction. He avoided eye contact and kept a foot of distance between, trying to play it cool.

"No thanks!" Selena shouted over Michael Jackson's "The Way You Make Me Feel" while shaking her head.

The man moved on to the next line of women with no objection. Selena remained six people back in line, watching the bartender pour a line of shots with complete ease. The line moved faster when no payment was involved, and she ordered a vodka soda after another few minutes had passed.

She scanned the room, but found no empty tables, forcing her to stand along the railing that separated the dance floor from the rest of the club. People-watching never got old. She had done it ever since she was a child, and always tried to get inside the minds of those making a fool of themselves—something she attributed to her becoming such a skilled actress.

After making it halfway through her drink, someone tapped her on the shoulder. She turned to see a rather handsome man grinning. He had a strong jaw, and jet-black hair slicked to the side. Beads of sweat decorated his forehead, but his dark eyes drew her in.

"Hey!" he shouted over the music. "I'm Eli."

"Hi," Selena replied, turning her attention back to the dance floor.

Eli had a thick, groomed beard that stood out in contrast to his light complexion. If she wasn't on a mission, she just might have had an interest in conversing.

"I don't mean to intrude," he shouted from behind her, his hot breath blowing in her ear, causing her to recoil. "But you are one of the most beautiful women I've ever seen."

Selena turned over her shoulder and said, "Thank you."

"Are you new to town? I've never seen you here."

"No."

Conversations amid loud club music were already awkward enough, and she knew giving curt responses only made the man feel like more of an asshole. In due time, if he didn't get the hint, he'd ask if they could speak "somewhere more quiet."

"Do you have a boyfriend?" Eli persisted.

"Yes." With that, she turned her head, assuming that was what Eli needed to hear to leave her alone.

"I saw you walk in alone. Is he not here?"

An observer, Selena thought. *He might take a little more work to get rid of.*

"He's not. I'm meeting some girlfriends."

"Can I keep you company until they show up?"

"No thanks, I'm okay."

"Okay. If you change your mind, or if you and your friends want a good time tonight, come find me in the VIP area."

He pointed toward a corner of the bar that had cushioned booths behind a red-velvet rope.

A line right out of my dad's playbook, Selena thought, smirking at her mother's voice warning her in her mind.

"Okay, thanks," she said dismissively.

She saw Eli return to his friends in the VIP section. A strategy she liked to use in these situations was to hide in the bathroom for a couple of minutes. This allowed time for whatever poor soul was trying to hit on her to move on to the next woman and forget all about her.

Selena pushed her way through the crowd to reach the bathrooms in a sectioned off area next to the bar. The small lobby served as a waiting room. The space was dimly lit despite lights running along the baseboards on the wall.

She entered the ladies' room and was relieved to see no long lines inside. A bathroom attendant sat on a stool at the far end of the sinks, handing a woman a clean towel to dry her hands. The attendant looked college-aged and appeared to hate her job—a stern expression was stuck on her face.

Selena shot her a soft smile before stepping into the stall and sitting down on the toilet. She didn't need to go, but just wanted to kill some time and finish her drink in peace. She debated getting one more drink before calling it a night. The club was too crowded. It was impossible to get from one side to the other without catching an elbow in the gut from squeezing through the herd of people. The clubs she used to frequent in Hollywood had limited capacity to keep it comfortable for the patrons inside. Apparently, these smaller towns didn't believe in such things.

She spent a couple of minutes in the stall before stepping out to wash her hands. The attendant slouched on her stool while squirting the soap into Selena's hands and completely avoided eye contact or conversation.

"Hey," Selena said. "Keep your head up. It will get better, I promise."

The attendant finally looked at Selena, and the slightest sign of a grin touched the corner of her lips. "Thank you," she said, just above a whisper.

Selena felt the pain in the girl's voice and wished she could invite her out to the club to chat. She could only hope her few words would help lift her spirits for the rest of the night.

Selena gave the girl a fifty-dollar tip, and that turned the hidden smile into a full-blown grin, revealing pearly teeth. "I can't take this," the girl said, shaking her head. "This is about what I make in a whole night."

"It's yours. Treat yourself to a nice dinner this weekend."

Selena turned and left the bathroom before the girl could say anything else.

She stepped back into the dark lobby, where the crowd had grown even more. A hand grabbed her by the elbow, and Eli's voice and hot breath returned to her ear from behind. "Hello again, beautiful."

She felt his hand run along the small of her back, and she lunged forward to get out of his reach, pivoting to face him. "You can't take a fucking hint, can you?"

"Whoa, I'm just trying to talk to you."

"And I don't *want* to talk to you. Why is that so hard for you to understand? Are you not used to girls being able to resist big muscles and cheap pickup lines? Not everyone likes you. Did that ever occur to you?"

Eli grinned, his teeth glowing in the dim lobby. "Well, damn, baby, you got a mouth on you. I got some ideas for what you can do with it."

"You're fucking gross."

Selena spun back around, and Eli snatched her arm before she could walk away. She wasted no time in swinging her free arm down on his wrist as hard as she could, promptly loosening his grip as Eli grunted and clutched his arm.

"You *bitch*!" he shouted, and Selena shoved through the crowd and toward the exit. Her night was done, once again ruined by a cocky man who couldn't accept rejection.

Once she stepped outside, her mind immediately felt more focused thanks to the silence. Loud music had a way of making everything seem more chaotic, and she already felt more at peace.

She had parked two rows from the back of the lot and rummaged in her pockets for her keys. The music from the club grew loud for a moment as the door opened and closed. She looked over her shoulder to see Eli making a beeline towards her.

"Are you shitting me?!" Selena shouted, hoping to catch any passerby's attention. She had no problem fending for herself, and was hoping to do Eli a favor by letting someone else mitigate the situation.

She saw a group of smokers huddled in the parking lot at a bar across the street, but the traffic on Main Street must have blurred her shouts.

"Are *you* shitting me?" Eli asked, his teeth clenched. "I was just trying to have a polite conversation."

Selena hadn't noticed in the club, but now realized Eli had a solid six inches on her. He was built and could certainly handle his own in a fistfight, assuming he knew how.

"I suggest you go back inside," Selena demanded.

Eli laughed. "You think I'm afraid of you? Just because you're pretty doesn't mean I'm intimidated."

Selena had reached her car and stopped beside the driver-side door, debating if she should attempt to grab the pistol in her glove box. Eli didn't slow at all, and once he was within an arm's reach, he extended his hands toward Selena's shoulders.

She dropped to the ground, catching all her body's weight on her hands, and thrust her feet into Eli's knee, hyper-extending it. He wobbled backwards as he screamed into the night sky, catching himself on the hood of Selena's car.

"You're gonna pay for that," Eli said, the slightest suggestion of fear now weaved into his voice. He gathered his footing and limped toward Selena, pain clearly shooting up his leg with each step.

"Really, dude? Are you just mad you can't get into a bar fight with anyone inside? You're really trying to take it out on me?"

"You should have just come into my booth," Eli said, rearing back a fist and swinging it wildly toward Selena's head. His movement came quicker than she had expected, but she dodged it just in time, the breeze from his errant punch blowing over her face.

This put Eli in a vulnerable position with his entire side and right shoulder suddenly in front of Selena, crouched slightly to protect his busted knee. She grabbed the top of his head and slammed it into her rising knee, connecting squarely with the center of his face.

Blood spurted from his nose as both of Eli's hands shot to it, red streaks running down his hands and arms. He remained on his feet, and this is where his size was working to his advantage. It was going to take even more to get him on the ground.

Not too much more, she thought, and swung another kick to his already injured knee. This caused Eli's hands to leave his face and shoot down to his knee as he slowly crumpled to the ground. His face was no longer visible, smeared in the slick darkness of his own blood.

Selena wanted to kick him in the face for good measure, but saw a clear window to get in the car and speed out of the lot. She did so without saying another word, leaving Eli wailing on the ground.

Chapter 25

Friday had passed with no excitement. Arielle sat outside CreditConnect for the last time that week. Felix listened to Thursday's audio recordings from the Gregory household and still found nothing to report. And Selena followed Lindsay from a safe distance, never telling Arielle or Felix what had happened at the Paris Lounge on Thursday night.

Felix had dinner alone on Friday night, while Arielle and Selena followed their targets to the dance recital for Amanda Gregory. They would return later that night to report a typical recital. Mason and Lindsay attended together, and both parents stayed through the duration of the event.

They shifted their focus to Saturday night, when Mason was scheduled to attend the poker game.

On the morning of, Felix woke at six o'clock to get himself ready and prepare a hearty breakfast for the team. He cooked eggs, bacon, pancakes, and prepared a bowl of fruit salad. Arielle studied her map of Pueblo while eating, and Selena brushed up on her poker strategy from a book she had checked out from the library the day before, hoping to land a coveted invite to next week's game.

By eight o'clock, they were all out the door. Selena rode with Felix, and Arielle drove separately to the Gregory neighborhood. They needed the separate vehicles in case Mason or Lindsay left in the middle of the day and had to be followed.

The morning passed without so much as a bird shitting on the Gregory lawn. The front door remained closed, the curtains drawn, and both Mason's and Lindsay's cars remained in the driveway.

"A lazy Saturday morning," Felix said. "Remember what those were like? I'll bet the kids are watching cartoons and eating cereal in their pajamas."

Felix had parked across the street, two houses down. Arielle took a spot on the other block that ran perpendicular to the Gregory house.

"That seems like a lifetime ago, doesn't it?" Selena replied. "What I'd give to have a day like that."

At noon, Arielle left to grab lunch for everyone, sneakily dropping it on the sidewalk next to Felix's car. It wasn't until two when the front door finally opened, and the two Gregory children played outside on their front lawn. The oldest, Amanda, had fun blasting her little brother with water from the garden hose, and the two played and fought with each other over the next hour. Lindsay had made a brief appearance to mediate a dispute between the kids, but Mason never showed his face.

"Do you think someone picked him up before we even got here?" Selena asked.

"Doubt it. He seems like a guy who sleeps until noon on the weekends. Maybe he's just getting his day started, especially if he has a late night ahead."

"What time do you think he'll leave?"

"Impossible to know. We have to be ready the moment he steps outside."

There was a long pause before Selena spoke again. "Thanks again for standing up for me the other night. It really means a lot. That situation would have been a lot worse if you were attacking me like Arielle."

"Arielle wasn't attacking you. She just has a particular way she likes things done. You challenged that, and she didn't know how to react. You're one of the few people in this world who can say they've startled the great Arielle Lucila."

Selena grinned. "I suppose that's one way of putting it. You're quite the neutral person. A calming presence."

"I just like to have control over my emotions. In this line of work, I've seen far too many people ending up with their lives destroyed, all because their emotions got the best of them. I just try to think slowly and see things from all angles. And that includes different people's perspectives. That other night, I understood perfectly fine where both you and Arielle were coming from. No one was right, no one was wrong."

"I wish I could be more like that. I guess I developed a chip on my shoulder after my parents separated and played tug-o-war with me across the globe."

"If you can recognize *why* you let your emotions run you, then you shouldn't have a problem taking control back from them. It sounds to me like you're very in tune with yourself."

"I guess I'll have to work on it."

They swapped more stories about their childhood for the next three hours. At five o'clock, Mason Gregory appeared for the first time, stepping out of the front door with his keys in hand. His wife and kids had filled the doorway, and he planted kisses on all three of their foreheads before shuffling toward his car in the driveway.

"Shit, it's time!" Felix said, jamming the key into the

ignition, but waiting to turn on the car.

Mason pulled out of the driveway, and Felix fired up the engine. Mason turned at the stop sign, and they saw Arielle pull onto the road behind him. She insisted on leading the way, since she already had a feel for Mason's driving style.

"Stay as close to Arielle as you can," Selena said.

Mason took his time exiting the neighborhood, and this caused Arielle and Felix to drive at a painfully slow speed. He could have jogged faster than they were driving.

They followed Mason to the main roads, where he eventually got onto the freeway.

"Where the hell are we going?" Selena asked, but Felix didn't respond. He wouldn't dare break his concentration on the task at hand.

The drive took them through parts of Pueblo none of them had yet visited. After ten minutes on the freeway, they left the Pueblo city limits and were on their way south of town on I-25.

Tailing on the highway was easy, especially since Mason stayed in the middle lane for another ten minutes before getting over to exit at Colorado City.

"Colorado City?" Selena asked. "Do we have anything in our notes about this place?"

"Not ringing a bell," Felix said.

All three vehicles exited, Mason leading the way. Colorado City was deserted compared to Pueblo. They passed a gas station, two campgrounds, and a pizza parlor as they moved deeper into town.

It took them another ten minutes on Highway 165, a county road with trees lining the left and open fields on the right. Everything was spread across the stretch of highway. They passed a bank, grocery store, and even a golf course. The Rocky

163

Mountains glowed a majestic blue, fluffy clouds decorating the horizon above.

Once they reached the other side of town, Mason turned on a side road and drove another mile, passing a handful of barns.

"Where the hell are we going?" Felix asked. Arielle had slowed her pace now that they were isolated on a dirt road. It would be obvious to Mason that he was being followed.

Towering trees lined the sides of the road as far as they could see.

"I'm getting a bad feeling about this," Selena said. "This isn't really a poker game, is it?"

"Let's not jump to conclusions," Felix said, trying to push away his own worries. They were in the middle of the woods. And while they passed some barns, it was clear they were in deep enough isolation where, if something went wrong, no help would come.

The road curved and winded as they continued, and Mason eventually hit his brakes as he slowed to a complete stop. The tree coverage stopped suddenly, prompting Arielle to slam on her brakes as a house came into view, cars piled next to each other in the long driveway that led up to the property. She had remained about 500 feet behind Mason, and that had bought her enough distance to turn around without being noticed.

If he had thought he was being followed, he showed no signs of it, parking his car next to the dozen others.

Felix had stopped the car and waited for Arielle to circle back. She pulled up next to him, facing the other direction, and they both rolled down their windows.

"The house is literally the end of this road," Arielle said. "There are a *lot* of people there. I think we should drive back and pull off the road. Maybe even go all the way back to the highway. When it gets darker, we'll come back."

"Should we just leave, though?" Selena asked. "What if he doesn't stay long?"

"It's a poker game, right? He'll be there at least four hours. That gives us about three hours to kill before the sun goes down. We can probably head over a little sooner. We'll stay right by the turn for this road in case he leaves early. Follow me."

Arielle drove off, leaving Felix and Selena staring at each other.

"Goddammit!" Selena shouted, slamming the dashboard. "We're wasting valuable time. We need to find out who all those people are. One of them is definitely the murderer. To hell with Arielle, let's go."

Felix couldn't have been more grateful to be in the driver's seat. Had the roles been reversed, they would undoubtedly be on their way to crash the party.

"I'm gonna trust Arielle on this one. We need to move in the dark. Besides, more people might show up behind us."

He turned the car around and sped away.

Chapter 26

By 7:30, the sun flirted with the horizon over the mountains, turning the sky a bright orange. What sounded like hundreds of buzzing cicadas reminded Arielle of a distant fire alarm.

"I think it's safe to go," she said from the backseat of Felix's car. They had agreed to drive back to the property together, one less vehicle to worry about when they tried to creep toward the house.

"About time," Selena said from the passenger seat.

They had passed the time by eating a pizza from the parlor. The car reeked of garlic, thanks to Felix insisting on breadsticks with the meal.

"No one has come in or out of this road in the last hour," Selena said. "We should have been in there already."

"Relax," Arielle said calmly. She would no longer let Selena's emotional outbursts get the best of her. Would they get under her skin? Absolutely. But no more letting the young Angel sway her day. "We still need to be careful. There are a lot of people. Some might be hanging out outside. Some might even be leaving. Selena, what do you suggest our cover story be if we get seen?"

Arielle figured if she could get more input from Selena, she might encounter less resistance later on when split-second

166

decisions needed to be made.

Selena pursed her lips. "Since there are three of us, it will need to seem like we were invited. We can say that Mason invited us to the game."

"But we'll be arriving so late," Felix said.

"Then we say we had the wrong time. We thought it started at eight."

Felix snorted. "Wow, you sure can make up a lie on the spot."

"Acting is a weird mix of skill, truth, and lies."

"That should work," Arielle said. "And to be clear, we are *not* going inside the house under any circumstances. Our main goal is to get all the license plate numbers we can. Let our team at HQ do the heavy lifting of finding out who all these people are. We have to avoid being seen, but if we do, we'll stick to these talking points from Selena and get the hell out."

Felix turned on the car and flipped it around to take them back onto the dirt road, into the thick of the woods.

"Any thoughts on who might live out here?" Arielle asked.

"I think Mason just has a rich friend. Not much else to explain it."

"It wasn't a barn like these other properties. It was a regular house. Two stories, big from the glance I got. Not quite a mansion, but pretty damn close."

"Only rich people can afford that much privacy," Selena said. "Doesn't even have a street name. It's just a house in the middle of nowhere."

Darkness crept into the sky, a purple glow clinging to life before the moon and stars took over. The tall trees made it even darker on the road, and Felix turned on the headlights.

They cruised along until Felix recognized the curve in the road where they had stopped earlier. He slowed to a crawl; the

ANGEL ASSASSIN

gravel crunching beneath the tires.

"Let's creep up to the property," Arielle said. "We might be able to park behind another car and go unnoticed."

Felix obliged, letting the car coast as they rounded the corner and the house came into sight. Cars lined the sides of the driveway, about twenty in total.

"This is quite the crowd," Selena commented. "And house. Wow."

The house was stunning, even at night. It had a white exterior, a four-car garage, and a roundabout near the main entrance. The house was built in an L-shape, so the entrance was out of sight, tucked on the other side of the massive garage.

"Definitely a rich person," Felix said. "Wouldn't be surprised if there's a swimming pool and helicopter pad in the back."

"We're in luck," Arielle said. "I don't see anyone. They're inside or in the backyard. Just park behind the first car you see."

Felix wasted no time pulling to the side of the driveway and parking the car behind a windowless black van.

"Roll the windows down," Arielle said. She wanted to listen to the surroundings and was pleased to find the only sound belonging to crickets. No voices or shouting that might suggest an outdoor party, even from the backyard.

"Everyone have a notepad?" Felix asked, opening the center console to pull his out. "Keep an eye out for motion-sensor lights the closer you get to the house. If one comes on, hide behind a car and wait."

"Good call. Are we all ready?" Arielle asked.

Selena and Felix nodded, opening their doors. Arielle followed suit and welcomed the fresh mountain air, albeit a tad

168

warmer than she preferred.

"You two take the left, I'll take the right," Arielle whispered, pointing across the driveway where more vehicles lined up.

Felix nodded and led the way, with Selena trailing behind him. Arielle started with the black van directly in front of her and crouched down to read the white letters on the license plate. She pulled the notepad from her back pocket and flipped it open to write. Felix and Selena were doing the same, each of them already moving on to their second cars.

Arielle moved on, looking up and scanning the area after each license plate number she had written. As she got closer to the house, she moved slower, more cautiously. Someone could step around the corner at any moment, and she needed to be ready to hide. They had the darkness to their advantage, and they had dressed in black to blend in.

A light glowed from the other side of the garage, presumably from the home's entrance, yet the silence remained thick. The echo of her own footsteps kept making her look over her shoulder, but she pressed forward, nearly to the car parked closest to the house.

"Shit!" Felix gasped from across the way.

Arielle listened as his and Selena's footsteps pattered away from the house, back toward the direction of their car. She saw nothing, but crouched next to the car on her left.

What the hell are they doing? she wondered, and her gut instinct told her to head back. Neither Felix nor Selena would abandon a task for no reason. She pivoted around, taking soft steps to allow her ears to focus on any potential sounds coming from the house.

Practically lunging back to the car, she found Felix and Selena behind the trunk, crouched as low as her. "What's going on?" she demanded.

Felix was panting and held up a finger while catching his breath. "They have cameras. Surveillance cameras on the garage."

"Are you kidding me?!"

"I saw them. I think they caught us."

"How sure are you?"

Selena watched the exchange with worry plastered across her face.

Felix nodded. "I'm very certain."

"Okay, let's—"

A gun fired, cracking the silence like a lightning strike.

Selena shrieked out of reflex.

"Who's out there?" a voice called from the house. "We saw you."

Arielle extended her arms and grabbed Felix and Selena by their shoulders. "We need to get out of here right now," she whispered. "Get in the car and drive like hell. Okay?"

A second gunshot rang out, and Arielle identified it as a shotgun.

"Now!" Arielle snarled, shuffling around the car and diving into the backseat.

The noise level rose as more people stepped outside of the house, chattering. Footsteps marched on the ground like soldiers, just as Felix made his way behind the wheel. Selena moved a step slower, but made it safely inside the car.

"Go!" Arielle shouted as she swung her door closed.

Felix twisted the key into the ignition and spun the car around, flooring the accelerator as dirt flew in every direction.

"Stay low!" Arielle barked, just in time.

The next gunshot blast caught their back window as Felix

sped away, shards of glass scattered across the back seat, and in Arielle's hair. Selena screamed, the sound drowned out by the roaring engine and subsequent shots showered in their direction.

None of the other shots landed, and Felix swung around the curve, out of sight from the house.

"Keep going!" Arielle shouted. "They might follow us."

Felix had no intent of stopping and barreled down the dirt road. Arielle sat up and looked through the space where the back window was moments ago. No one was visible. Not yet, at least.

"Ahhhhh!" Felix cried, slamming on the breaks.

Arielle spun around to see a deer in the middle of the road, its head low as it ate something off the ground.

The car slid, tires screeching for an eternity as they inched toward the animal. The stench of burning brake pads filled the car as the rear wheels started drifting at an angle, positioning the car sideways as it continued toward the deer.

For a moment, Arielle saw her life flash before her eyes. And in the deer's eyes. She was on a direct path to the creature, and if they hit it at the wrong angle, they'd be lucky to walk away alive.

Instead, the deer came to its senses and darted into the woods. The car came to a stop inches from where the animal had just stood.

Selena gasped for breath, hands on her chest. "Are you *kidding* me?!" she wheezed.

Felix had his shoulders elevated in a shrug position, arms extended and stiff as he clutched the steering wheel.

Arielle sat up after having been flung around the backseat, and gently touched his shoulders. He was in shock.

"Felix," she said. "You did incredible."

He gulped and shook his head. "I can't believe that just happened. How are we still alive?"

"That was the past, wasn't it?" Selena asked, gaining some control over her breathing.

"It might have been," Arielle said. "Hard to know for certain. It's not like a deer in the woods is uncommon."

"It totally was. We haven't seen a deer this whole time, and *that's* when it shows its face?!"

Arielle sighed, her own tension dissipating. "All that matters is we're still alive."

Chapter 27

"It might have just been a poker game," Felix said as they sat around the table for breakfast the next morning. They had returned home, relieved no one had followed them. Felix had no energy to cook after last night's drama, so they each enjoyed a bowl of Cheerios.

Arielle shook her head. "I don't know. Something just felt *off*. Don't you think?"

Felix shrugged. "I don't usually get this involved in a mission. The whole thing felt off for me. But I'm also used to snooping around someone's house when I know they're not home."

"No one was outside when we got there," Selena said. "It really could have been a poker game inside. I assumed we've already checked out Mason's bank records. Does he have the money hidden somewhere to play in a high stakes game?"

"Why are you so convinced it has to be high stakes?" Arielle asked.

"Selena's right," Felix said. "I used to play in college. Friendly games have people up and out of their seats in the middle of the game. They get snacks, take smoke breaks. It's more of a social gathering than serious poker. You get into hundred-dollar buy-ins, and it's a lot more focused. People are there to win and make money, and couldn't care less about the snack tray in the kitchen."

Selena nodded in agreement. "That's why I ask."

"The Gregorys live paycheck to paycheck," Arielle said. "Unless Mason keeps a stash of cash under his mattress, there are no signs he has extra money for high-stakes gambling. I think we need to stop worrying so much about it, and wait for the results to come back from headquarters. I called in the list of license plate numbers first thing when we got home last night. I let them know it's urgent and to have info sent back by 10 A.M. today."

Felix checked his watch. "That's in half an hour. I didn't realize we slept in so late."

"Time flies when you're surviving," Selena said.

"So how are we supposed to get this information?" Felix asked.

"They're going to call," Arielle said. "Our teams work efficiently across time. All of my communication is with the Denver team here in 1988. I called them last night to relay the license plate numbers. From there, they'll research their existing database, while also sending an agent into the future to run the plates, along with names they find during the initial search. That helps pinpoint if anyone at the poker game either currently has a criminal record, or gets one in the future. That will tell us what kind of trouble we're dealing with. Once they gather all that information, the agent returns to 1988 and will call back with their findings."

"And what time are you heading to the Gregorys'?"

"As soon as I get the call. That's why I told them I need all the info early. I'm leaving at ten, regardless. So if we don't hear before then, you'll need to field the call and take down all the notes."

The phone rang, and all three of their heads shot up like alert cats. "Right on cue," Arielle said, standing to pick up the phone on the kitchen counter.

"Hello?" she answered, grabbing the notepad and pen next to the phone, leaning onto the counter with an elbow while cradling the phone between her head and shoulder.

Felix and Selena watched as Arielle jotted down notes, nodding and offering a brief "Okay" every few seconds.

Selena craned for a better view of the notepad. Her eyes bulged as she turned to Felix and separated her hands a foot apart. "It's long," she whispered.

Felix couldn't see much. He hated when people read over his shoulder and refused to do the same to Arielle.

After three long minutes, Arielle said, "Okay, so around noon?" she checked her watch, then pointed at Felix. "Felix will be here. . . Perfect. Thank you so much."

She hung up and scribbled a few more notes down.

"Well?!" Selena asked impatiently.

Arielle turned to them, notepad in hand. "We have quite the mess. There are a handful of people with backgrounds. Drugs, prostitution, robbery. One man will be on the America's Most Wanted list by 1992 for operating one of the biggest sex trafficking rings in North America. Our team believes the house belongs to him, and that he is already operating the ring here in 1988, although not as grand of a scale as it will become."

"Sex trafficking?" Selena asked. "I don't understand how Mason is tied to all this?"

Arielle pursed her lips. "That's where our mission becomes a bit . . . gray. They are going to keep looking into it, but so far, there is no concrete evidence that Mason *is* involved in the ring."

"Wait," Felix said. "So we're potentially trying to save a sex trafficker? You've got to be shitting me."

"How the hell did our scouting team not catch this sooner?" Selena asked, her tone drifting toward anger.

The scouting teams found the missions for the Angels to work on. They focused on crimes or tragic events that had wide-rippling effects on the community. Scouts worked all throughout time and all across the continent. Once finding a potential event, another team of scouts dug deeper to figure out who was all affected by the event, persons of interest, police reports (if available), and virtually every detail possible to determine if a mission was worth the organization's time.

From there, a panel of Angel Runners reviewed the data and files, and served as the last checks and balances before either throwing out the mission, or pushing it forward for assignment.

"It's too late to dwell on that," Arielle said. "We have to adjust on the fly."

"Adjust?" Felix asked. "I think we need to *abort* this mission. Why should we risk our lives to save a monster?"

Arielle raised a hand. "We have a lot of angles and options to consider. And trust me, aborting the mission is on the table. However, this mission wasn't so much about saving Mason Gregory as it was saving his children's future and the community. And we can't change the mission, either. I know stopping the trafficking altogether seems tempting, but we have no preparation around that."

"What's happening at noon that I need to be here for?" Felix asked.

"Someone is driving down from Denver with complete files

on all the people who were at that party last night. Rap sheets, mugshots, addresses. Everything they could get their hands on."

"I'm with Felix," Selena said. "I don't think we should continue."

"Of course. All you two do is side with each other against me. Frankly, I don't give a shit anymore. *I'm* the lead on this mission and *I'll* make the final decisions. If *you* have a problem with that, call Commander Briar and take it up with him."

Arielle returned to the table and sat down, Selena still standing with her jaw hanging open. Felix sat unfazed, staring at the ceiling as if calculating something to say, but coming up with nothing.

"Now, are we ready to talk business?" Arielle asked Selena.

She stood for another twenty seconds, glaring at Arielle, a burst of outrage swimming beneath her surface. Her jaw bulged as it clenched, and she finally gave in, sitting down and pushing her breakfast back to cross her hands on the table.

"Thank you," Arielle said. "I understand there are some strong emotions toward this news. I have the same feelings as you both, but we need to look at the big picture. I'm not ruling out calling off this mission, but I'm also not going to jump to that conclusion. There are a lot of moving parts, and we need to drill them down to weigh the pros and cons. I'm happy to consider your input, but ultimately I will make the last call—probably after a chat with Commander Briar."

"What are we factoring into the decision?" Felix asked.

"A few things. We should all read through the mission report again. We need a deeper understanding of the effects of Mason's death. We know his kids spiral out of control later in life, and that's something that really hurts the community.

That's just the future. The immediate aftermath of his murder sends quite the ripple through Pueblo. The problems that stem from this simple murder are much bigger than Mason's family. It has societal impacts."

"That's always been Commander Briar's focus since he defeated the Revolution."

"Exactly. He took a trip into the future and witnessed a dystopian, fascist government running the country. His major focus as Commander has been to learn from that future and understand ways to stop evil from flourishing before it gets the chance. That is literally what drives his every decision. I think we're going to have to stop this murder still, no matter how wrong it may seem. This murder caused division. Some people used it to launch anti-gun campaigns. Others blamed gang activity in the area. There was a day of very heated protests outside of Town Hall. It may seem like a blip on the radar in the grand scheme of things, but enough incidents like this over time, and around the continent, lead to major divisions."

"That's a stretch," Selena said, crossing her arms, a cue Arielle had picked up on: Selena was ready to argue. "The death of a middle-aged account manager from Pueblo, Colorado leads to the rise of fascism? Get real."

"You're thinking too broadly. I've had lots of conversations with Commander Briar about this, and have made the same arguments. The murder itself is insignificant outside of Mason's family and friends. The ripple effect is what we're trying to prevent. The protests may have only been one day, but they were emotionally charged. People dug into their opinions and solidified their stances. In time, these beliefs get passed down to the next generation, and the cycle of division continues and strengthens. Division leads to extremism. I've grown a much deeper appreciation for our work. Sometimes the missions seem ridiculous on the surface, like this one. But it has a much deeper effect. One we can't quite understand. We can only trust the process and keep working. Enough of us Angels influencing the past just might save the future."

Felix nodded. "The future is never safe. Even after what Commander Briar accomplished. The work never ends."

"So we're just trying to make sure people never have arguments again?" Selena asked. "Seems impossible and a tad utopian."

"Not at all. Think of the old assembly line workers who built cars. Many of them had very boring tasks, maybe attaching the mirrors onto the vehicles. Meaningless in itself, but so important to the big picture. If that person skipped a car, that one car could make it out to the road one day and get into a serious accident. I know that's a silly example, but that's exactly what we're doing. Some missions might not feel as important as others, but they all play a role."

"Sounds like we're continuing the mission then."

Arielle stood up. "Most likely. Like I said, let's review things and get on the same page. Understand the driving force behind Commander Briar, because for a mission to be canceled, we would need his approval. I need to get going—I have a long day of sitting outside Mason's house and reading these files. Felix, if you come across anything major in what they're bringing over, bring them to me. Selena, if you can help him read through it all, I'll let you stay home today. No need for two of us to sit outside the house today—I don't expect much action, if any."

"Will do," Felix said.

Selena agreed to the terms, and Arielle left for the rest of the day. The week of the murder was upon them, and with it, plenty of drama awaited.

Chapter 28

Felix enjoyed a lazy Sunday reading through files while the Dodgers played on the TV for background noise. He still had an unpleasant taste in his mouth from the near-death encounter the prior night and had no interest in cooking dinner. The thought of standing in front of the stove seemed so far out of reach, especially with all the reading he had done during the day.

He ordered takeout from a nearby Chinese restaurant.

Selena took some files to her bedroom and agreed to follow Felix's method of sorting the documents into separate piles of importance. There were eighteen total people at the poker game on Saturday night, or rather eighteen vehicles they could pull information on.

Felix made three stacks: urgent, moderate, and insignificant.

When Arielle finally returned shortly after 6:30 that evening, they gathered around the dinner table with takeout boxes and papers scattered about.

It was these moments Felix liked to shine. He'd have Arielle's undivided attention for the next hour as he discussed the day's findings. And there were plenty of juicy details to share.

"So what do we have?" Arielle asked, sitting opposite Felix

and Selena.

"Let's start from the top," Felix said, grabbing a stack of papers and tossing them to the center of the table. A portrait of a man with scraggly gray hair and a matching beard stared at the ceiling, his brown eyes bulging, lunacy swimming behind them. "This is Nathan Baldwin. He is the leader of the entire sex trafficking ring, referred to as the 'National in Charge.'"

"These people have official titles?" Arielle asked.

"Sick, isn't it?" Selena replied, shaking her head.

"Yes," Felix continued. "They are highly organized. They have to be, to not get caught. Anyway, Nathan here runs things across the United States. Our team believes he owns the house we were at last night. Nathan will eventually get caught and prosecuted in 1999, ending a fifteen-year operation—he's already been at this since 1984. Being in charge, Nathan makes the most money. By the time he's caught in 1999, he will have accumulated over ten million dollars. We believe he has just become a millionaire now in 1988."

Felix returned to his stack of documents and grabbed the next pile to toss in the center. This one showed a younger man with a long face and droopy eyes, hair freshly buzzed.

"And this is Anton Romanovich. Moved to the U.S. from Russia with his family when he was twelve years old and had a rough time through high school. In and out of juvie, suspended six times in four years. Somehow graduated, but didn't go to college. Spent some time in jail for stealing electronics, and that was the end of his record. We suspect he fell in with these people while in jail and started working with them once he got out. He is the head of the region and oversees Colorado, Wyoming, Nebraska, Kansas, Oklahoma, New Mexico, and Utah. He rents low-priced apartments in all the states mentioned, so we suspect he moves around a lot for the business. He wasn't present during the sting that took place in 1999, so he never gets caught in the future. We believe he is the most likely suspect for killing Mason Gregory, or at least ordering the hit."

"Why so?" Arielle asked.

"That sort of duty would fall within his responsibilities. He's also a ruthless man. Some of the prison records say he was constantly getting in fights, and even paralyzed a man with his bare hands, although there was no direct evidence to link him to it. Just eyewitness accounts. Wouldn't be surprised if that's who was shooting at us last night, but that's just my speculation."

Felix shoved more papers across the table. Multiple photographs of different suspects. "These are everyone else. Nothing too different across these people. Low-level crimes before they joined the operation, some with minimal jail time, some just with fines. Anton and Nathan should be our primary focus, unless Selena found anyone else?"

Selena cleared her throat and rummaged through her stacks, pulling out a candid portrait of a dark-skinned woman who had just stepped out of the backseat of a car. "I came across Cynthia Narine. She runs a brothel in Santa Fe. She's from Trinidad and Tobago, and used to be married to Nathan. She used to help him lure vulnerable homeless women when they were in their earlier days. They've since divorced, but it looks like Nathan keeps her employed. That might be something worth looking into. If he still has feelings for her, we can use that to our advantage."

It relieved Felix to hear Selena talking about the mission in a more serious tone. No one had brought up the possibility of aborting it again.

"Did either of you find any connections between Mason and any of these people?" Arielle asked.

"I did," Selena said, reaching out to flip through the photos on top of her stack. "This guy." She slid the photo forward, a man with a wide grin, glasses, and a receding hairline.

"What is this? Looks like a picture someone takes for their work badge."

"That's exactly what it is. His name is Rusty Kirk. Mason used to work with him at an accounting firm in 1982. Rusty still lives here in Pueblo, and his only job is to manage the books for the operation. He was at the gathering last night, but we believe he's never had any involvement with the actual trafficking portion."

"That's probably how Mason is involved," Arielle said. "Especially if there are no obvious ties, and his name never leaks in the future. Selena, when you go to dinner tomorrow, try to figure out what skills Mason might offer to a group of thugs like this. Rusty is an accountant. We know Mason does account management, but I doubt that's something a trafficking ring would require." She chuckled at the thought. "Especially since we know he doesn't spend a lot of time involved in their scheme. From what we've gathered, it's just a few hours every Friday night."

"Can Mason and Rusty still be taken down if we bust this ring?" Felix asked.

"Absolutely," Selena said. "They have knowledge of what's going on, and can be charged as an accomplice. Not to mention, the other crimes that go along with handling the money for a criminal organization."

"That might be a good place to start," Felix said. "He's

probably the easiest person to intimidate within the group. He's just the numbers guy. Wouldn't know what to do if we cornered him."

"Let's slow down," Arielle said. "I know it may seem tempting, but we can't make any plans to break up this ring. This is good information, but not enough to pull something off at such a grand scale. We're not equipped, either. Would need a lot more guns and ammo, and more people. I did some reading today, and I feel comfortable keeping our mission as is."

"Just saving Mason?" Felix asked. "We're not going to influence any of this other mess?"

Arielle tossed her hands in the air. "We can't. We don't understand the consequences if we do. The past is sensitive. We don't even know how much we'd be able to do. This is a trafficking ring that affects thousands of lives over the next decade. It has too wide of a reach. We would get so much resistance from the past. It's too risky."

Felix and Selena nodded. That's what made Arielle the top-ranked Angel. She had a firm grasp on all the factors at play, and knew how to weigh them for any situation, including the random wrenches like this one.

Arielle sifted through the documents and froze, looking up at the other two. "I know who our killer is."

She tossed a vehicle registration form to the center of the table.

"How?" Felix asked, standing up to lean over the table and read the form. It showed a 1967 Camaro registered to one Nathaniel Joseph Baldwin.

"Unless any of these other people own a 1960s muscle car, Nathan is our guy. When I visited the night of the murder, I couldn't completely make out the vehicle, but I'm positive it fell in that range. A 1967 Camaro fits the description perfectly. It was black or a dark blue. We need to find Nathan and confirm what car he's driving."

"We can't go back to that house," Felix said. "Especially after what happened last night."

"I'm not saying we go back, but maybe we wait near that side road for him to come out. Selena, what do you think? We can probably pull you off watching Lindsay after your dinner tomorrow night. I now highly doubt she has any involvement with his death."

Selena licked her lips, and her legs bounced below the table. Felix heard the rapid rhythm of her shoes jackhammering against the hardwood floor. He rarely saw her nervous and understood she was taking a moment to think this through.

"Okay," she finally said. "I can handle that."

"We'll shuffle around our tasks for the week, but I think this is the right call. Tomorrow will still be helpful. Learn everything you can about Mason—there has to be something we're not seeing. I'll still follow him around in case something comes up, otherwise we need to find the right time to intervene with whatever situation comes up between Nathan and Mason. This is finally it. We're in the home stretch."

Chapter 29

Mason Gregory drove home in silence on Monday evening. Fielding sixty phone calls during the day, each about five minutes, made his brain itch with fatigue. *I'm so fucking sick of this job,* he thought. Just a few more years and he'd finally reap some financial benefit from the dirty work he'd been doing on the side.

All he had done was set up private credit card scanners for Nate and the gang to process payments at their brothels all around the country. Transactions went undetected thanks to Mason's knowledge of CreditConnect's system, assigning himself as the lead account manager for a phony business that operated under the name of The Puzzle Piece. On the application, they were a puzzle and board game shop with locations near major cities. In reality, they were a chain of brothels with a constant flow of customers. And girls.

Nate saw himself as a visionary. He wanted to modernize prostitution. And allowing his clients to pay with a credit card provided opportunities for more expansion and better repeat business. Snooping wives would see cash withdrawals on the monthly bank statements and question their cheating husbands. Now they'd see transactions for a game shop. He was even on the hunt for someone who could get him puzzles and board games at a wholesale price. Or less. That way, his clients could return home with proof to match the bank transactions.

What Mason did was highly illegal. A federal felony. But after years at the same company, thanks to a referral from his old friend and co-worker, Rusty Kirk, he had gained the trust of his superiors and got to overlook their more lucrative accounts. He virtually flew under the radar, and at a slow-paced company with towering cubicle walls across the bullpen, Mason had carved out his own little world.

While he had done this shady work for Nate, he had yet to see the financial rewards he had hoped. So far, he received an extra three hundred dollars each month for the last year, enough to buy him into the weekly poker games held at Nate's house. He played a conservative game, never leaving with less than two hundred, sometimes with nearly seven hundred dollars. He'd tell Lindsay he received a cash bonus for outstanding performance at work and take her and the kids out to a fancy dinner in Colorado Springs. She never questioned it.

Nate had promised a raise as soon as the credit card trans-actions started coming in. Not just a flat raise, but a three percent commission from each transaction. Right now, they were meeting a lot of pushback from clients. They didn't want any paper trail tied to their activities, no matter how much they were promised full discretion and a fake business name to appear on the statements. Nate expected this, but believed the future of money was changing.

"In twenty years," he told Mason at their first meeting, "There won't be any cash or checks. It's all about the plastic." He held up his credit card like it was a literal piece of gold. And Mason believed him.

Rusty cooked the books for Nate, and being an old friend, had no problem sharing numbers with Mason. In 1987, they made two million dollars in revenue. Of that, only five thousand dollars had come in from credit card transactions. Nate was practically losing money by paying Mason the three hundred each month.

Sometimes Mason wondered if he had been conned into the illegal activity. *Invest now and reap the rewards in twenty years!* It was a classic, sleazy sales pitch. But Nate didn't bullshit. Ever. He was a calculated man who studied his numbers closely, but more importantly, studied the world and its economics. If he said everyone would have credit cards by 2007, then that would be true. Mason would be retired by then, and could move to Florida, Arizona, or even Costa Rica if he really wanted. Assuming Nate's projections came true. As the business grew and more people started using their credit cards, Nate predicted Mason could have north of $800,000 in the bank, off commissions alone, by the year 2010.

Mason daydreamed about this bright future, perhaps the only thing that helped him get through the slog of his workday. "One day, me and Lindsay will sip margaritas on the beach, and never have to check our bank account again," he said to the empty car. "The kids will have their college paid for, and it won't even put a dent in our funds."

The concept had always seemed so absurd. He had to speak it aloud to make sense of it all.

For tonight, he'd push his dreams aside and enjoy dinner with his family, and some new friend Lindsay had met at the park. He hated having company over for dinner. Mason just wanted to come home, enjoy a delicious dinner, and take off his pants to watch TV and enjoy a beer until bed time. It was a routine he appreciated ever since working at CreditConnect. If he didn't have the chance to unwind, he just might implode from the constant nagging and complaints he fielded from his clients.

He often thought of Nate's mansion and fancy cars. His parties with top-shelf booze and the finest women available. The ones he liked to "scout" for his more affluent clients. All was fair game at a Nate Baldwin gathering, but Mason didn't care for the extra-curricular activities. He just wanted to make some extra cash and go back home in peace.

When he pulled into his driveway, he saw a car parked along the sidewalk. Their guest had already arrived, meaning he wouldn't get a single moment to kick back and chat with the kids and Lindsay about their days.

"Please eat and leave," he said as he killed the engine. He hated when guests lingered, especially once the sun went down.

Mason sighed before grabbing his lunch pail and stepped out of the car, trudging up the pathway where he entered the house, the smell of baked chicken oozing into the living room.

"I'm home!" he shouted, and immediately a rumble came from down the hallway as both kids rushed him. Amanda jumped into his arms and David wrapped himself around Mason's leg.

"Hi, Daddy!" Amanda cackled, a wide, toothless grin on her face. She had lost three teeth in the past two months.

"How are you guys?" he asked, putting Amanda down next to her brother. "How was your day?"

"Good," David said, turning and running into the kitchen where Lindsay stood over the stove.

"Good, Daddy," Amanda said. "I went to dance, had lunch

190

with Mommy, and helped her pick up the toys in the yard."

"Very good! Thank you for doing that." They had been working with Amanda on actually telling them about her day, and not giving the simple one-word response like David had.

Amanda skipped away, back down the hallway to her room, where she likely had a meeting of Barbie dolls set up.

Mason turned into the kitchen and stopped when he saw the most beautiful woman he'd ever seen standing next to his wife. She had a slender figure, long brown hair, and an innocent charm behind a shy smile. *She looks like she stepped out of one of those* Swimsuit Edition *magazines,* Mason thought, immediately fantasizing about what lied beneath her clothes.

"Hello," Mason said.

"Hi, hon, have a good day?" Lindsay asked, turning toward him and walking over to give him a kiss. He couldn't keep his eyes off the stranger in his kitchen.

"Yeah, just another day. Who is this?"

"This is the young lady I told you about. Selena. I met her at the park last week."

"Nice to meet you, Mr. Gregory," Selena said, sticking out a hand.

Mason grabbed it, her skin as soft as satin. "Pleasure to meet you. You can call me Mason. No need for formalities."

She grinned and stepped back. "Can I help you set the table?" she asked Lindsay.

"That would be great! Plates and cups are right above you," Lindsay replied, pointing to the cupboard behind Selena. "Dinner's ready, hon. Would you mind getting the kids washed up?"

"Sure," Mason said, suddenly not caring how long their guest wanted to stay tonight. He gathered the kids from their bedrooms and had them wash their hands before taking their places at the dinner table. Lindsay had prepared a feast with baked chicken, steamed veggies, mashed potatoes with gravy, and a small chocolate cake from their local bakery.

"This looks fantastic," he said, sitting down at the head of the table. "You've really outdone yourself, Linds."

Lindsay always put together quality meals, but enjoyed upping her game when company was over. He genuinely believed his wife could open her own restaurant and often encouraged her to. But she believed that would take all the fun out of cooking. They didn't *need* the money to justify the hassle of startup costs to open a new business. Never mind the long hours required to run a restaurant.

Once Lindsay served everyone's food, the kids dove into the mashed potatoes while she and Mason cut up their chicken. Selena watched for a moment before taking her first bite.

"So, Selena, what do you do?" Mason asked.

"I don't have much of a set job. I do some part-time work bartending and babysitting."

"Selena recently graduated from the university and stayed in Pueblo," Lindsay said.

"Wow, I don't think I've ever heard of such a thing," Mason said. "Most of those kids run for the hills when they're done."

Selena shrugged. "I like it here. Pueblo has a certain charm. I grew up living between New York City and Paris."

"Oh, wow, so you come from money?"

"Mason Gregory!" Lindsay gasped, smacking him in the arm. "We don't ask visitors about their finances."

Mason waved his hands over his plate. "My apologies. I didn't mean it like that. It's not every day you meet someone who's lived in such big places."

"No offense taken, Mr. Gregory . . . er, Mason." Selena said, poking at the food on her plate. "My dad has always been rich. My mother not so much. They divorced, my dad moved to Paris, and that's why I spent time in both cities."

"And they're still there?"

Selena nodded. "They like the lives they have. Those places are home for them. I invited my mom to move out here with me. I guess some people just like the chaos of New York."

"Well, from a Pueblo native, welcome to town. Happy to have you."

"I didn't realize you were native to Pueblo. What do you do for work, if you don't mind me asking?"

"Not at all. I work for a company called CreditConnect. It's not the most exciting job, but it pays the bills. I work as an account manager, so do things like customer service, a bit of sales."

"Very nice," Selena said. "I haven't quite figured out what I want to do for a career. I've been doing side jobs ever since college. Even used to make some decent money on the weekends playing poker in the dorms. I was one of the few girls who played. It was so fun taking money from the guys."

"Mason plays every week," Lindsay said. "Maybe he can invite you one of these times."

Mason nearly choked on the piece of chicken in his mouth. While they played poker at their gatherings, it was meant more as a weekly meeting for Nate and all the leadership to get on the same page. They had strict rules about bringing outsiders in. Not even spouses were allowed. Nate understood the delicacy of their work, and while most of the crew didn't have families, he would shuffle things around if it meant keeping the secrecy alive. Just as he had done for Mason this past weekend.

"Oh," Mason said. "We have kind of an exclusive club. I would need to talk to the guys."

Lindsay rolled her eyes. "God forbid a lady tries to play cards with the boys. I'm sure our tiny brains couldn't possibly calculate the odds of hitting a flush."

Selena laughed, and Mason felt like he was being ganged up on. The kids continued eating their food, uninterested in the conversation.

"It's not that *I* don't want you there," Mason said. "It's not my game. Not my house. If I ever host a game here, you're more than welcome to come."

"Well, thank you," Selena said. "If you get the chance to ask your friends, I'm free this upcoming weekend and would love to play."

"I'll let you know," Mason lied. He already knew the answer without having to ask Nate. In fact, Nate would probably howl like a loon if he brought up this question.

"So, since you work for a credit card company, do you have any sort of accounting background?" Selena asked.

Why is this chick asking me so many questions? he thought.

"No accounting background. I didn't go to college—couldn't afford it. I had to do things the old-fashioned way. Started at entry-level positions and worked my way up."

"What skills did you need to get where you are today?" Selena asked.

"I'm sorry, but why do you have such an interest in my work background?"

"Just curious. I've always enjoyed math. Like I said, I'm still trying to figure things out for my life. I'm trying to see what might be feasible."

Mason took a drink of water, suddenly craving a beer and

once more wishing his guest would leave. He didn't care how fun she was to look at. She talked too much.

"Well, I wish I could give you more insight. I don't really have any special skills. I've just learned my jobs on the fly and use that experience whenever I've had to apply for new positions or companies. I have a background in sales, customer service, administrative work, and am learning some new things on computers. None of that compares to a college education, though, so you'll automatically have an advantage whatever you decide. What was your major, anyway?"

"Finance," Selena said, not offering any further details as she shoved food into her mouth.

Mason did the same, grateful for a moment of silence. Lindsay must have sensed the awkward tension because she was the next to speak.

"Who's ready for dessert?"

Chapter 30

Arielle and Felix waited anxiously at home while Selena was at dinner. They tried to pass the time by reading through the files, but concentration proved difficult. Too much was at stake over the dinner. Arielle hyped it up as the night that could swing the entire mission in a different direction.

When they saw the headlights pull into their driveway, they both rushed to the front door like puppies excited to see their owner arrive home.

"What is taking so long?" Felix asked after an entire minute passed and Selena remained in the car. She had cut the headlights, but no other movement came from the car. "Should we check on her?"

The door finally opened and Selena stepped out, and she danced up the pathway to the front door.

"Hey, you two. How are things?" she asked. "Why are you standing at the door?"

"Because we need to hear all about tonight," Arielle said. "What were you doing in the car just now?"

"Relax, *mother.* A good song was on and I wanted to finish listening to it."

"Of course," Felix said, showing a rare glimpse of frustration as he rolled his eyes and tossed his hands in the air.

"You guys need to chill," Selena said. "I didn't get anything that's going to help us."

Arielle's stomach dropped. She had put so much emphasis on this dinner. Such high expectations. *Maybe Selena was the wrong person for the job,* she thought. "You didn't ask about the poker game?"

"Of course I did," Selena said, frowning. "Do you actually think I just went over for dinner to shoot the shit with these people? I tried. And if you'll let me come inside *our* house and sit down, I'd be happy to tell you about it."

Arielle and Felix parted ways to let her pass through, and Selena smirked at Felix as her shoulder brushed his chest on her way to the living room. She found the wine rack and poured a glass of red before taking a seat on the couch.

"Are you coming?" she asked, Arielle and Felix not having moved from the door. They snapped out of their trance, Felix sitting on the opposite end of the couch, Arielle leaning against the wall and crossing her arms. "I probed as much as I could. So much that Mason asked me why I was asking so many questions. I arrived about twenty minutes before him and helped Lindsay in the kitchen. I asked if they had other friends, hoping to get some names we could look up. But she gave me nothing. Said there is a couple from church they like to spend time with."

"Church?" Arielle asked. "They didn't leave the house yesterday?"

Selena shrugged. "I know, but I couldn't act like I knew that. Anyway, when he got home, we had some pleasantries. He couldn't stop checking me out—was kinda weird, seeing as I'm young enough to be his daughter. During dinner, I told them how I used to play poker in college. Lindsay got all excited

197

and told Mason I should join him. He played it off that it wasn't his home to invite someone over. An 'exclusive' game is what he called it."

Arielle laughed. "It's exclusive, all right."

"Then I asked him about his background and work, trying to figure out what the hell this sex ring uses him for. He has no college education, and nothing special on his work resume. Says he's spent his career starting from the bottom and working his way up. Has lots of corporate skills, but nothing I can tell that translates into a criminal operation. After all the probing, it was clear he wanted me out, so Lindsay served dessert and called it a night. Here I am, nowhere further than when I arrived."

Arielle shook her head. "Dammit."

"I'm sorry. I did what I could."

"I'm not upset with you, just the situation. We were really counting on this, and who knows what this may have done to the relationship. They might never have you back if Mason felt uncomfortable."

"Hard to say. Mason hugged me before I left. Maybe he just wanted a reason to touch me, but it felt like we were all on good terms. Just bad, awkward conversation, but I didn't have much choice with only one night to figure out everything. Normally, I'd use the entire two weeks to sprinkle in these types of questions."

Arielle paced back and forth. "We did what we could. We'll have to re-evaluate our strategy for the next mission. But where do you guys suppose we go from here?"

"Arielle," Felix said, standing up, pointing a finger at her. "You need to relax. No, we didn't get the golden ticket we wanted tonight, but we're still in good shape. We know who the killer is."

"To be fair, we don't know with complete certainty. I'm taking a leap of faith with the matching cars. We can't get sloppy and base our actions off an assumption. I've also found it's important to understand the *why* behind a murder like this. It helps pinpoint better times to interrupt the act."

"We're closer than you think. We know Mason's schedule. He doesn't go anywhere besides work and this weekly poker game. He either does all of his duties the night of the poker games, or he does them during work hours."

"It sounds like he has some freedom at work," Selena said. "Or at the very least, he's well respected. This could mean he has some leniency from his superiors should he decide to take time to himself during the day."

Arielle shook her head. "That may be so. But why do something illegal at work? Seems too risky. He's definitely a family man and keeps his wife and kids as his main focus. Do you not agree after having dinner with them?"

"Sure, it *seems* that way, but is he really that dedicated if he's doing this kind of sketchy stuff on the weekends? How could a man with a daughter be involved, in any capacity, with selling off other young women?"

"Money," Felix said. "Money runs the world, don't you know? People will happily throw away their moral compass for a few dollars. We should have had Selena get a job inside his office. Maybe if we could understand what's going on inside that building, we'd know more. Maybe his job status is shaky and he's desperate for cash. Don't forget, we're in an era of raging masculinity. Men don't just go home and tell their wives the income might cease soon. Instead, they make up for the funds any way they can. Gambling, selling drugs, looking for a job during their free time. It doesn't always have to be so drastic. Did he seem secretive at all around Lindsay?"

Selena shook her head. "They were fine. From what I could tell, at least. I didn't exactly have a norm to compare it to. But Mason was engaged in the conversation, didn't seem to be off in his own world."

"Have you tried going into his office, Arielle?" Felix asked.

"Of course. You need a badge to just open the main doors. From what I could see, you need to swipe it again to get through another set."

"Sloppy preparation," Felix said, and Arielle took this personally.

"Excuse me?! I've done nothing but prepare—"

"Not you," Felix cut her off. "The scouting team. *I* can make a fake work badge. Not that difficult. I don't have my machine with me, or else I could have put one together."

"Don't worry about it. We could hack his computer after hours, but we likely wouldn't have a way of knowing if he was in trouble."

Arielle knew they probably could have found this out by hacking his manager's computers and seeing what notes they stored. But there was no point in them dwelling over the matter.

"Let's worry about Friday night," she said. "That's all we can do now."

"What are we supposed to do all week?" Selena asked.

"The same thing we've been doing. Although, I'm serious about taking you off Lindsay. I think that's a waste of time at this point. Maybe a couple of days tailing Nate and another two following Anton."

"That's fine with me, but how close can I realistically get?

We know Nate has security cameras outside, and I can't exactly hide across the street like I've been doing with Lindsay. The logistics are going to make it difficult to get much done."

"That's fine. I don't want you approaching him at all. That alone might start the wheels in motion for tampering with the past. Observe. Hang out on that main road and wait for him to leave. Follow him, see where he goes, who he spends time with, that sort of stuff. Same with Anton. Felix, I don't suppose you'd be able to bug their houses."

Felix let out a hearty, almost exaggerated laugh. "Not a chance. I have to know exactly when a subject will be gone, and for how long. That's where good scouting comes into play. If we can get into Mason's office building, I can probably bug that place."

Arielle thought during her pacing. While it seemed productive on the surface, it wouldn't yield any results. Bugging the office would only explain Mason's motivation behind joining the criminal underworld, assuming the issue stemmed from his office job. It had no bearing on his actual murder.

"Let's not worry about the office. We know where Mason is going to be on Friday night. We know some of the people who will be there."

"And what they're capable of," Selena added.

"Indeed. We know where Mason will be murdered. Maybe you can drive the possible routes from Nate's house to the warehouses and look for potential areas we can set up to interfere. Maybe we park on the side of the road and pretend we need help. Those warehouses are kind of in the middle of nowhere."

"I can do that."

"Good. The most important thing is to remain diligent. I'm

not expecting too much on this mission, but the days leading up to our targeted event are usually when the past will start intervening. Don't get caught off guard—it can cost you your life."

Chapter 31

Mason hung up his work phone, fuming. How he wanted to rip the cords out of the wall and hurl the damn machine across the office.

That motherfucker, he thought.

Earlier in the day, Mason had pulled up the transactions received by The Puzzle Piece, and to his delight, saw the organization had a monster week. Mason naturally grew excited at the prospect of earning more than three hundred dollars from Nate for the month of June.

Three hundred dollars per week, now that's more like it.

He had wanted to call Nate on his lunch break to let him know the good news, but couldn't contain his excitement that long. He was already spending the money in his mind. At this rate, he might even take the family to Disneyland before school started up, something that had only been a wild fantasy up to this point in their lives.

He called, shared the numbers, and reminded Nate that he waived the processing fees for every transaction that had occurred. Another way to ensure he put more money into Nate's pockets that would eventually come back his way. Nate sounded grateful, but distant.

"That's great, Mase, keep up the good work. You'll see that

money in due time. We just have to cover some other charges first."

"Bullshit!" Mason had snapped, cupping his hand over the receiver so his conversation wouldn't carry to his colleagues in the neighboring cubicles. "That's *my* money. We had a deal."

"We *have* a deal. But something has come up and I need to pay some other people. Do you think that bump in sales happened by accident? I have guys on the streets pushing the credit cards. They're the frontline soldiers. They get their money. Then you'll get yours."

"Well, you're not a frontline soldier, and I'm sure you still got paid."

"What the fuck did you say?"

"You heard me. This is complete *bullshit*. I've spent enough time with the others to know that you pay out when the money comes in. Everyone gets their cut. Why am I the only one being fucked over? I got you the credit card machines and watch the accounts every damn day."

"I suggest you watch your mouth, Mason. Don't forget who you're talking to."

"And don't forget who made this all possible."

Those were the last words Mason spoke before slamming the phone down to hang up the call, his body trembled with steaming rage. The stress of doing such illegal activity every single day had long taken its toll on his psyche, but to not receive the financial rewards for doing the dirty work? Now that was a whole new level of fucked-up.

Mason had no options. Nate was the top dog, and whatever he said was final. There was no negotiating with the man, especially over money. If someone had a serious concern and wanted to take up the matter with him, they usually met his revolver.

Mason had heard the stories, and while he didn't know how true they were (he suspected the stories were made up to keep the peasants at bay), he had no plans to find out.

He planted his elbows on his knees and held up his face in the cups of both hands. Next to his computer monitor stood a family portrait. He and Lindsay in the backdrop, Amanda and David with cheesy grins just below them.

"What am I doing?" he whispered to himself. One mistake by anyone within Nate's group, and they could all go under. There were a lot of moving parts, and too much trust to leave with a collective of criminals. The little money he had been receiving so far had made a difference in his family's life, but was it worth it? If Mason went to prison, they'd be left with absolutely nothing. Lindsay didn't have an income. She'd have to find work and cut back on all unnecessary expenses. She would pull Amanda out of her dance classes. David wouldn't get to play baseball next summer. They'd never get to leave the house for pleasure and would be reduced to basic meals. All while Mason rotted away in a jail cell.

Mason's stomach swirled. They made it plenty clear to him when he joined the group that leaving wasn't an option. "When you're with me," Nate had said, slinging an arm over Mason's shoulder. "You're with me for life."

As long as he had been a part of the gang, Mason had yet to see someone leave. No one had even entertained the thought.

"I'm not like these guys," he muttered. Their gatherings brought together drug dealers, murderers, kidnappers. And there were Mason and Rusty—the white-collar workers who ensured things ran smoothly behind the scenes. *Am I closer to a mob leader than a drug runner? Only a few people get to keep their hands clean in groups like this.*

All things considered, he had the cushy job.

Can I actually get out? Or am I really stuck? What would happen if I just stopped showing up to the meetings, or answering my work phone? Will they come to my house? Threaten my family? Would they actually kill me for wanting to return to a normal life?

These thoughts pressed on his conscience, and he grew overwhelmed with the considerations. If he waited for a couple of days to pass—he'd have to wait now, after how he ended his last conversation—would he be able to have a civil conversation with Nate and tell him exactly how he was feeling? He could explain himself from a position of gratitude and regret. Grateful to have received the opportunity for life-changing money, regretful for putting his family in a risky position. He hadn't truly weighed the gravity of the situation from the onset, but things had come into focus. And no, it wasn't because Nate had just stiffed him of the funds he deserved—although that was certainly a factor. He could find work picking up a weekend shift. Hell, CreditConnect might even approve some overtime, and he could get the extra cash that way.

Mason slouched in his seat, his limbs feeling hollowed out while his head spun. The thought of picking up the phone and calling Nate—no matter what mood the man was in—to have this discussion made him nauseous. While he didn't think it likely, it was still *possible* he could end up dead at the close of that phone call.

At least if that happens, Lindsay would collect insurance and have some cushion.

He shook his head free of the morbid thoughts, suddenly concerned about putting together the living will he had long kept on the back burner.

Mason slouched further, on the verge of spilling out from his chair and collapsing under his desk. He had reached a cross-roads, and could either commit to leaving the organization or jump all the way in. He supposed Nate would reward him if he showed a little more initiative. *Maybe even a parting gift,* he thought. *A token of appreciation before sailing into the sunset and never looking back.*

He thought of the Selena girl who came over for dinner last night. Maybe she was a godsend to get him out of this mess. She was stunning. Way more attractive than any of the girls they deployed to the brothels and street corners.

Nate had always spoken of expanding the business with a high-end escort service. The girls multi-millionaires would pay up to fifty-thousand dollars to have for one night.

Selena was the perfect candidate. Beautiful. Young. Alone in a city with no family. And she needed money. Nate would know how to convince her. He would sell her on the dream of making twenty-thousand dollars a weekend. And none of it would be a lie. She really would make life-changing money.

"I just have to get her to Nate, and he can seal the deal," Mason muttered under his breath. "Good thing she likes to play poker."

He picked up the phone and dialed Lindsay to ask for Selena's number.

Chapter 32

Felix ordered a meat lover's pizza for dinner on Tuesday night. The stress and pressure of the week were taking their tolls on all three Angels, and cooking no longer seemed a pressing matter. Not after the phone call Felix received earlier in the afternoon.

He expected both Arielle and Selena home by six, as had become the norm since their arrival in 1988 Pueblo. The pizza sat on the dining room table while Felix paced circles around it.

Why would he call here? What does he want?

The front door jiggled and swung open, Arielle stepping into the house.

"Dammit!" Felix spat.

"Well, happy Tuesday to you, too," Arielle replied.

"No. It's not you. It's Selena. We need her home ASAP. He called here today asking for her."

Arielle dropped her duffel bag with a loud clatter. "Mason called *here*?!"

"Yeah. He asked who I was, so I said a roommate. I don't know what all Selena has told anyone, so I hope that didn't throw anything off."

"Did he say what he wanted?"

"Nope. Just to relay that he called, and would like her to call him back."

Selena turned into the driveway and Arielle immediately waved her arms, urging her to hurry and come inside.

Selena, who had spent the day trying to follow Nate, didn't waste any time singing in the car this evening, and hurried up the path to meet them. "What's wrong?"

"Mason called for you today," Felix said. "Wants you to call him back."

Selena narrowed her eyes, suspicious. "Just him? Not Lindsay?"

Felix nodded. "It was around two o'clock, so he would have been at work."

"Well, this adds some excitement to my boring-ass day. I sat on that main road all day and no one ever came out. Nate must have not had any business that required him to leave his house. Of course, right?"

"You don't know what this could be about?" Arielle asked, grabbing Selena by the shoulder and forcing her into the kitchen where the phone waited on its cradle.

"No idea. He didn't say anything about reaching out to me. It can't be too secretive—he would have gotten the number from Lindsay. She's the only who has it."

"Then call him. Right now. They're probably having dinner over there, but I don't care. We need to know what he wants."

Felix had never seen Arielle so excited. But it was more of an anxious excitement. Urgency. Borderline chaotic.

"Okay, relax. I'm going." Selena placed her bag on her seat at the kitchen table before picking up and dialing the phone on the counter. "Hi Lindsay, it's Selena. How are you?"

Selena's leg started bouncing while she leaned against the

counter. She looked at her friends and mimicked a blabbering mouth with her free hand.

"Well, that's good," she finally said. "Mason called here for me earlier, so I was just returning his message to call back. Is he available? Okay, thank you."

Selena nodded and gave a thumbs up. Mason Gregory was on his way to the phone.

"I'm good, Mason," Selena said after a few seconds. "How are you?"

She nodded her head for about thirty seconds while Mason spoke, then said, "This Friday night? Um, let me check my schedule real quick."

Selena slapped her hand over the receiver and spun around to face Arielle, eyes bulging. "He's inviting me to the poker game on Friday night. What should I do?" she whispered, but the words still spilled out of her mouth like she had no control over them.

"Holy shit!" Felix gasped.

Arielle nodded. "If you're comfortable being there, go for it. We'll be there in case anything goes wrong."

Selena took a moment before uncovering the phone and placing it back to her ear. "Looks like I am available that night. Should I plan to meet you there? . . . Okay, understood. See you then. Thank you."

She hung up the phone and drew in a deep breath. "Alright, guys. I don't know what the hell is going on, but this is really happening. He told me to meet at his house and we can drive over together. Said the house they're going to isn't the easiest place to find." Selena let out a nervous chuckle.

"Look," Arielle said. "I know this is critical to the mission, and being handed to us on a silver platter. But my number one concern on any mission is the safety of our Angels. Knowing what we know about that place, and who all is there, I'm not going to force you to go. I completely understand if you want to call him back tomorrow and make up an excuse. We still know he's going to be there Friday night, regardless if you are. At this point in the mission, that's really all we need to know."

"But we still don't know one-hundred percent for sure who kills him. Or why."

"The *why* doesn't matter anymore. We just need to stop the murder and go back home. I really don't like the way this mission is turning out."

"How is the past going to react to this?" Felix asked. "Selena obviously wasn't there the night Mason was killed. Could her presence lead to some problems?"

"It definitely will," Arielle said. "Be on high alert all week, Selena. Your presence itself could lead to the murder not happening, and the past might push back against that. Might even try to prevent you from showing up. Maybe you should stay home until Friday night. I'll have to think about the best approach for that. But definitely be ready for anything."

Selena gulped and nodded. "Okay, I understand. Would the past have let me come this far, though? Why allow this invite to happen in the first place?"

"We don't have a full understanding of how other people can affect the past. This wasn't a matter of you inviting yourself to the poker game. *Mason* did it. Mason isn't a time traveler, he's living in his original timeline for these events. There have been a few theories. Some argue the regular people can still receive pushback from altering the past. Others say they are protected since they are in their Original Time. I guess we'll have to see what happens with Mason, but that doesn't mean *you* should be any less careful."

"Got it. Okay. I feel alright about this. I'll be ready to enter the belly of the beast. And I'll be damned if anything is going to happen to me."

"You don't suppose . . ." Felix began, but trailed off. He wondered if Mason might try to kidnap Selena, or have the thugs at the poker game kidnap her. They could either want her as a sex slave, or maybe they just wouldn't like if Mason brought a guest along, and wanted to ensure her silence. But they wouldn't ever get away with that with Arielle Lucila on the scene. "Never mind. Do you think Mason asked Nate if he could bring Selena? Or is he planning on just showing up?"

"He said he would ask the host when we talked about it at dinner," Selena said. "I didn't think he actually would, but here we are."

Arielle's brow lowered as she entered deep thought, and Felix could only wonder if she was thinking the same thing he just had.

"Irrelevant," Arielle said. "Let's enjoy some dinner and call it a night. The rest of this week is going to be exhausting."

Chapter 33

Mason hadn't slept six hours combined between Tuesday and Wednesday night. He had mentally committed to the decision to tender his resignation to Nate on Friday evening, and leave him with Selena as a peace offering.

The guilt already pricked at him. He had never committed such a heinous crime against a fellow human being. He thought of his own daughter, and how he might react if she were to go missing one day, forever lost in the underground world of human trafficking. His heart ached, his stomach wrenched, and his limbs shook. He supposed the latter was because of the lack of sleep and amounts of caffeine he had consumed over the past two days to stay a functioning adult.

Mason had debated calling in and taking personal days until this all passed, but decided going to work would be best. Stewing at home wouldn't be any better. Worse, in fact, since Lindsay would prod him and ask him how he was feeling, and probably convince him to not go to the poker game on Friday night. In his current state, he just might agree with that decision, and that would leave him trapped under Nate's thumb for the rest of his miserable life.

At least from work, he could distract himself with tasks, even if that meant mindlessly staring at the screen for hours at a time. He was in his own world—his own personal hell—within the confines of his cubicle. His manager might check in with him a couple of times throughout the day, but he otherwise expected no visitors or distractions.

All alone to swallow this pill like a man, he thought. Mason would never understand the folks within their ring that did this portion of the job for a living. They navigated the streets, scooping up homeless women sleeping on park benches, bringing them to safe houses to get cleaned up and polished to market.

"You'll never have to sleep on a bench again," they'd tell the women. "You'll be in a bed every night, in fact, with a complete stranger. Just spread those legs and we'll change your life forever."

They needed little beyond a sleazy sales pitch when trying to attract women who had absolutely nothing. About ninety percent would join after hearing about the life-altering money they would make on top of the benefits of sleeping in hotel or brothel rooms with a roof and heating. And food. Another five percent would require more convincing, while the last five would still refuse and be released back to the parks they called home.

They rarely forced women into the trade, but sometimes Nate allowed a kidnapping. They typically took these women across the country, far from where they had been captured, in case anyone searched for them. This happened with women who had the highest earning potential. Ones who might qualify for the high-end escort service but couldn't see the exorbitant value they could provide. And earn.

Selena fit this mold, and that was the only reason he thought Nate would let him live.

A knock on the cubicle wall startled Mason from his wandering thoughts, and he jumped in his seat.

"Whoa, sorry to startle you," his manager, Brian Rogers, said with a chuckle. Brian was a tall, heavy man with a thick mustache that often caught the crumbs of his morning doughnuts. Brian was an asshole. "Do you have a minute to chat in my office?"

Under normal circumstances, Mason would have spun into a complete panic attack after hearing these words. But he was already in that phase, so he felt nothing of significance as he stood and said, "Sure."

He had been so consumed with his impending doom that he felt like he was walking in a dream, following Brian down the hallway, passing cubicles where his colleagues continued with their days. Brian led the way, his pudgy ass stretching his slacks to their limits. Mason always thought his boss would sit down one day at a meeting and the button on his pants would burst free, blasting across the room like a rocket ship. The thought brought a much needed grin.

"How's the week going?" Brian grumbled over his shoulder as they stepped into his office. He closed the door behind them once Mason took a seat in front of the cluttered desk.

"It's been fine," Mason replied, now feeling the pressure to act cool. He couldn't recall having made any mistakes in his work.

"Glad to hear. Family okay?" Brian asked as he sat in his office chair, the hinges screeching as they begged for mercy.

"Yes, everyone is doing well."

"That's great. You've been doing great work, and because of that, we want to reward you. We are doing an audit of everyone's accounts and will reassign some of the higher profile ones your way. Companies bringing in at least fifty thousand a month. All the rest in your portfolio will be things of the past."

"*All* the current accounts?" Mason replied, suddenly light-headed. His secret account was nowhere near earning fifty thousand.

"Yes. We want to maximize the talent on our team, and you have the highest retention rate. Naturally, we want to place the bigger accounts with you."

"Are there any I can ask to keep?"

"I'm sorry, Mason, are you not understanding? You're about to earn at least an extra twenty thousand dollars a year, the way we are looking to structure your portfolio. Why on Earth would you want to keep accounts that will lower that number?"

Mason took a moment to let those words settle in. He had been so focused on working under the radar and keeping things afloat for Nate, that he hadn't realized the quality of work he'd been doing. He had just received a generous opportunity, yet still felt a resistance to jump for joy around Brian's office.

"I don't know what to say."

"You don't need to say anything," Brian replied. "Congratulations. You've earned it. Once the audits are complete, and we confirm everything with your existing accounts is sound, we'll make the announcement next week."

Mason grew queasy. "What does the audit consist of?"

"The usual. A second look at all the numbers to make sure everything lines up. We look for inconsistencies in accounts, fee waivers, cancellation reasons. That's why it can take some time."

Mason became dizzy and worried about standing up. "Okay," he said, the lone word forced. "Thank you. Is there anything else?"

Brian furrowed his brow as he planted his elbows on the desk, studying Mason from behind the glasses perched on his wide nose. "No, that's all. Are you sure everything's okay?"

It was the most concerned, on a personal level, Mason had ever heard Brian sound. He nodded. "Yes. Just a little tired, I suppose."

Mason stood on wobbly legs, reached out a hand and gave the weakest handshake of his life. He mustered a lazy grin before turning and exiting the office, sure to close the door behind him as he hurried down the hall toward the bathrooms.

Mason heaved as he pushed open the bathroom door, grateful to see no one else present as he stumbled into a stall and slammed the door shut, falling to his knees. He caught his reflection in the toilet bowl's water seconds before his guts released the tension and forced vomit of a sickly off-yellow color.

His body shivered while he spat out what remained in his mouth, tears flowing and combining with the mucus pooling on the tip of his nose. The raise, and even the promise of a future fortune from Nate, all seemed irrelevant. Depending on how this audit turned out, there was suddenly an increased chance that Mason was going to prison.

He closed his eyes and pictured it all. Brian receiving a report of the excessive fee waivers applied to The Puzzle Piece. There was a chance Mason would only receive a slap on the wrist, but a closer look at the details was more likely. A full investigation would launch, as CreditConnect needed to ensure no money laundering was taking place. It would only take a matter of days before they discovered The Puzzle Piece wasn't an actual business. The feds would get involved and march into the office building—or Mason's home—to take him away where he'd face a jury on charges of fraud, accessory to sex trafficking, and a slew of other criminal charges.

All for an easy buck, he thought, and puked once more.

He couldn't face a trial. Couldn't face his wife and kids. Couldn't even face himself, if that's how everything played out.

Mason had no chance in prison. He imagined himself in the bright orange jumpsuit, terrified to shower, leave his cell, or take a quiet walk during their outdoor hour. Hopefully, the movies made it seem worse than it really was, but he suspected the reality reflected plenty in the art.

"What the hell am I supposed to do?" Mason moaned, wiping away what he hoped was the last remnants from his insides. His head spun, his stomach now empty.

Do I pack up and move? Do I tell Lindsay?

If he told Lindsay everything that had happened, and she stayed with him, then maybe she would agree to move away. Pack up their bags and disappear into the night before Credit-Connect had time to piece it all together. Perhaps his sudden disappearance from work would prevent the audit from even happening. His accounts would all shift to different colleagues in a move that would leave Brian scrambling. This seemed the best scenario to pursue, but was it overreacting?

It was entirely possible they would complete the audit, and nothing would come from it. They might dismiss the fee waivers as something Mason did to accomplish a high retention rate. Hell, they might even adopt the practice, praising him for such a brilliant idea. They might find the waivers and question him about it, and he could try to bullshit his way out of it. He'd seen it plenty of times. Respected employees could get away with more. They wanted him to manage their biggest accounts. There were likely many parts already in motion in the background to make that happen. A minor wrench like the waivers could easily be dismissed to ensure the company's plans moved forward.

Mason stood at a fork in the road, one that determined the rest of his life. The most disturbing part was that his decision didn't guarantee a particular outcome. Both roads could lead to dead ends.

Mason still had a looming conversation with Nate.

I just hope he's willing to listen.

Chapter 34

The three Angels sat around the living room in stunned silence. It was eight o'clock at night. They had just finished a dinner of homemade cheeseburgers, Felix willing to cook the meal he saved for lazy days.

Dinner had gone well. Until the phone rang.

Felix had answered and handed the phone to Selena. She listened for just under a minute, her responses terse as she shook her head. After hanging up, she said, "He just uninvited me from the poker game."

After the phone call, they moved into the living room. Unfinished burgers and dirty dishes remained in the kitchen, scattered between the table and sink. It was the messiest they had ever left the kitchen.

Selena poured them all a glass of wine.

"I should have seen this coming," Arielle said, taking her first sip.

Felix nodded. "We often get tricked into believing the past pushes back with some dramatic event, but that's rarely the case. The past works efficiently. Remember, it wants to maintain its original chain of events. It wants to correct the changes we've made to ensure the same outcomes happen. Selena was never supposed to be at that poker game, so now the past is working to make sure that doesn't happen."

"So if I still go, what will happen?" Selena asked.

"We *can* still go," Arielle said bluntly. "If our goal is to observe the mansion, we shouldn't meet any resistance. Selena wasn't in the house the night of the murder, so that's all the past is reverting to. We still know where the murder will happen. We're going to have to split up. Someone needs to be at that warehouse, waiting to intervene. And whoever we decide that is, will need to be there first thing tomorrow morning. We have to cheat the past, and I'm afraid that's the only way to do it."

"How do we decide?" Felix asked, a tinge of fear in his voice. "It should be you, right, Arielle?"

Arielle knew damn well it should be her. Everyone in the room did. They also didn't know *how* she wanted to play this situation, nor could they.

While her fellow Angels were the best at their given roles, neither of them understood the intricacies of dealing with the past. Neither of them had played out the night of June 24th hundreds of different ways. She was still leading this mission, and would position her team in the best spots for success and safety. She had made enough mistakes in her early days as an Angel to learn how to cheat the past. That's *why* she was the best.

"Felix, you'll be waiting at the warehouse tomorrow."

"What?!" he gasped, jumping off the couch. "Why the hell would you pick me? I don't kill people."

Arielle raised a hand. "Stop worrying. I'll be nearby, but you'll need to step in if something prevents me from getting there. I've already mapped this out. You're decent with a rifle and scope, yes?"

"I, uh, I'm decent, sure. But nowhere good enough to be left with this responsibility. Is this one of those mind games to trick me into some sort of false confidence?"

"I don't play games. You can handle the job. It's that simple."

"Well, do you mind sharing *why*?" Felix scoffed.

Arielle indeed didn't play games, but she utilized strategy. Felix and Selena were now pawns in the chess match she was playing against the past.

"Actually, no."

"Whoa," Selena said, standing beside Felix. "You can't do that. We've been working together this whole time. You can't just decide what to do without discussing."

"I understand your concerns, but you need to understand where I'm coming from. I know what it takes to beat the past. Don't ever mistake who our enemy is. It's not Mason, it's not Nate. It's the past. Every mission, we have to beat the past. I'm putting us all where we need to be, and I just need you to trust me, no matter how little sense it makes to you."

"This is bullshit," Selena snapped. "You're being a dictator." She stomped around the living room, returning to the wine rack and pouring another glass.

"I'm happy to answer any questions *after* the mission, but for now, I need to keep the strategy to myself. Felix, do you have a problem with any of this?"

He had crossed his arms and fell silent while Selena lost her cool, returning to his seat on the couch. He shrugged. "Not much I can do about it. You're in charge, and if we don't comply, I'm sure we'll get banished from the Angels."

"It shouldn't be that way," Selena muttered under her breath.

"Look, guys," Arielle said. "We have structure and protocol. I was afraid of this happening—"

"Then go back to working by yourself," Selena cut in. "Do all the prep work yourself, bug the houses, kill the bad guys. You've never needed us, and you still don't, apparently."

"Selena, sit down and listen!" Arielle shouted. She had never risen her voice toward another Angel.

Selena returned to the couch and sat next to Felix, his eyes bulging as they remained fixed on their leader.

"It's go time," Arielle said, sliding over to stand directly in front of them. "I'm not playing games with either of you. There are a lot of moving parts I need to consider when planning out missions and how to best approach them. I don't have time right now to go over all the little details. We can do that after. I've learned from thousands of these missions and witnessing firsthand what can go wrong. Again, I don't have time to go over the errors I've made in the past. I just need you both to trust that I know what I'm doing. Are we on the same page?"

Felix was the first to nod, and Selena reluctantly gave in a few seconds later.

"Okay, thank you," Arielle said. "Now Felix, you will be at the warehouse tomorrow. You're going to have a boring day, so come to terms with that now. Bring a book. I need you to head there first thing in the morning. The past won't understand your presence there so early in the day, so don't plan on encountering any resistance. You should be able to show up, park among the other vehicles, and hang out all day. I only want you there as a last resort. If things go our way, Selena and I will be there as well. If you don't see us, then you'll need to take the shot. I've circled a perfect hiding place

223

on this map."

Arielle shuffled into the kitchen where she kept the duffel bag, rummaged for her binder, and pulled out a printed map of the area surrounding the warehouse. She tossed it on Felix's lap, and he looked down like it was an ancient scroll.

"Selena. You're going to Nate's house in the morning and will wait along the main road as you've been doing. I'm going to Mason's house and will follow him all day again. Once you see us arrive—I'll leave about a hundred yards between us—follow us down the side road where you and I will pull off to hide. We know where the cameras are now, so we can avoid them. I want you there in case we get caught. Your presence can be a simple explanation, since Mason invited you at one point. I can be your friend you wanted to bring along. This might seem silly, but it *will* work. From there, we will figure out how to proceed. We may try to enter the house, or we might wait outside."

"So you might shoot Nate at his house?" Felix asked.

"Not likely. Way too many people there to try that and expect to outrun them all. Besides, we still need that visual confirmation that Nate is who enters his car and drives to the warehouse. Just another detail we need to confirm before stopping anything."

"And if it's someone else?" Selena asked.

"Then we follow them and still carry out the mission."

"Then why bother? Can't we just blast whoever sits in that car first?"

"Never leave a detail untouched," Arielle said. "We'll stop whoever carries out this murder, regardless of who it is. But we need to make sure our notes and story are all correct. Remember, we have teams that look into the missions long after the fact. If it were to come out later that we stopped the wrong person, that could get very messy for all of us. Possible expulsion from the Angels. You should never act on a whim in these missions."

Felix nodded. "Okay," he said. "I feel better about all this. Still hoping I don't need to pull that trigger tomorrow night."

Arielle shrugged. "Get that out of your head. You need to imagine that you *will* do it. Mentally put yourself in that scenario. Listen to the sounds around you, breathe in the air, feel the rifle in your hands. If you don't do this sort of mental prep, you're doomed to collapse under pressure when the time arises. And I am not trying to do this mission again."

A failed mission would be disastrous. While they could start over, the past pushed back much harder on a second attempt, often making it impossible to change anything. The past, in all its wisdom and glory, strongly believed in the old *Fool me once* proverb.

"So we're good?" Arielle asked.

"As good as can be, I suppose," Felix said.

Selena stared distantly at the wall.

"Selena?" Arielle said.

"We're good."

"Okay, let's call it a night," Arielle said. "Tomorrow will be plenty eventful."

They parted for their rooms in what would be their last night in the house.

Chapter 35

Mason Gregory left his house Friday morning with no idea about the long night that awaited. Perhaps the human soul detected dangers beyond the brain's comprehension. His body felt sick all over, despite having no actual symptoms. After he kissed his wife and kids on the way out, a monsoon of sensations flooded him. He was hungry (he hadn't eaten a complete meal in three days), but also entirely full. He felt both cold and hot. His legs and arms trembled beyond his control. As he drove to work, he swore the car ran on autopilot. He spent the first hour at his desk wondering how he had safely arrived. He couldn't recall putting the key in the ignition or driving on the highway. It was like he had teleported to his desk.

It was a hot summer Friday—scorching, in fact—when he stepped outside of the office building at five o'clock. He released the top button of his collared shirt, its grasp around his neck suffocating. Part of him had expected to be hauled off to prison today. That didn't happen. He still planned to speak with Nate, and while he drove straight to Nate's house after work, a deep worry brewed within his subconscious, wondering if he'd actually survive the night.

I'll still tell him about Selena. If he gets really upset and wants that parting gift, it won't be hard to get her over for the poker game next week.

He mulled over this, but deep down he knew he'd never be able to contribute to a kidnapping. He had mentally checked out of his role with the trafficking ring and wanted nothing further to do with them. Tonight would be the last time ever he saw Nathan Baldwin. He hoped.

His palms sweated as he clutched the steering wheel. Beads formed around his crown. He had survived the day without so much as an encounter with his boss.

He didn't *want* Brian to check on him, but he also wanted to believe his new pay raise might shift their relationship to a more bearable level. As he had learned plenty of times in corporate America, the idea of a company truly caring for its employees was as common as stepping in unicorn shit.

The drive across town, which still felt surreal to him, dragged forever. Traffic was slightly heavier than usual, common for a Friday evening when most workers wasted no time leaving their offices at five sharp to get a start on the weekend. He passed plenty of bars on his way to the highway, many of them with lines out the door, and the outdoor patios jam-packed.

How he wished he had a normal life to do something like that.

He couldn't recall the last time he went out with co-workers for a drink after a long day. It hadn't happened once during his time at CreditConnect. Rusty had made it clear he was to avoid social interactions with any of his colleagues. Workplace friends only increased the odds of his little scheme being noticed. Too many times, those same friends could turn into enemies, and that's when probing into another's work began. A disgruntled colleague was more likely to find out

Mason's dirty deeds than management. And if not for the upcoming audit, that logic had proven true over the course of two years. He made zero relationships with those in his office. His colleagues avoided eye contact when passing him in the hall, and had developed the ability to walk right past him as if he didn't exist. Not so much as a grin or subtle head nod to acknowledge him.

Mason expected this of upper management, but grew delighted once colleagues treated him the same way. It meant he closed off any potential relationships from flourishing. No one at the office *hated* him, but they understood he wanted to be left alone.

He came in, did his work, and went home. A typical worker bee that punched in and punched out right on schedule. An ideal employee in the eyes of management. An invisible presence to those in the surrounding cubicles.

None of that mattered as he exited the highway and started his drive through the mountains. His fate waited less than two miles away. It would be hard to get Nate alone, but he hoped to portray a sense of urgency. Their leader was always swarmed by those on his team.

"Can I have a word with you in private?" Mason rehearsed, staring at himself in the rear-view mirror. "Can I have a word with you? In private?" he practiced again, softening his tone. He hoped his calm would rub off on Nate.

His mouth pooled with saliva as he turned off the small highway and onto the private dirt road. The bumps seemed exaggerated as his Civic cruised along, bobbing up and down on the uneven road.

"I can do this. I can walk away from this all and live a normal life. I will get my raise at work and can take the kids to

Disneyland with it. I don't need this blood money anymore."

His eyes kept jumping from the rearview and back to the road. He wished he had a mirror to speak in front of. It was a trick he had learned in high school, and one he had used in his professional career. Before any presentation or speech, he'd lock himself in the bathroom and rehearse the entire piece. He didn't know how well that might work. Hell, he didn't even know exactly what he wanted to say to Nate, but wanted to maintain a cool tone.

"Hi, Nate. How's it going?" Mason chuckled, practicing his response to whatever Nate might respond. "Oh, that's good. Can I have a word with you in private?"

Mason shook his head. "Fuck!" It all sounded fake leaving his lips, and he feared the nerves had become too strong. How was Nate supposed to take him seriously if he couldn't even *sound* serious?

He rolled down the window, needing fresh air, not giving a shit about the flying dirt from the road that would soon make its way into the car.

Within a minute, he reached Nate's house, vehicles already lined up and filling the driveway. He parked behind the first car he saw and killed the engine, leaning his head onto the steering wheel to draw in a deep breath.

"Change your life," he whispered. "It's your life, and no one else can control it. You just want out. That's all. He'll understand."

Mason nodded, balling a fist and punching the dashboard. His adrenaline had reached a tipping point, and he needed to let some out.

He stepped out of the car and closed the door, catching his full reflection in the backseat window. Having rarely looked at himself, he wondered when he had aged so much. His five o'clock shadow was peppered with gray. Bags hung under his eyelids, and pimples had sprouted across his cheeks.

I'm in bad shape, he thought, figuring at least some of it had to do with the complete lack of sleep and food over the past couple of days. He didn't feel as tired as he looked, and decided that Nate would take him seriously based on his appearance, no matter how rehearsed his words ended up sounding. He had the look of a man battered by emotional distress.

Mason gulped before turning away from his car and trudging up the driveway. His shoes crunched on the gravel. Birds sung their final evening tunes from high in the surrounding evergreens. But Mason heard none of it. He could only focus on putting one foot in front of the other as he marched to Nate's front door.

The growing commotion of chatter grew louder once he reached the door. Judging by the amount of cars in the driveway, there were already a dozen people inside, drinking and eating to celebrate the end of another week, and the beginning of a new weekend with lots of money to make.

Mason knocked on the door and waited, oblivious to the car pulling up and parking behind his own.

Chapter 36

"He's in," Arielle said.

"What now?" Selena asked.

They parked right behind Mason's Civic, and immediately exited the car, hiding in the confinement of the surrounding woods. They were about one hundred feet away from the house, and both studied the front door through a pair of binoculars.

"Think we can get in there?" Arielle asked.

"What the hell for?!" Selena asked, Arielle waving her hand to hush her.

"Quiet. Someone might hear us."

They both spun around at the sound of an approaching vehicle further down the road. The car parked behind theirs, and a man stepped out wearing a shiny leather jacket, tattoos covering his neck.

"Henry Freeman," Arielle whispered, recognizing the face from the file they had received last week. "I think he does a lot of the questionable business on the streets."

"Why are we dealing with these people?" Selena asked.

Arielle didn't answer, instead focusing on the man entering the house. The door swung inward, and he disappeared inside. She wanted to know if Nate answered his own door during these gatherings, but could never tell from their angle. They had eyes on the cameras and discovered a couple more on the front of the garage that overlooked the front entrance.

"I think if we wait for nightfall, we can sneak in around the back. We'll need a clearer view."

Selena shook her head. Arielle knew this was so far out of her fellow Angel's comfort zone. She was supposed to deal with people in the days before a tragedy, not be thrust into the middle of a dangerous scenario on the night of. In fact, Selena rarely stuck around for the night of the interjection, her work finished well before then. She would hop around from mission to mission, gaining information and developing trust with those involved before disappearing from their lives as quickly as she had arrived.

"But why?" she asked, desperation dripping from her in a *please-don't-make-me-go-in-there* tone. "We can get involved out here. Wait by their cars. Follow them. We have no reason to go in there."

"I'm not saying we kick in the front door for some grand entrance. We can *sneak* in. Snoop around. Imagine listening to the conversations."

"There have to be cameras around back. This place is protected like the White House. Why would he have cameras only in some spots? You saw how fast someone came out last time. Another reason to worry—they might be on high alert this week."

Arielle hadn't considered that. From these people's point of view, someone had snooped around the party only six days ago and got away. With so much at stake, Nate wouldn't spare an expense to ensure his mansion remained safe, his secret concealed.

"You might be right," Arielle said. "We're stuck here until

dark. I still say we entertain the thought. In the report, they mentioned there might be girls trapped in the basement. If we can save more lives, then we should. I can't stand the thought of innocent women terrified for their lives down there."

"You're just mentioning this now?"

Arielle shrugged. "It's not part of the mission, but if we can help, then why not? I wish I could say us killing Nate would set them free, but the rest of his crew might have specific plans in place should such a thing happen. Most likely, in fact, and the absolute last thing they'd want are their prisoners to be discovered in the basement."

"Is this why you won't tell us the plans for tonight? Because we would want to help them?"

"No, I'm not telling you in order to keep you alive, and I intend to keep it that way."

* * *

Across town, Felix sat in his car. He had read Michael Crichton's newest book, *Sphere*, to pass the time since he had arrived at eight o'clock in the morning. He had walked over to the sandwich shop a half-mile away where many of the employees from the warehouse enjoyed their midday meal, and took a cold Italian back to his car.

Felix had done a lot of dull work in his time with the Angels, but none of it compared to the torture of sitting in his car for the past nine hours, knowing he still had four more before anything happened. If it did.

He looked into the backseat and saw the blanket draped over

the rifle Arielle insisted he bring. Felix spent a couple of hours in the afternoon visualizing the night's events. He wanted to stroll over to the area on the map Arielle had marked for him, but she had given strict instruction to not venture that way until the parking lot had cleared. People might have seen him wandering the area, and that was the last thing they needed if a murder were to occur later.

Felix thought he would have been better utilized bugging Mason's car during the day, or even working on a way to circumvent the cameras at Nate's house, but it became plenty clear Arielle knew exactly what she wanted to happen. By the minute.

"Plan for a late dinner tonight," she had told Felix before they parted ways from the house. "A late dinner in 2022."

He leaned back in his seat and grinned at the thought.

Chapter 37

"Mason, my man!" Nate greeted him, throwing an arm around over his shoulder and pulling him in for a sideways hug. He kept a cigar between his teeth, blowing puffs of smoke toward the ceiling every minute.

Mason found Nate in the dining room where a table had been covered with cheese and fruit platters, and boxes of catered pulled pork and chicken. A typical feast for Nate's weekly gathering.

"How are things?" Nate asked, grabbing another cigar from the counter and offering it to Mason.

Mason waved his hand. "No thanks. Things are good."

"Boy, are they!" Nate cackled. "I know you've seen our numbers from the credit cards. Give us a few more months and you'll be making money you've never dreamed of."

Mason nodded, refusing to show any emotion. He was unable to. He thought he might faint right there on the dining room table. Apparently, Nate was going to pretend their last phone call never happened. Water under the bridge. "Yeah. I've seen. Looks good."

Nate puffed his cigar and craned his neck upward to blow smoke. His eyes returned to Mason and studied him. "Something's the matter with you. Talk to me, Mase. What's on your mind?"

Mason hadn't expected to run into Nate so quickly, let alone be questioned right off the bat. He had budgeted at least twenty minutes to settle in and get mentally ready for the tough conversation.

He looked around for anyone who might have been snooping on their conversation. But the house was too crowded. People were lost in their own discussions. Some shuffled through the dining room to fill their plates, others hovered near the fridge where the beer was kept, and the rest had gathered in the living room where they watched Ozzie Smith and the Cardinals take on Mike Schmidt and the Phillies.

Mason had the exact moment he had wanted.

"C-can we talk in private, Nate?" he asked in a hushed voice. His tone earned a glance from Rusty at the table.

Nate plucked the cigar from his mouth and studied Mason with questioning eyes. "Sure, man. Let's head to my office."

Nate led the way out of the dining room, through the living room, and down a long hallway. They passed three doors before turning into Nate's office, where he closed the door behind them.

The office was a cluttered room with shelves full of books and stacks of paper surrounding a small desk, with more papers spilling over the edges. It reeked of tobacco and marijuana.

"Did something happen at work?" Nate asked, placing his cigar in the ashtray on his desk, leaning against the front of it while Mason stood awkwardly at the door. Putting the cigar down was a sign of concern for someone like Nate. He rarely let a situation change his course of action.

Mason debated telling the truth about the upcoming audit. But that would only lead to more questions. And possibly threats from Nate toward CreditConnect. Threats that could easily become reality.

The audit wasn't the point. He still wanted out.

"Do you ever reflect on your life, Nate?" Mason asked, surprising himself at how calm he sounded. The same couldn't be said for his emotions bouncing all over the walls.

Nate scrunched his face in confusion. "What is this? You have some coming-to-Jesus moment? I sleep at night just fine, if that's what you're getting at."

"No, no. Not you. Me. I've been thinking about *my* life, and what I want from it."

"Are you asking to leave my organization?"

Nate always called his group of criminals an *organization*. He believed he ran a legitimate business, regardless of what society—or the law—had to say.

Mason forced a slow head nod.

"I don't know what you expect me to do," Nate said. "You're kind of a big deal for our operations. Critical, in fact. It's not like you're some street hustler I can replace within the hour."

You sure pay me like one, Mason thought, knowing he'd earn at least a broken jaw if he spoke those words aloud. "I understand that, and I'm willing to hang around to help train whoever you'd like to replace me."

Nate grinned and stood up tall from the desk, tossing his hands in the air. "Well, Mase, we don't exactly let people leave because they feel like it. Sure, I've had some guys with a sick mom or kid who really needed to step away. Those guys leave and never think about us again. But people like you, who want to leave because they think they found their morals." He shook his head. "That's dangerous, you see."

"I just don't want to go any further than I already am,"

Mason said. "I don't want my family to be at constant risk. I promise you I have no malicious intent for leaving."

Nate chuckled, shaking his head. "That's what they always say, and that's too bad for you. I want to believe you, but I've heard too many horror stories, and been burned too many times in the past. Each time started with a conversation just like this. 'Oh, sorry, Nate, I just want a normal life again.' Then six months later, they're still thinking about how much better they are because of their bullshit morals. And BAM!"

Nate raised his hand and slapped the top of his desk. Pens and paperclips bounced while a couple of sheets of paper fluttered to the floor. "They turn on you. Tell their mutual friends what you do. Tell the police. Then it's *my* problem to figure out how to stay a free man."

"Look, Nate, I understand where you're coming from. But I'm not having some moral objection to our work all of a sudden. I've just been afraid of what happens if we get caught. Any one of us. We're all going down if that happens, and it's not fair to my family. I just want life to be a little more . . . secure."

Nate laughed through his nose and elevated his hands wide apart above his head. "This is as safe as it gets. This house isn't registered on any government document. We are literally off the grid. No one knows about this place except for the people who need to. Do you think I would really expand our business to use credit cards on a whim? Buddy, I've grown. I have people on my payroll for the lone reason of protecting all of us. Lawyers, district attorneys, judges. Why do you think I've been slow to pay you? These guys ain't cheap, but they're worth it in the long run."

"Are you serious? Judges?"

A wide grin took over Nate. "Oh yeah. This is America, man. Land of the greedy, home of the hustlers. Anything in this country can be bought. *Anything.* Sometimes you just need to ask the price."

"Well, then," Mason said. "What's your price?"

Nate's eyelids fluttered as he stared down Mason. "Excuse me?"

"You just said you can buy *anything.* I want to buy my freedom back. What will it cost?"

Confusion gave way to another smile for Nate. "I'm impressed, Mase. You have a hustler's mentality. That's why I'm not setting a price. Not yet. I need to think about it. But I also want *you* to think about it. We're on the verge of big money. Shit, we have the big money already. I just need to pay off these fools and we'll get to pave our own road. Made of gold. Think about what you really want. You and your family will be safe if you stick with me."

"I have a girl," Mason said abruptly.

"I know . . . and a boy, yes?"

"I'm not talking about my kids. I have a girl, and I can get her right in this house if you want her. She's a knockout. A stone cold ten in any book. She's a Killer Whale."

Nate liked to use a ranking system for the girls. It was all based on their earning potential. Puppies were the everyday girls who earned anywhere from twenty-five to one hundred dollars per night. Horses earned around three hundred per night, but usually only worked on weekends. Whales brought in one thousand per night. And Killer Whales could net five thousand dollars or more for one session. So far, Nate had one Whale, and was still on the hunt for his first Killer.

"You sure about that?" Nate asked. "What do you even know

about our rankings? It's a lot more than looks."

"I understand. This girl is physically perfect. And her personality matches. She's sweet and gentle, but I get the sense she can lay down the law, if needed. She's everything you'd want in a Killer."

"You got a picture? How can you get her here?"

"No picture. I've only met her once. She finished college and said she's been looking to play in a poker game. Also, she needs money."

Nate pursed his lips and stroked his chin, fumbling with a match to relight his cigar. The mood had shifted for the better, and Mason tasted freedom on the horizon. "And you think she'd be interested? I'm not looking to kidnap some random girl. We don't play that shit anymore."

Mason shrugged. "She sounded desperate for money. No local family. Works multiple jobs. I think she's a prime candidate. And you're the right guy to convince her."

He hadn't meant to stroke Nate's ego, but it seemed to benefit him. The leader of the trafficking ring paced around his desk, cigar fully lit, and faced the wall, turning his back on Mason.

"I'll admit, this is an interesting offer. Are you sure you really want to leave this all behind?"

Mason grew uneasy. Speaking to someone's back was something he couldn't recall having done before. It was odd. Intimidating.

"Yes. I've gone back and forth all week. Ultimately, I decided this is what I want. I understand what I'm walking away from, but I'm thinking long-term. This is the best decision for my family."

Nate nodded slowly, cigar smoke gradually filling the room

to create a light haze. "Tell you what. I'll take you up on the offer. Let's meet later tonight. Do you know the warehouses off 40?"

"Yes."

"Meet me at the parking lot outside of the Big Z Home Office warehouse around nine o'clock."

"Tonight?"

"Tonight."

"What about everyone here? We can't just leave."

"They'll be fine. I'm going to give you a generous parting gift, but I can't do it near everyone else here. Have you ever held a briefcase full of cash?"

Mason felt his face flush. This all sounded too good to be true. Not only was Nate open to the idea of him leaving, but he was going to pay a severance package, too? "Can't say I have."

"They're heavier than you think. And I can't just have you lugging it around here. You didn't arrive with a briefcase, and someone will definitely notice. Our guys pay attention to these things."

Mason wanted to ask why they were driving so far. They could have just gone out to the main road and met at a gas station. He didn't want to press the matter—money was on its way, after all. If he needed to drive to Vancouver to pick it up, then that's what he'd do.

"Okay. I'll meet you there."

"Leave here around 8:30. I'll leave at 8:45. Don't tell anyone where we're going, or even that we're meeting. If any of these guys found out what I'm doing for you, all hell would break loose around here." Nate finally turned around, his cigar a small stump between his fingers. "You're a good man, Mason. It's a shame you're leaving."

Chapter 38

"We need to get back to the cars," Arielle said. She checked her watch to find a time of 8:22. "They're going to leave any minute now. I'll follow Mason. You wait around and follow whoever leaves after him."

"Is the car here?" Selena asked. "The one the killer drives?"

"Haven't seen it, but if it's Nathan's, it's probably in the garage."

They had made their way to the opposite side of the property, remaining in the trees and out of sight from the cameras under a powerful glow from the night's full moon. Arielle really wanted to find a way into the house, but from the rear side, they saw through the kitchen window where people kept walking in and out. Some even stepped outside onto the back patio for a quick cigarette break. They stared toward Arielle and Selena, oblivious the two women were there, just waiting to pounce.

Arielle led the way back to their cars, tracing back their earlier steps. Having grown up in Colorado, she'd heard plenty of stories of mountain lions attacking people in the middle of the night. She feared little in this world, especially with her pistol by her side, but something about a wild mountain cat kept her on edge as they navigated the dark woods.

Their shoes crunched on the rocks and twigs, the sound

exaggerated amid the silence. But they were far enough from the house to garner any attention. Even if they did, it wouldn't end well if one of them ventured into the woods to confront the Angels.

They reached the cars a couple minutes later, crouching next to the passenger side of Arielle's, staying out of sight from the main road. Mason's car remained in front of theirs.

"I still think we should intervene right now," Selena said. "What if he comes out by himself?"

"If that happens, I'll consider it. But we need to stay hidden."

"How do you think Felix is doing?"

"I'm sure he's fine. He's in a much safer place than us."

Arielle sensed the angst in Selena's voice. Despite all the preparation that went into these missions, it was impossible to avoid the emotional jitters on the day of the big showdown. One mistake could throw all the hard work down the drain. One misstep could result in death. But just as equally, one well-executed plan could change the world for the better. It was a twisted seesaw of good and evil.

"Someone's coming," Arielle whispered, crouching lower. "Stay still."

She had heard the chatter of voices from around the garage, and listened as steady footsteps made their way down the driveway.

Arielle craned her neck enough to make out the figure walking their way and knew it was Mason Gregory. She had watched him enough over the past two weeks to recognize his silhouette against the floodlights pouring from the garage. She turned over her shoulder to Selena behind her. "It's him. He's alone."

She hadn't expected it to be this easy, so Arielle's heart

started drumming much quicker. They could grab Mason right now, throw him in the backseat, and drive off. But that still didn't guarantee his survival.

If Mason didn't show, there was no saying what Nate might do for being stood up. The man's life might only be spared for a few extra hours.

These thoughts raced through Arielle's mind as she contemplated her next move. They had a few options to consider, but all required at least having Mason in their possession.

He was fifty feet away when Arielle looked back over her shoulder and nodded. She had no idea if Selena understood that as a cue to make a move right now. At the least, she'd follow her lead.

Once Mason was twenty-five feet away from his car, Arielle stood up, confident the surrounding darkness wouldn't reveal her. She stood in the shadows, watching and waiting. Arielle took one step forward and immediately stopped, collapsing to the ground like she had dropped something important.

"Mason!" a voice shouted from the garage.

Selena remained in her crouched position and helped Arielle get back on her feet.

"Who the hell is that?" Selena whispered.

Mason stopped and turned around. "Rusty? That you?"

"Where you goin', brother?" Rusty called back, trudging down the driveway to meet him.

Arielle couldn't make out his appearance in the night, but could tell he was a tall, skinny man.

"Just calling it an early night," Mason said once Rusty had reached him. They both shuffled toward Mason's car and stopped next to the door.

"Everything alright?" Rusty asked. "You seemed a bit out of

sorts today."

"Yeah, everything is wonderful. I'm just tired from work. Been having some long hours at the office. Getting more accounts dumped on me."

"Those fuckers. No one ever said the work was glorious, but you're about to get paid for your efforts. It'll all be worth it in no time."

"I sure hope."

"Alright, amigo, I'll let you get back to it. See you next week."

"See you then."

Mason entered his car and closed the door as Rusty walked away.

"Dammit," Arielle snarled. "Too good to be true."

The engine in front of them fired up, the headlights flashing on.

"We can still try," Selena said.

Arielle rocked her head. "Not while he's in the car. Too dangerous. And he'd be able to honk the horn to get attention. I'll follow. You wait here and follow Nate."

Selena took the instruction in stride and shuffled backwards to be next to her car. Mason had already turned his car around and was on his way down the dirt road.

Arielle dashed around and jumped into her driver's seat, jamming the key into the ignition in one swift motion. Mason had already turned around the curve, which was fine. Arielle kept her headlights off, the moon providing just enough light to see safely.

"You know where he's going. No need to drive like a maniac," she told herself. She often had to recite this reminder because she loved driving fast. Racing lessons were her absolute favorite from her early days of training with the Angel Runners.

Driving fast was second nature, a skill she had used plenty of times in the past, but unnecessary in the current moment.

She cleared her mind as she tailed Mason, but more importantly, cleared her soul. Perhaps the biggest advantage Arielle had over her peers was her understanding of time and the universe.

The universe was omniscient. All living creatures were bound to its rules.

We all come from the dirt of this planet Earth, she recalled a philosophy teacher explaining once. *We all return to the dirt at the end of our lives. There has never been an exception to this rule. The Earth floats in the universe, bound by the rules of gravity and physics. Because of this, the universe knows exactly where the Earth will be at any given time. It knows where the moon will be, the precise axis it will be tilted. It even knows when disasters will strike. The universe gives us life. It takes life. The universe understands its living creatures to their very core. And that includes us. There have been plenty of people in our existence who have spoken of being one with nature. Sensing a shift in the world. These people have a unique gift. They can speak the language of the universe, even if not completely fluent. The universe knows what we will do, even before we do it.*

It was this last line that lingered with Arielle for many years since college. A line that has proven itself true over and over. It provided her with an understanding of how to deal with and manage time. No one could master time, as it was part of the grand universe. But they could understand it enough to anticipate its next moves.

That's exactly what she did on her missions. The hardest part of her job—and the thing that made her unlike anyone else in the organization—wasn't her ability to fight, drive, or shoot guns. It was her ability to remove her inner soul's ambitions.

The universe, via time, couldn't put up roadblocks if it didn't know what she had planned. Through all the preparation and reading about her missions and subjects, she had to force the information into her brain while keeping a neutral heart. It was like keeping a secret from the universe. A secret she would later use against time.

She often dropped into recruit training camps to offer words of wisdom. "The universe is the core of existence," she liked to say. "Every living thing, from us humans, to the trees, to the little ants on the sidewalk, are all extensions of the universe. Time is an extension of the universe. Understand this basic principle and you will go far."

Her words always motivated, but she felt no one truly understood her message. It was far from a simple concept to understand, let alone implement. It wasn't something that could be taught. She thought of it more as a sixth sense than anything. She wanted to teach her new teammates about this understanding of the universe. They would need to grasp it if they were to work together long-term. But she couldn't do it ahead of time. Her soul was clear, her mind focused on the task at hand.

Arielle could cheat the past, but she was not immune to its foolery. The bigger the mission, the harder the resistance. For everyday missions like this one, she just might cheat time once more. As far as the universe knew, she was just a girl driving on the highway late at night. It didn't see her as a threat to interject with its plans to kill Mason tonight.

They finally reached the highway, and she grinned as they sped up.

Chapter 39

Just before nine o'clock, Selena watched the garage door creak open, more bright light spilling across the driveway. From her location she could see three sports cars inside, and one black Camaro clearly from the Sixties.

She licked her lips as she watched, legs clenched with anticipation, palms clammy with sweat. It was impossible to get a clear look inside the garage. Doing so would have left her standing in the open, directly between the cameras.

But she saw shadows moving within the light. Tall shadows that stretched twenty feet across the ground.

"Two people?" she whispered, craning her neck over the hood of her car. There had never been a mention of multiple people in any of their reports.

The shadows remained for a couple of minutes, swaying as they clearly carried on a conversation. One shadow disappeared, then the headlights on the Camaro flicked on, the engine roaring into the silent night. The car crept carefully out of the garage, turning wide and slow to avoid hitting any of the cars parked in the surrounding roundabout.

Selena opened her car's passenger door and climbed over to the driver's seat. The Camaro sped away, leaving a long trail of dust that bent around the corner.

"Shit!" Selena gasped, fidgeting with the keys, and eventually dropping them into the dark pit near her feet. "Gah!"

She patted around the floor until finding the keys, drawing a deep breath before guiding the car key into the ignition. *Slow down,* she thought. *The past is going to start fighting.*

Selena got the engine turned on, only to battle with the stick shift. It was stuck in park and wouldn't budge. "What the *fuck*?!" She put all of her force into it, and it finally gave way, dropping straight into drive, where she made a quick U-turn to get on the dirt road.

She wondered what Nate told his guests before leaving. Probably a blanket statement like *I have a quick errand to run. Be back in thirty.* Or her favorite line her dad used to say all the time: *I have business in town. Food is in the fridge. Don't know what time I'll be back.*

She never knew if he really had business, or if that was his cover to meet women during those summer nights in Paris.

Selena floored the accelerator, the Camaro already out of sight on the dirt road ahead. Her car had no business driving at high speeds, and she could only pray a deer wouldn't wander into the middle of the road, as it had done last weekend.

None did, and when she approached the highway a minute later, she saw the Camaro just turning onto it.

Selena had to slam on her brakes just before turning onto the highway, catching the slightest glimpse of a reflector from a cyclist zooming down the street.

"Are you kidding me?!" she shouted. "Who the hell rides their bike in the middle of the night?!"

She gripped the steering wheel tighter, knuckles whitening as her body clenched with frustration. Selena rarely dealt with resistance from the past. Tonight, however, was a different story. She hadn't quite realized all the minor nuances occurring directly resulted from the past pushing back against her. The past sensed her main objective to stop the murder of Mason Gregory, and was throwing out obstacles left and right.

She had only ever heard about the chaos that ensued right before the end of a mission, and now, witnessing it firsthand, she felt completely helpless. And clueless as to how to work around it.

When the bicyclist passed, she had to wait for a semi-truck to steamroll past her.

"Of course!" she grunted, turning onto the highway where she'd remain stuck behind the semi for the next few minutes. The truck belonged to City Supermarket, a regional chain of grocery stores. The trailer's doors had a cartoon banana smiling and giving a thumbs up, next to the words: *Serving the Rocky Mountains since 1947. Count on us!*

The banana and its oversized, cartoonish eyes wouldn't stop staring at Selena.

Creepy-ass fruit!

Selena giggled, briefly wondering if she was losing her mind. She weaved into the opposite lane for a view ahead, but couldn't see in the darkness. These small mountain highways had no street lights, and she knew better than to chance racing around the semi. The road could curve without warning and send her tumbling into a ditch.

Much to her increasing frustration, the semi was driving exactly the speed limit, if not a tad slower. Her left leg bounced as she rode the truck's bumper.

"C'mon, c'mon!" she screamed.

The highway was only one lane, and she remained stuck behind the truck for another seven minutes until they reached the interstate where she could finally get around it and speed up.

The Camaro was long gone. Selena gunned the accelerator, the car's measly engine whining as it flew down the interstate. Traffic was nearly non-existent heading northbound.

Five minutes later, she exited and blazed down the road that led to the warehouse. The only positive out of this drive was that she hadn't seen Arielle anywhere along the way, trusting she had reached their destination safely and on time.

The clock on the radio showed the time was 9:13, leaving less than twenty minutes until the murder. She hadn't achieved a single thing to slow it from happening, watching helplessly as the Camaro gained a head start and never looked back.

Selena pressed down on the accelerator until it touched the floor.

I really hope Arielle and Felix are okay.

Chapter 40

Arielle parked in the lot nearest the warehouse, around the corner and out of sight from Mason. She saw Felix's car parked nearby and him not in it, meaning he had made his way to the spot she marked for him on the map.

Arielle stepped out of her car and tiptoed toward the corner of the building, peering around the edge, hidden in the shadows. She watched Mason's car sitting idle, the parking lights turned on while the engine ran.

Roughly seventy-five feet separated her from Mason's car. She already knew which way the Camaro would pull up from, and could clearly see the light illuminating a ten-foot radius, enough to cover Mason's car and the Camaro once it arrived.

Dressed in black, Arielle could get fairly close, possibly even hide behind the rear of one vehicle once the two men stepped out to have their conversation. They would speak for five minutes before Mason returned to his car. She could step in at any point.

Arielle had put on a utility belt equipped with everything she needed: pistol, baton, flashbangs, pepper spray, and three throwing knives. When dealing with the past, she couldn't solely rely on a single weapon. A gun could jam, the pepper spray could malfunction. She'd even heard stories of batons snapping in half upon initial impact.

The throwing knives were the ace up her sleeve. They were virtually foolproof against the past. They had no mechanical flaws that could be exploited. All Arielle needed was her precision and a powerful throw to make them lethal. She could hit a target from fifty yards away about half the time. She rarely missed under twenty-five yards.

Where she stood was already within her comfort range, but the closer she could get only increased the chances of everything going right.

Arielle stepped away from the building, taking one slow step at a time. She moved in a stealthy crouched position, ready to turn and run if needed. She remained in the shadows, and would for as long as possible. The parking lot had smooth pavement, no crunching steps as she placed her foot down with the gentleness of a cat walking on carpet.

She continued toward the idle car, stopping ten feet away from the outer edge of the light. The Camaro's headlights could easily expose her, but she'd navigate around Mason's car to stay out of their path.

Arielle saw Mason through his windows. He sat forward, drumming his hands on the steering wheel, bobbing his head to the tune of whatever song he had playing on the radio. After having watched him extensively for the past two weeks, this moment caught up to her. Despite what they learned about his involvement with the sex trafficking ring, she saw a man who loved his wife and kids. She didn't know what happened inside his office building, but he punched in and out every day, going through the slog of life to provide for his family. She suspected his involvement with the ring was financially motivated. Even from afar, Mason Gregory seemed a genuine, well-intentioned man. Sometimes good people found themselves in bad situations, and Arielle could only hope their work on this mission would help put Mason back on the right path.

Headlights appeared from the nearby road, zooming toward the lot. It was the Camaro, and Arielle promptly shuffled to position herself more behind Mason's car. Mason killed his engine and turned off the lights, adding to the darkness.

They both waited for the Camaro to park in front of Mason, where it eventually did, cutting its loud engine before it drew any attention.

The doors of both cars opened, Mason stepping out first.

Arielle felt her legs tense. Through it all, this moment in any mission still caused her great anxiety. Her hand subconsciously shot down to her pistol in the holster, gripping the handle.

The Camaro door swung open, and out stepped a tall, skinny man.

"Rusty?!" Mason asked. "What the hell are you doing here? Why are you driving Nate's car?"

Arielle heard the panic in Mason's voice. It was clear he sensed something wrong. She felt it, too. Death was thick in the air, an invisible sensation she had learned to recognize from the day she climbed over her dead family in the mall.

"Hey, Mason, brother. How's it going?"

"I . . . uh. What the hell is going on? We just talked before I left."

"I know. Nate chatted with me right after that. Said you're thinking about leaving us behind." Mason took a step back toward his car, his hand reaching out for the handle. Rusty tossed up his hands. "Easy, brother—I'm just here to talk."

"Why didn't you just talk to me over there?"

"Nate said you'd be here. Told me about the deal he worked out with you. I guess he wanted me to find out how serious you were. Said you have a girl he might be interested in."

Arielle frowned as she stepped left to see around Mason's car. *Who the hell are they talking about?*

She could hear every word of the conversation clearly and wouldn't move an inch. She could take down Rusty with ease from this distance.

"Well, yeah. She's real. Did he think I was making this all up?"

Rusty shrugged. "Not my job to figure out what the boss thinks. When can you get her to us?"

"Wait. Do you have the money?"

Rusty reached into his shirt pocket and pulled out a pack of cigarettes, then sat on the hood of the Camaro. "Want one?"

"Sure," Mason replied quickly, reaching out a hand to grab the cigarette. He leaned toward Rusty to let him light it.

"Have a seat. I'm just here to talk. You're acting too strange."

"Talk about *what*? You and I have nothing to discuss."

"Dammit, Mason, I'm trying to help you. Will you just relax?" Rusty chuckled before taking a long drag, Arielle able to see the orange tip of the cigarette. He blew clouds of smoke into the night sky.

Mason nodded. "Sorry. I've been on edge all week about this."

"I understand. We've probably all gone through similar thoughts, but what can you do about it?"

"Well, I'm leaving. That's what I'm doing about it."

"Sure. But can you really ever leave this life behind? You'll see us, hear about us. We're going to be millionaires. All of us. At some point, you'll realize it was a mistake and want back in."

"Are you supposed to be some sort of last resort?" Mason asked. "Nate sends my closest friend to make this sales pitch so I'll stay? Seems desperate. I understand my value with the credit cards, but I'm sure you guys can find someone to replace me."

"Oh, we will. That's not the point. We can do that, but it's a hassle. Why not just stay on? What's *really* pulling you away?"

"I already explained myself to Nate. Can't you just give me the money and let me move on with my life?"

"That's not what I came to do. I have orders."

"Listen to yourself. You have orders? Is this the military?"

"Look, brother. I grew up with nothing. Lived in a trailer park with my parents and five siblings. That's a lot of nights sleeping on the floor. I came into this opportunity and I'll be damned if I mess it up. I'm just here doing my job. That is all."

"I thought you were my friend."

"You are. But you don't pay my bills. I gotta do what Nate asks."

"Fine. Let's cut through the bullshit, then. There's nothing you can say to convince me to stay. I want out of this life. I'm not going to snitch on you guys. I just want a normal job, and to spend Friday nights at home. That's all there is to it. Can you please pass over the money and be done with it? I'll arrange for the Selena girl to be at the mansion next Friday."

Hearing Selena's name caught Arielle off guard. Maybe Mason was a monster, after all.

"Okay," Rusty said. "Suit yourself. I need to call Nate real quick and confirm he still wants to give you the money."

Mason sighed and threw his hands up. "Are you kidding me?"

"Not at all, brother. I'll be right back—he has one of those fancy phones in his car, so I'll just be a second."

Arielle watched as Rusty turned away and sat back down in the Camaro. She had no idea if the car really had a phone, or if he just said that as an excuse to grab his gun. All she knew was that the next time he appeared, he'd have every intent on shooting Mason Gregory in the head.

Mason remained on the hood of his car for another minute, arms crossed as he stared at the Camaro. He finally gave up, flicked his cigarette butt into the darkness, and returned behind the wheel, never turning the car back on.

Arielle considered causing a distraction. Maybe throwing a rock at Mason's car to get him back outside. But that wouldn't guarantee anything.

Instead, she waited two long minutes before the Camaro's door swung open again. Rusty appeared, no gun in hand. She raised her pistol and waited for Rusty to come around toward Mason, who had just rolled down his window.

"Sorry, brother," Rusty said, his arms twitching. "Nate isn't too happy with you and doesn't want to give you the money."

"Are you kid—"

Arielle pulled the trigger, a slug blasting through Rusty's back and chest. He looked down, blood already forming a dark splotch on his shirt. Rusty clasped his hands over his chest and looked at Mason with bulging eyes. Mason had an equally shocked expression and flailed his hands to open the car door.

"What the fuck?!" he shouted, catching Rusty as he collapsed, easing him toward the ground. Mason spun around, looking everywhere, but was too panicked to let his eyes focus

257

on the woman standing in the shadows.

Arielle stepped forward, no longer concealing her footsteps, entering the glow from the above light.

Mason recoiled when he saw her, backing away from Rusty until he bumped into his car. "Wh-who are you?" he asked between heaves for breath.

"This man was going to kill you," Arielle said, nodding at Rusty's dead body. "He has a gun in his pants. Nate sent him here to kill you."

"Who are you? How do you know this?"

"I guess you can call me a guardian angel. We'll take care of Rusty's body. It'll never be found, and because of that, Nate will leave you alone. He'll know better than to mess with you. Just promise to live a clean life."

Mason nodded, still gasping for air, as the panic had surely taken over all his senses.

"I will."

"Get out of here and don't speak of this night to anyone." Arielle spoke in a threatening tone meant to intimidate, and it worked.

Mason scrambled to his feet and climbed into his car, refusing to break eye contact while turning on the car, fastening his seat belt, and driving away. He drove much faster than she had witnessed over the past two weeks, but seeing his tail lights disappear gave her the sense of accomplishment that always came at the end of a mission.

Applause echoed from the distance, followed by a cheerful whistle. "You go, Arielle!"

It was Selena.

Arielle looked into the void, and after a few seconds saw two figures moving through the dark.

"That was the most impressive thing I've ever seen," Felix said. "How did you do that?"

"Do what?" Arielle couldn't help but smile. She had never performed in front of a live audience before, and the instant praise was gratifying.

"All of it. I was out there in the trees trying to not throw up, and you just creep right up to these guys. Hiding like a ninja."

"And then your patience," Selena said. They all stood under the light, grins wide across each of their faces. "I would have shot him right when he stepped out of the car. But you waited so long. And how the hell did you not get any resistance from the past? It almost took me half an hour to get here because shit kept happening. Barely made it in time to see the show."

Arielle laughed, her body relieved to release the nerves and tension that had built up over the day. "I have a lot to teach you guys. We should get out of here, though. Let's call HQ and tell them to send the clean-up crew." The Road Runners had a team called Housekeeping, and their job was to visit the site after a mission and erase all evidence from existence. "Have them leave the Camaro. That way, the police will find it and trace it all back to Nate. That should be enough to help them bring down the trafficking ring."

"Do you think Mason will be safe?" Selena asked.

"He will be. I told him that once Nate realizes Rusty is missing and never coming back, he won't bother him. I know these types of guys—it's pretty much who I always hunt down. They don't clash with people they consider on their same level. And if it looks like Mason killed the man sent to kill him, *and* made his body disappear . . . he won't hear a peep from Nate. No doubt about it."

Felix wandered toward Rusty's dead body and stood over it,

looking down and shaking his head. "I still can't believe it was Rusty this entire time."

Arielle shrugged. "I don't get too surprised any more. Did you know Mason was planning to invite Selena to the poker game next week and offer her to Nate?"

"What?!" Selena gasped.

Arielle nodded. "It's a sick world we live in. Obviously, none of that would have gone according to plan had it played out. But it's safe to say now that Mason won't ever dip his toe into the criminal underworld again. He'll be there for his family, and they won't have to suffer."

"So, what do we do now?" Felix asked, returning to the ladies. Arielle leaned against the lamppost, ready to relax.

"We go to the house and pack, then we go home."

"Such beautiful words have never before been spoken," Selena said, prompting a giddy round of laughter from all three of them. They were slap-happy, delighted to be done with a grueling two-week mission.

"Then it's on to the next mission, right?" Felix said.

"We'll get a couple of days to unwind," Arielle said. "But yes, we'll jump right into preparation for whatever we're doing next. Let's get out of here."

Chapter 41

They had mostly packed before heading out Friday morning, and just had to pick up a couple of things before hitting the road after the mission. They opted to drive to Denver while still in 1988 to avoid the traffic that seemed a constant in 2022. After dropping off Arielle's and Selena's cars at the local rental agency in Pueblo, they all crammed into Felix's car and started the two-hour drive north.

Arielle leaned against the window while they cruised, watching Pueblo disappear. She imagined Housekeeping had already arrived and was preparing to take Rusty Kirk's body into a different year, where they could take their time cremating it and disposing of the ashes.

Another killer off the streets, Arielle thought, still disturbed that Nate lived and continued operating his sex trafficking ring for the time being. Part of her wanted to request a new mission to come back and put him out of business, but she knew that would be shot down. Especially if the Futures Report came back with positive news.

She often forgot just how wide the butterfly effect could spread. Saving Mason and eliminating Rusty could very well have led to Nate's downfall. Not immediately, but eventually.

Once they arrived in Denver, Felix parked at a meter one block away from their future offices and killed the engine. Crime and a massive homeless population still overran downtown in 1988, making it dangerous for anyone to wander the streets in the middle of the night.

"This is it," he said. "Any last errands to run here in 1988 before we head back?"

"Just get me back to my cell phone," Selena said, wasting no time fetching the flask of Juice from her bag. The others followed, and they each raised their flasks before taking the small sip and thinking of their return to the present day.

Within a minute, the world fell dark, and they arrived back in a busy downtown Denver. A warm summer night.

Felix stepped out of the car first and drew in a deep breath. "Missed that modern smog." Arielle and Selena joined him and laughed while they started down the sidewalk in search of a restaurant.

"Look at these beautiful lights!" Selena said, spinning in a circle as she danced down Sixteenth Street mall in downtown Denver. Street lights lined the sidewalks, and music poured out of buildings as the nightlife scene formed. People hurried down the sidewalks while horse-drawn carriages moseyed down the road that was closed to vehicular traffic. The city bustled, and Selena felt right back at home.

"Must have been a Rockies game tonight," Felix said, nodding to a dozen people strolling down the sidewalk in their purple and black attire. "I know we're all starving. Let's go eat."

"Oh, how I've missed it," Selena said. "Look at all these people with a sense of fashion. And they're going to *real* clubs and bars. Not some ghetto hole-in-the-wall."

"Relax, Selena," Arielle said. "You have plenty of time to

tear up downtown."

"You have no idea. I'm ready to dance with a man who *knows* how to dance. But first I need a big drink. Maybe you should have one, too, and I can convince you to come out with me."

"Good luck. I'm just ready to crawl into my bed and sleep for two straight days."

"This should do," Felix said, nodding to the restaurant they were approaching. "Mexican sound good?"

"Um, a margarita or four sounds perfect," Selena said. "And they're already dancing!" Her mouth hung open while she led the group into D'Corazon, where half of the restaurant had been transformed into a nightclub for salsa dancing.

Elvis Crespo's voice boomed from the adjoining room while they sat in the dining area and devoured a basket of chips and salsa, margaritas freshly served.

"So, how did you pull it all off?" Selena asked. "I really have to know."

Arielle took a sip from the frozen margarita in front of her and smiled. "It's very complicated, but it's why I didn't want to tell you anything ahead of time. Long story short, the universe knows your intentions. And if you take these missions to heart, it's going to know what you intend to do, and will stop you."

"Are you saying you don't take the missions to heart?" Felix asked, frowning. "I feel like that would come as a surprise if you asked any Road Runner."

"I don't take them to heart. I take them seriously, but they don't consume my soul. I've learned how to separate myself from my work. Kind of like a coroner has to do. We're surrounded by so much doom and death. My God, the whole sex trafficking thing really tried to bother me. I kept thinking about the innocent girls those people were ruining and exploiting.

263

But I couldn't let that be my driving force. Too much emotional investment and you're screwed—my gun would have definitely jammed if I was thinking about those girls."

"So what do you think about?" Felix asked. "Surely you don't just have a blank mind."

Arielle nodded. "I always try for a blank mind, but it's not always possible. I think back to the day I lost my family. The day I survived. It helps keep things in perspective. If I survived that, I can survive anything. Nothing else is really relevant compared to that. At least for me. I'm not even supposed to be here. I'm playing with house money every day."

Selena shook her head. "Don't say things like that, Arielle. That's survivor's guilt talking. You got lucky that day, yes. But you're right where you're supposed to be."

Arielle patted at the tears forming in her eyes.

"Selena's right," Felix said. "You better people's lives. Even if you don't know it. You've turned your tragedy into something beautiful for the world. Because of you, people don't have to suffer through their own grief. The Gregory family won't fall into drugs and addiction. All because of you. I'm sorry you lost your family—I'm not going to pretend I can understand—but you survived. That's the simple fact. You're here, every day, changing lives. I can't speak for Selena, but my life already feels changed after working with you on just this one mission."

Selena nodded in agreement. "It's true."

"Thank you both," Arielle said, her throat tensing with a swell of emotions. "That means a lot. Maybe working together will be good for us all."

Selena grinned. "I'm gonna dare to say it. We just might become friends."

Felix slapped his hands on the table, startling the two women as the silverware and glasses jingled. "Don't say the F-Word!"

Selena burst into laughter, followed by Arielle.

"We can't be *friends*," Selena said, still giggling. "We are colleagues. Teammates. Right, Arielle?"

Arielle smiled, shaking her head as she took another sip of margarita. "I don't put labels on relationships." She pinched her lips shut, trying to not laugh.

"Booooo!" Felix howled through cupped hands over his mouth.

"Weak!" Selena cackled, grabbing a tortilla chip and tossing it at Arielle.

They all burst into more laughter.

"You know what," Selena said. "I'll take it. Don't you remember at the beginning, Felix? Arielle acted like we were going to be business associates for the rest of our lives. I guarantee if we had gone out to this same dinner then, Arielle would have come up with some excuse."

"'Oh, I have too much work to do!'" Felix mocked in his best Arielle impression, batting his eyelashes.

"Woooow!" Arielle said. "You guys are so funny."

"What?" Selena said. "It's not every day you get the number one Angel to *not* deny having new friends."

"She's right," Felix said. "We'll take it. Maybe by the end of the next mission you can say . . . the F-word."

"Maybe," Arielle said, conceding the argument that had spiraled well beyond her control.

They each took sips of their drinks before Felix asked, "When are we going to find out how the mission turned out?"

Arielle stuffed a chip into her mouth, expecting this question to come up, eventually. "I don't do that anymore. We are done. I've been burned too many times in the past. Finding out things turned out the same, or sometimes even worse. That's not common, but after reading a few of those reports, it's just deflating."

"So we'll never know?"

"Do whatever you want. You can get the Futures Report and find out what happened. I'm sure you can look up some of the names on your phone right now—just to see what comes up. But I don't want to hear about any of it."

"Really?" Selena asked. "You're not even a bit curious about what happened to Nate? I hope he got taken down so hard."

"Curious, sure. But what would happen if we found out he never got caught? Maybe he's still in operation today. We already deal with the past enough. No sense in dwelling over it further."

"I'm going to look it up. Later, of course."

"Speaking of later," Felix said. "Any rumblings about the next mission? Just wondering where and when we might be going."

"I haven't even checked my email since we got back," Arielle said, reaching into her pocket to pull out her phone. "I'm sure there's something in there."

Felix and Selena watched in anxious anticipation.

"Well, I have almost 800 unread emails—that will be fun. Let's see."

Arielle scrolled through her crowded inbox until she found a message from the Scouting Department. "Well, this looks interesting."

"What is it?!" Selena pleaded. Felix shifted forward in his seat and drummed his fingers on the table.

"Looks like a local mission in 1991. An unsolved robbery

homicide. A bank robbery."

"In Denver?" Selena asked.

"Sure is." Arielle continued to read through the email that provided high-level notes on the potential mission. "Wow. This case had a suspect and a trial, but the jury found him innocent."

"So we're just going back to find out who did it?" Felix asked.

Arielle chuckled. "We're not detectives. We're going back to stop it from happening. Four people died. Two-hundred thousand in cash stolen. Sounds like a fun one."

READ THE FUTURES REPORT!

Just because Arielle Lucila doesn't want to look at the Futures Report to find out what happened after the mission, doesn't mean you can't!

Enjoy an exclusive look at the official Futures Report for the Mason Gregory mission that is prepared for the Commander's office following each mission.

All you need to do is join my e-mail Reader Club by signing up at bookhip.com/LDXKFDR

Author's Note

Thank you for reading this first book of the new Arielle Lucila series. If you're not already familiar, Arielle first appeared in the fifth book of the Wealth of Time Series, so this is very much a spinoff/continuation with new characters in the same universe.

My plans for this series are extensive. I'd like to take it at least 20 books, assuming you'll stick around for the ride. Alex Cross, John Milton, and Jack Reacher are three main characters with book series spanning over a dozen books, and my hope is for Arielle, Felix, and Selena to reach that same level of longevity.

Planning to write such a long series opens up many new doors that aren't possible when writing a shorter series or standalone book. This allows a much slower, gradual progression for the main characters, and makes them a bit more lifelike. They will all face their own tragedies and triumphs, romance and heartbreaks, and the overall growth and change we all face as humans living in a world that seems to go a little madder with each passing day.

My hope for you, the reader, is to enjoy a few hours of escaping reality, as this trio does their best to make the world a better place one mission at a time.

In future books, starting at the second, these three Angels will tackle real-life and historical events, either trying to prevent tragedy or learning the truth. In this first book, I didn't want to take on a real event yet. It's important for an author to gain a full understanding of the characters, and in this type of story, that task is much easier when not having to worry about historical accuracy for the overall plot. They explore a fictional, unsolved murder. And while they succeeded, my main goal was to learn how they work together and complement each other. This is critical because future books are only going to crank up the chaos the three of them will face together.

I feel I have built a solid foundation, and I can't wait to see how they develop in the coming books, both as individuals and as a team learning to work together in a high-stress environment.

I want to take a quick moment to thank those who have helped make this book a reality.

My editor, Stephanie Cohen-Perez. We worked together on the entire Wealth of Time series, and I know we're both equally excited to start on this new project. Stephanie always offers additions (and subtractions) that will make the story stronger. Behind every great book is a talented editor, and this is no different.

My wife, Natasha. Aside from reading my books and finding more things that need to be tweaked, she helps run our publishing house and keeps things afloat while I vanish into the writing cave. Nothing would be possible without you.

And finally, to my kids. They continue to inspire me every day and keep my motivation tank filled to the brim. Not only do I want them to see what is possible when they chase their dreams, I hope they find a bit of themselves in these characters who will be around for many years to come.

Thank you, again, for reading. See you in the next book!

Andre Gonzalez

May 25, 2021 – February 21, 2022

Enjoy this book?

You can make a difference!

Reviews are the most helpful tools in getting new readers for any books. I don't have the financial backing of a New York publishing house and can't afford to blast my book on billboards or bus stops.

(Not yet!)

That said, your honest review can go a long way in helping me reach new readers. If you've enjoyed this book, I'd be forever grateful if you could spend a couple minutes leaving it a review (it can be as short as you like) on the site you purchased you this book from, or on Amazon if you bought it in-person.

Thank you!

Also by Andre Gonzalez

Wealth of Time Series:
Time of Fate (#6)
Zero Hour (#5)
Keeper of Time (#4)
Bad Faith (#3)
Warm Souls (#2)
Wealth of Time (#1)
Road Runners (Short Story)
Revolution (Short Story)

Amelia Doss Series:
Salvation (#3)
Nightfall (#2)
Resurrection (#1)

Insanity Series:
The Insanity Series (Books 1-3)
Replicate (#3)
The Burden (#2)
Insanity (#1)
Erased (Prequel Short Story)

The Exalls Attacks:
Followed Away (#3)

Followed East (#2)
Followed Home (#1)
A Poisoned Mind (Short Story)

Standalone books:
Snowball: A Christmas Horror Story

About the Author

Born in Denver, CO, Andre Gonzalez has always had a fasci-
nation with horror and the supernatural starting at a young
age. He spent many nights wide-eyed and awake, his mind
racing with the many images of terror he witnessed in books
and movies. Ideas of his own morphed out of movies like
Halloween and books such as *Pet Sematary* by Stephen King.
These thoughts eventually made their way to paper, as he
always wrote dark stories for school assignments or just for
fun. Followed Home is his debut novel based on a terrifying
dream he had many years ago at the age of 12. His reading and
writing of horror stories evolved into a pursuit of a career as
an author, where Andre hopes to keep others awake at night
with his frightening tales. The world we live in today is filled
with horror stories, and he looks forward to capturing the raw
emotion of these events, twisting them into new tales, and
preserving a legacy in between the crisp bindings of novels.

Andre graduated from Metropolitan State University of
Denver with a degree in business in 2011. During his free time,
he enjoys baseball, poker, golf, and traveling the world with
his family. He believes that seeing the world is the only true
way to stretch the imagination by experiencing new cultures
and meeting new people.

Andre still lives in Denver with his wife, Natasha, and their
three kids.

Printed in the USA
CPSIA information can be obtained
at www.ICGtesting.com
LVHW012044280923
759516LV00003B/134